THE
PEOPLE'S
POLICE

BOOKS BY NORMAN SPINRAD

The Solarians
Agent of Chaos
The Men in the Jungle
Bug Jack Barron
The Iron Dream
Passing Through the Flame
Riding the Torch
A World Between
Songs from the Stars
The Mind Game
The Void Captain's Tale
Child of Fortune
Little Heroes
The Children of Hamelin
Russian Spring
Deus X
Pictures at 11
Journals of the Plague Years
Greenhouse Summer
He Walked Among Us
The Druid King
Mexica
Osama the Gun
Welcome to Your Dreamtime

THE
PEOPLE'S
POLICE

Norman Spinrad

TOR

A Tom Doherty Associates Book
New York

THE PEOPLE'S POLICE

A Tor Book
Published by Tom Doherty Associates
175 Fifth Avenue
New York, NY 10010

www.tor-forge.com

Tor® is a registered trademark of Macmillan Publishing Group, LLC.

The Library of Congress Cataloging-in-Publication Data is available upon request.

ISBN 978-0-7653-8427-0 (hardcover)
ISBN 978-0-7653-8429-4 (e-book)

Our books may be purchased in bulk for promotional, educational, or business use. Please contact your local bookseller or the Macmillan Corporate and Premium Sales Department at 1-800-221-7945, extension 5442, or by e-mail at MacmillanSpecialMarkets@macmillan.com.

First Edition: February 2017

Printed in the United States of America

0 9 8 7 6 5 4 3 2 1

To
THE INDOMITABLE SPIRIT OF THE BIG EASY
Past, Present, and Future
Never let your song sing surrender

Acknowledgments

Who dat'?
The marching band of our Secondary Parade

Ben Abrass on camera
Simon Thoral on mike
Wilton Hymes on the road
And the ever-popular Dona Sadock
on tambourine and rhythm

THE
PEOPLE'S
POLICE

1

Some folks are still bitching that the Eternal Mardi Gras is a Disney version, what with the traditional Krewes' parading limited to the traditional lead-up to Fat Tuesday while the big budget corporate floats from Hollywood, Bollywood, and Pornywood parade all year, all long, all over New Orleans, which is sort of true, given that it was Disney I brought in first.

But whining that the Mouse has gone and done to the French Quarter what it did to Times Square, and oozed out into the rest of New Orleans like the annual dose of mud during the Hurricane Season, and calling yours truly, Jean-Baptiste Lafitte, a swamp rat traitor to the true soul of the city is going a tad too far, seeing as how the Quarter had fallen far off its fabled glory days even before Katrina.

You expect me to apologize for saving the city from drowning to death?

Oh yes, I did!

Everyone knows New Orleans had been on its economic ass for decades, barely able to pay the cops to keep the Swamp Alligators down in their lowlands swamps and out of the New Orleans Proper high grounds.

And the Hurricane Season wasn't going away, now was it, and what the Dutch were demanding in order to save what was left of the Big Easy from finally going under would've been about the total budget of the city government for the next decade or two. No high-priced, high-tech Hans Brinker seawalls and solar windmill pumping stations back then, need I remind you?

I guess I do.

Amazing what short memories ingrates have.

New Orleans featured itself as the Big Easy since before Mickey Mouse was even a gleam in Uncle Walt's evil eye, but just because the truth wouldn't look so good in the tourist guides doesn't mean we don't all know that it's always really been the Big *Sleazy,* now does it?

This city was making its living as a haven for pirates and slavers and the riverboat gamblers, saloon keepers and whorehouse impresarios like yours more or less truly, rollers high, low, and medium, who serviced their trade since before the Louisiana Purchase.

The Big Easy was *born* as the Big Sleazy. *Easy?*

Yeah, sure.

Born between a bend in the mighty and mighty ornery Mississip and a briny marsh presumed to call itself *Lake* Pontchartrain serving as an overflowing catch-basin for tidal surges when the major hurricanes hit and a giant mud puddle in-between.

Easy?

First built precariously on the natural levees of the Mississippi, expanding greedily and stupidly into the back swamps. Tossed around like a beachball between the French and the Spanish. Finally sold to the Americans by Napoleon on the cheap because he knows he's gonna lose it to the British anyway if he doesn't. Flooded every few decades even before Katrina, before there even was an annual Hurricane Season, squeezing what remained onto what high ground was left to it after the sea level rose. The population cut almost in half, forced to live off the tourist and entertainment trade alone when the Gulf oil dried up, just about surrounded by the Alligator Swamp and what crawled up out of it if its back was turned.

You call that *Easy*?

Those who adapt survive, like the Cajuns from icy Quebec said when they found themselves in the steamin' bayous of the Delta, like the Alligator Swamp nutria hunters turning a plague into protein. Those who don't ain't been heard from lately. So making legal what the Big Easy always was to pull our terminal condition from the mud is not "selling out the soul of the city" or "whoring ourselves to the mavens of show business."

Because the Big Easy has *always* been a whore, a charming, sleazy, free-wheeling, good-natured hooker with a heart of gold and an eye for the main chance, which is what makes her easy, and bein' easy is the name of the game in this business, which has always been the main game in town. And let an old bordello impresario tell you, who would ever hire a hooker who wasn't all of the above, and good-lookin' too?

In case you're forgetting, the Big Easy wasn't exactly looking as appetizing as a platter of Oysters Bienville back in the day before Mama Legba and Her Supernatural Krewe. She's all spiffed up and lit up and giving herself the star treatment now, to the point where ingrates and ignoramuses and Creole romantics looking back over their shoulders can afford to complain about how New Orleans is peddling her previously jazzy derrière to less than the genteel bohemian trade of their absinthe fantasies.

Whoever wrote that song about there being no business like show business sure got it wrong. As things stand now, there's no business *but* show business and we all are in it. Not that we haven't always been. The only difference now is that it's making the good times roll again after all those years in the deep dark shit, and that's good enough for me, and if it's not good enough for you, this ain't your town, you'd best leave and go somewhere more to your tight-assholed liking.

But y'all come back on vacation from the salt mines, y'hear! Whatever your pleasure, we got it, and if we don't, don't worry, no matter how pervo it may seem to your sweaty vestigial morality, we'll get it for you. Here in the Eternal Mardi Gras of the Big Easy, we make no such judgments, we're impossible to scandalize, de gustibus non est disputandum.

What pays here, stays here, and never fear, we do still want your money.

2

Patrolman Luke Martin had "enforced" more final eviction warrants than he could count or cared to, and while it didn't exactly make you feel like a hero kickin' folks out of their houses and into the street, it was far from the worst duty, sure better than dealing with pickpockets and muggers from the Alligator Swamp trying to work the Quarter or gangbanger patrol duty guarding the swamp itself.

There had been a few minor firefights when this dirty work got dumped on the New Orleans Police Department, but these days you did it with a partner, and the two of you were issued military body armor and M35s hung with enough scopes and grenade launchers and fancy doodads to scare the shit out of the civilians in question to the point where no cop he had ever heard of had ever needed to fire one of the things even when the former homeowner was armed with a sawed-off shotgun or a rusty M16. Sweet duty in a way, 'long as you didn't think too hard about it.

But—

"Is this some kind of fuckin' joke?" were the first words out of his mouth when he read the address and the name on the latest final eviction warrant handed to him.

"You find something *fuckin' funny* about one more poor sucker's eviction notice?" snarled Sergeant Larrabee, aka

Sergeant Slaughter, aka the Mouth That Roars. "You're not some kind of sicko Bourbon Street comedian, Martin, you're a cop, remember, or anyway you're dressed like one and this ain't Mardi Gras, so keep your black sense of humor to yourself, just take Moreau with you, hold your nose, and go enforce it."

There it was, the full legal form of his name on the final eviction notice, the exact same form on the mortgage contract he had so proudly and hopefully and stupidly signed less than two years before the onset of the Great Deflation, aka the Steroid Dollar, aka the Superbuck, aka Up Shit Creek.

"Don't you read these fuckin' things before you hand them out?"

"*Read* them? You out of what passes for your mind, Martin? Don't you know how many of them come down across my desk every fuckin' day? Of course you do, Martin, you must've enforced at least a hundred of 'em by now yourself."

"This is *my* house," said Martin Luther Martin.

"Say what?" grunted Sergeant Larrabee, snatching the poison paper out of Luke's hands. "Jesus H. Christ on an airboat!" he sort of moaned when he took a good look, in a tone of voice that made him sound almost human. "Martin Luther Martin!"

Almost. For a moment.

"*Martin . . . Luther . . . Martin?* Now where did an ol' gator like you get such a highfalutin handle? Yo daddy had himself a reefer dream?"

What Daddy had as far as Luke could remember was a bad smart-ass attitude. Martin Luther Martin had always loathed the official name inflicted on him at birth, and hearing it out of Larrabee's flannel mouth, let alone seeing it on this piece-of-shit paper sure didn't make him like it any better.

He was calling himself Luther about the time he learned to talk, transmuting it into Luke as his gangbanger tag in the Vu

Du Daddies, cool hand that he styled himself after seeing the Paul Newman movie on an ancient TV they had snatched, no Mohammed This or Barack That bullshit for him, no Rat Man or Baron Saturday or other such Vu Du mumbo jumbo either.

So Luke Martin was a self-made man from the git-go, who had a choice, Papa doin' long hard time in Angola for general bad-ass thuggery by the time he hit the first grade in what passed for school, Mama makin' her junkie ends meet by selling the shit and her pootie at street level, that is, to the extent that you could call anything a street in the Alligator Swamp.

Mudville, Stilt City, the Alligator Swamp, whatever.

Mudville because the so-called streets were unpaved pathways of mucky mud when they weren't underwater. Stilt City because anything that wasn't built up on a platform tall enough to keep it above the incoming surges during the Hurricane Season wasn't going to be there for very long.

The *Swamp* because it *was* what had been called the "back swamp" way back in the day before the young city called New Orleans started slithering down off the natural levees of the Mississippi and the Esplanade and Gentilly Ridge and suchlike into the sea-level lowlands and worse. And the poorest of the poor had been living there even then, squeezed between the levees and ridges and the *real* bayou swampland between the spreading city and the Gulf of Mexico, more or less, and sometimes much less, absorbing the tidal surges and keeping it from being flooded with salt water.

These days, what with the rising sea level, and the various canals stupidly dug down through the decades to connect the old natural harbor to Lake Ponchartrain and to the Gulf, the far back-swamp bayou land was now under salt water, and the more or less habitable front of the back swamp that wasn't, except during the Hurricane Season when it too was more or less under water, had moved inland all around what high ground remained.

So no one tried to build anything that wasn't stilted and platformed above the record high-water mark or if they were stupid enough to try it, got drowned out within a year, and during the Season, New Orleans Proper—as the proper folks living there had taken to calling it—was more or less surrounded by a cross between a Third World version of a country-mouse Venice and the long-gone true bayou country of zydeco-mourned forlorn Cajun lore.

Mostly wooden stilt-huts on mostly wooden platforms mostly clustered together in mostly self-contained villages like something carved out of clearings in the Amazon rain forest or on the low-lying shores of the Mekong Delta. One-room grade-school buildings in the bigger ones that the law still more or less required the city to provide. Outdoor markets selling swamp-grown vegetables, swamp-hunted nutria meat, swamp-caught fish, crab, shellfish, and crawdads. Liquor stores, clothing huts, and general stores selling most everything else, mostly tools, fishing gear, guns, ammunition, and more of them than not serving as fences for stolen goods.

During the relatively dry seasons, it was foot traffic on the muddy village streets, and not much better from village to village, and during the wetter days, which were about half the year, it was patched-up rubber zodiacs, homemade lightweight and shallow draft canoes and kayaks, and half-assed rafts pretending to be gondolas.

As America thought of itself, as New Orleans Proper thought of it, the Alligator Swamp might be a shameful rural slum that belonged somewhere in the deep Third World Boonies, but as a Third World Boonie, it was better than most.

Enough growing months when it wasn't Hurricane Season

and enough rich-soiled farmland to grow just about any vegetable, if nothing that grew on a tree or grew like a grain. Back away into the new bayou back swamps, there was abundant saltwater seafood fishing and trapping. The uncounted hundreds of thousands or even millions of nutria—amphibious rodents the size of beavers that banged like bunnies and reproduced like rats—that had once been a despised plague destroying the freshwater swamp vegetation had been driven closer in by the salting of their previous turf, right under the village huts during the Hurricane Season, and were now an abundant supply of easily hunted meat. Easy small-plot farming. Easy fishing and lazy-man's hunting.

A subsistence-level lifestyle, maybe, but a good one, almost a paradise if you were into it.

The *Alligator* Swamp not because the real reptilian deal had indeed managed to make its way up from the bayous but because it was a shithole if you weren't a teenage *human* alligator hungrily clacking your teeth at what you knew all too well was up there that you couldn't have in New Orleans Proper, as the mofos there called it.

The French Quarter, with its saloons, and bars, and music halls, and high life, the Business District and Magazine with their supposedly easy pickin's, and the burglar's dream Garden District hovering there on the high ground like the literal City on the Hill, had much more appeal to the boys in the hood than a lifetime of dirt-farming in the mud or hunting swamp rats or fishing for your food.

But knowing full well that their chances of honest gainful employ in New Orleans Proper were slim and none, the boys trying to become men, and the men who didn't know how to stop being boys and really didn't want to, became the top predators of this ecological niche, sharp-toothed and lizard-hearted young Alligators who would bring down their own fathers if they could find them and devour their own mothers if the bitches ever accumulated anything worth stealing.

For a teenage Alligator, the down-and-dirty economic base of the Swamp was low-level drug dealing and pocket-picking and drunk-rolling and such in the Quarter or the Magazine District one step ahead of the police if you had the brass balls to try it, but mainly joining one of the gangs preying on the softer targets in your own hood.

So young Luke took the path of least resistance, not that the resistance was insignificant, not that there was any other path to take, and managed to gain admission to a scruffy and scurvy low-level gang called itself the Vu Du Daddies, though what they knew or cared about voodoo would fill about five of their remaining brain cells, and as far as they were concerned what they might father by gangbanging some skank was none of their business.

What was their business was what more powerful Alligator gangs allowed to be their business, which wasn't very much. Muggings. Burglaries, but not of the more lucrative liquor stores, which were reserved for the dominant gangs—more like bottom-of-the-food-chain dealing.

Of course, you could always get a job and leave. That's what they told you in school if and when you bothered to show up.

Hah, hah, hah.

There weren't really enough "proper" jobs in "proper" New Orleans to keep much more than half of its "proper" populace above the official poverty line and their heads, uh, above water, so no one up there with a job on offer was about to lay it on something that slithered up out of the Swamp.

But one not so fine day not that long after the Hurricane Season, Luke emerged from the family hut toward sundown to join the Vu Du Daddies for a night of nothing in particular and had a vision that changed his life.

The streets were in the slow oozy process of emerging from the floodwaters, the worst time of the year for getting around, with the so-called village streets no longer flooded but up over your ankles in mud, and what was left of the waterways so shallow that proceeding by canoe or raft was like mud puppies flipflopping their way from puddle to puddle.

Nevertheless, or maybe because their meth-sotted brains saw this as some kind of advantage, a half dozen members of the Fuck Yo Mothers had boosted some out-of-date TVs and computers from somewhere and were fleeing with the loot in two wormy old bayou pirogues fitted with rusty electric outboards, here and there having to dismount, hold tight to the gunwales, and, cursing and bitching, push their overladen boats off a not-yet emergent mud bank.

The Fuck Yo Mothers were as high up the food chain as it got in the Swamp, which only made this sorry spectacle even more pathetic, and Luke might even have laughed at these addled buffoons were it not worth your life to be caught doing so.

And then Luke heard a rock and rollin' thunder like a low-riding helicopter gunship, and 'round a bend it came at about fifty miles an hour, with an actual *airplane propeller* whirling and roaring inside a wire cage behind some kind of racing car engine, planing a flat-bottomed boat like a huge water ski magically slip-sliding over mud and water alike and leaning over into the turn like a motorcycle—one of those high-speed airboats snapped up at cut-rate prices by the New Orleans Police when the Okefenokee and the Everglades became deep year-round lakes, kicking up a rooster-tail of mud and water behind it, and pushing a heady cloud of expensive gasoline fumes before it.

Whoo-ee! Enough to give a teenage Alligator a hard-on for hot iron, and it more or less did, and likewise in spades for the three cops riding it and having a high old time, at least as Luke was seeing it: one driving the speeding airboat, another standing up beside him waving a pistol, the third at some kind of long-snouted curdler mounted on a swiveling pedestal.

The police airboat caught up with the Fuck Yo Mothers in nothing flat, and took to gliding mocking circles around their two boats, then neato figure eights around and between them just to taunt them, hah, hah, hah, go fuck *yoselves,* muthas!

Now, of course, anything in the Swamp with descended testicles automatically hated the cops, Luke being no exception, but who could keep from laughing at this sarcastic display of police primacy at the expense of and over these feared lizard-lords of the Alligator Swamp?

And that was when it came to him, even before the cops began playing the tight beam of their sonic curdler over the Fuck Yo Mothers, causing them to scream, grab at their ears, and, it would seem, piss, and possibly *shit* in their pants.

Think of the Cops as just another gang and it was immediately apparent.

The *Cops* were the Supreme Gang of the Alligator Swamp. They had the top gear. They had the colors. Each of them got a top-of-the-line gun for nothing and plenty of ammo for it. Each of them made more money in a year than anyone else in the Swamp, without risking hard time in Angola like Papa.

Forget the Vu Du Daddies, Luke told himself. Forget trying to join the Fuck Yo Mothers or the Spades of Ace or the Darth Invaders.

The *Police* is the gang to get into.

That was when Luke knew that a Cop was what he wanted to be, had to be, and he never looked back. The Police were always looking to recruit a few gang members from the Alligator Swamp for their down-and-dirty knowledge, but rarely getting any takers, seeing as how they were the Enemy, not to mention that you couldn't even try to get into the police academy without being a high-school graduate.

But if you looked at the Cops as just another gang, as the toughest, best-armed, best-equipped, richest gang of all, you took advantage of the invitation to try your stuff at the police academy.

Bummer that it was, Luke actually started going to the local one-room school regularly enough and studied just hard enough to get into Brad Pitt High School, a long, hard, and somewhat dangerous daily commute from his own hood in the southeast edge of the Lower Ninth Ward through sometimes hostile territory by a ratty kayak he stole and defended with a rusty Bowie knife by waterway when he could, slogging through the mud when he couldn't, and squeezing through to a high-school diploma.

After all, looked at the right way, it was better than having to make your bones, or get banged by the whole gang, or go through some disgusting punk vu du ceremony, which was the sort of thing you had to do to join any other gang worth getting into.

3

Let me tell you, New Orleans was knocked back on its soggy ass by Katrina, and much worse by the advent of the Hurricane Season, and so was I. Katrina was nothing compared to what followed, like a pug got knocked down in the first round by a haymaker, managed to crawl more or less to his feet on the eight count, only to get socked again, and again, and again, each roundhouse right stronger and stronger.

Before Katrina, ol' J. B. was riding high on the return from three saloons, one of which was actually in the Quarter, and a couple of cathouses, one of which was a fancy three-story establishment in the Garden District. None of 'em was washed away by Katrina, and all of them were high enough to survive even the annual Hurricane Seasons.

But the same could not be said for the tourist trade, knocked back down after it had just about recovered from Katrina by one Category 3 or 4 storm after another during what came to be called the Hurricane Season, by at least one Category 5 hurricane a year, by the rising seawater of the Gulf surging up through the waterways and canals and down over the banks of Lake Pontchartrain, squeezing what was left of the Easy part of the Big Easy up onto the levees and ridges.

It finally got through to the powers that be at the time, or

THE PEOPLE'S POLICE * 25

anyway to Cool Charlie Conklin who was then the mayor and well known for knowing which side of his bread the butter was on, that this situation was going to be permanent, and the only way to save the city from completely turning into a series of islands in the watery muck was to draw borders around what could afford to be saved by permanent pumping operations and internal levees, and giving up on trying to save the rest of the city by letting nature do its stuff and turn it back into the buffering marshland that had once been known as the back swamp.

Charlie Conklin also knew where the votes weren't, which was in the lowlands first depopulated by Katrina, and turned into isolated faux Third World villages by the Hurricane Season, inhabited by fragmented tribes of blacks who had been there for generations, Cajun refugees from the bayou country now permanently under water, Vietnamese fish-folk, and the like, the sort of population highly unlikely to get it together to vote as a constituency, so he was able to get away with this bottom-line political calculation.

Which was cool, if you were among the electorate up on the Quarter, or Metarie, or the Business District, or the Garden District and so forth. What was not cool if you were in the saloon and bordello trade was creating an urban bayou land known all too far and wide thanks to the less-than-favorable media coverage as the "Alligator Swamp," legendarily infested with human reptile life whose gangbangers slithered out of it of it whenever they could to seek their pickings in the turf of honest sleazy impresarios like me.

So in practice the tourist district, aka the Zone, was more or less reduced to the areas bordered by the Mississippi and Canal Street, and maybe as far north as Rampart or maybe Claiborne, and as far east as Esplanade or maybe Frenchmen. And after a passel of nationally and internationally colorfully reported unfortunate incidents, it sort of became official via hotel and tourist board pamphlets and maps, and by the concentration of the majority of police patrols and sometime checkpoints guarding its periphery.

Well, as you might imagine, the two saloons whose premises I rented outside the Zone became the giant sucking sounds of expenses over receipts gurgling down the drain. I owned the building the one in the Quarter was in, or thought I more or less did because I had twenty-three years left on a fixed-rate mortgage I could easy afford thanks to a federal loan shark subsidy I didn't really understand or want to, or so I thought at the time. It ran at a small profit, and I had a nice apartment with a balcony above the bar.

The bordello in the Garden District was further in the black, and I owned that too along with your friendly government subsidized and regulated mortgage packager, but the whorehouse outside the Zone became a den of meth and heroin-addicted hookers half a step up from street traffic, and what they attracted is something you don't want to think about, and neither did I.

Those who adapt survive, so I closed everything that I was renting space for, leaving me with the nameless bordello house known only by its address and phone number, and my Bourbon Street saloon, Lafitte's Landing, and a much-reduced monthly nut to carry.

If it was no longer exactly cocaine and cognac and Antoine's for lunch and dinner every day, at least it was only a few cuts below the lifestyle to which I looked back so fondly to have become accustomed to.

No one expects the Spanish Inquisition or the Banking Crash of '08 or one disastrous hurricane to be followed by an endless line of bigger and bigger brothers and sisters or an alligator to come up through the toilet and bite you on the ass.

So how was I to foresee the Great Deflation Scam?

How was anyone except the sons of bitches who ran it, whoever they really were?

And there is smart or not-so-smart money claiming that, in the end, they really didn't even know what they were doing either.

4

With a diploma from Brad Pitt, Luke found getting into the Police Academy mysteriously easy and when he found out how right he was about the Cops being the top gang in the Alligator Swamp, he found out the reason why.

The tourist street crowd life in the Zone being such a big slice of the economy, the police force had always been under-manned in venues not involved in the tourist trade when it came to keeping the peace in poor and mainly black neighbor-hoods like the Ninth Ward or northeast Tremé.

Post–Hurricane Season, with where the money was to be made more or less surrounded by the Alligator Swamp, the most important job of the NOPD was to keep the Alligators down there where they belonged and, above all, from invad-ing the Zone.

Completely cordoning it off would have required a police force far larger than anything the city government could af-ford, so the only viable tactic was to make the gangbangers live in fear of the cops, and the only place to do it was inside the Swamp itself.

This had long been accomplished by arbitrary airboat patrols, arbitrary billy clubs laid upside arbitrary heads, the occasional terminal elimination of gang leaders who got too big for their britches, and other assorted acts of forthright police brutality, busting such would-be perps and treating them to prolonged free food and shelter in jail cells being counterproductive to the municipal budget.

But now some asshole in the mayor's office had persuaded Sam Bermudez to set up a so-called Experimental Community Outreach Unit in the Lower Ninth, and recruit a few Alligators from the Swamp itself to partially man it.

So soon as he had the badge Luke found himself dropped right back into the Alligator Swamp, into the Lower Ninth Ward, into one of the crummiest of the Brad Pitt Houses converted into what was laughingly called a new district police station.

The Brad Pitt Houses were originally a noble development godfathered by an idealistic movie star close up to the section of the Industrial Canal levee breached during Katrina, something like a hundred single-family homes made available with all kinds of subsidies to those who had lost theirs in the flood.

Pitt had commissioned world-class architects to do their stuff, the main rules being that the houses had to be built up on stilts or pylons to survive the further flooding, which the advent of the Hurricane Season turned out to supply in abundance, and have energy-wise solar panel roofing. Most of the results were artistically stunning, but the new Ninth Ward Community Police Station was not one of them.

One of the earliest built, it resembled an outsized aluminum shipping container propped up on metal piping of the sort used to frame staircases in parking garages. It was also outside the electrified fence of what was now a gated community besieged by the Alligator Swamp and the lowlife wildlife within to which it was an all-too-tempting target.

The ward room of this dump was where Luke Martin found

himself dropped along with the other eleven cops who constituted the new unit to be greeted by a lieutenant whose orders
were delivered in jaundiced terms that were brutally clear.

"The New Orleans Police Department does not have the
men or the money to adequately protect this place from what
periodically tries to short out the fencing for the purpose of
sacking it, but the Brad Pitt Houses are a political sacred cow,
and if that were to happen, there would be holy hell to pay
at City Hall, and as y'all might be aware, shit flows downhill,
meaning from the mayor to the police commissioner, and
from there to you. So your mission is to keep that from happening and nobody gives a fuck about how. Just make it so and
don't bother filing reports. Screw up and nobody ever heard
of you."

So saying, higher authority departed, leaving the Experimental Community Outreach Unit all on its own. You didn't
exactly have to be a political sophisticate to figure out that no
one in the police department had a clue as to how it might
accomplish its mission, and that the higher-ups probably believed it was impossible and really didn't give a shit if it failed
because its very existence was some sort of political ass-
covering operation and nothing more.

Twelve cops in a unit supposedly ordered to pacify the immediate area besieging the Brad Pitt Houses or maybe even
the whole fucking Lower Ninth—yeah, sure. Three veteran
cops a few years from retirement, and probably assigned to
the unit as a garbage dump, seeing as how the three of them
were overweight and out of shape drunks, and Sergeant Rick
Harrison, who had no idea of what orders to issue beyond
"Bring that bottle over here."

The eight other cops in the unit were, like Luke, recruits
from the Alligator Swamp straight out of the academy, unable
to get into a Swamp gang of significance and hoping they could

be better positioned to line their pockets under the colors of the Police.

Only Luke took the mission seriously and only because no one else did and it therefore afforded him the first opportunity he had ever had to become a gang leader himself.

He set up a firing range close by the gate to the electrified fence and easily enough persuaded his fellow Alligators to blast away. He organized mass nutria hunts in the surrounding swamp and left piles of the dead rodents around to rot as calling cards. His Alligator squad took to doing likewise with the real-deal reptiles, chopping off the heads and impaling them on poles as exclamation points.

To his gang of Alligator Swamp Cops, this was just good dirty fun, but Luke had a point to make, that there was a new gang on this turf, namely the Alligator Swamp Cops, and they were trigger-happy badasses not to be fucked with and out to rule.

Toward this end, he took advantage of a half-assed attempt by some local gangbangers to breach the electrified fence to bullshit Sergeant Harrison into bullshitting the higher-ups into supplying heavier weaponry, hoping for an airboat, which was not forthcoming. But they *were* issued M35s, stun grenades, two handheld sonic curdlers, a couple of crates of tear gas grenades, gas masks, riot shields, and electric billies.

Fully dressed in these colors, the Alligator Swamp Cops trudged and canoed around the swampland, blowing away nutria and alligators in the process of showing the flag, violating the turf of the local gangs with swaggering impunity, and all but calling them pussies and daring them to come out and fight.

Luke didn't really expect them be stupid enough to offer themselves up as target practice for this level of ordnance. He expected them to bitch about it sooner or later one way or another and waited for it to happen.

It finally did in the form of Ally X, honcho of the Fuck Yo Mothers, the acknowledged top gators in this neck of the Swamp, who swaggered into the police station decked out in twenty pounds of cheap steel bling and piercings, packing a pair of rusty revolvers, and doing his best not to look nervous as he shouted at Sergeant Harrison, who was in the process of washing down a shot of bourbon with the last of a six-pack of beers.

"Yo mo, bobo, what the fofo goin' on?"

Harrison shouted for Luke, who had long been waiting for something like this, had watched Ally X enter the building, and had assembled his posse just outside.

"Get yo ass out here, you wanna know what the fofo goin' on, mofo," Luke shouted back.

When Ally X did, he found himself surrounded by a semi-circle of fully armed and armored Alligator Swamp Cops and backed up uncomfortably close to the electrified fence.

"I'm gonna tell ya, mofo, and you gonna tell yo' bobos, and y'all gonna spread the word from the bird fuck' far an' fuckin' wide—"

"Wish is—"

"Wish is there's new colors inna Swamp, an' you lookin' at 'em, and the name of our gang is the Alligator Swamp *Po*-lice, and the deal is *we rule*. We the top of the food chain in this here turf, and we do not take shit, an' shit is what we will get from what's up the food chain from *us* if they get the idea we not doin'our job. And *our* job is to tell you how to do *your* job, so here's how it is. . . ."

Luke's Alligator Swamp Cops flipped their M35s down into firing position and pointed them at Ally X before he could do more with his mouth than drop his jaw wide open, and Luke laid it out:

"Look, the po-lice don't want no trouble and trouble for

us is getting shit from upstairs because you motherfuckers are making trouble down here, like any you mofos get so much as in sight of the Brad Pitt Houses, like any you mofos try to cross the canal into the Zone, like any you mofos fuck with anyone but other mofos down here—"

"Oh, yeah, bobo?"

"Cor-rect, mofo. These are the rules now, we find you disobeying them, we come after y'all and we do not stop till we got no more targets."

"Well, what the fuck does that leave us to do, mofo? Chase fuckin' nutria an' pray t'Jesus?"

"Look, my man, the police don't want no trouble from what goes on in the Swamp as long as it *stays* in the Swamp and don't make any trouble for us—"

"Meanin' *what*?" Ally X demanded belligerently. But Luke could smell it was turning phony, turning into a necessary face-saving show.

"Meaning don't make trouble for us and we won't make trouble for you. We not gonna be runnin' no hos, we're not gonna deal no stuff, an' if we steal this and that once in a while, it's just gonna be for personal use. Meaning the police are not here to be bad for business. Who goes along, gets along . . . ain't there enough shit in this city already? We don't have to make no more for each other, now do we?"

5

Don't expect J. B. Lafitte to explain what really caused the Great Deflation because the smart money—what's left of it—says the what is a who, and the why is to make money off it, what else, and if the suckers who are born to be screwed every minute in this great nation ever find out who and why, there won't be enough tar, feathers, railroad ties, and rope in all of Dixie to do the necessary justice.

On the other hand, there are also those who point out that the Loan Lizards of Wall Street or whatever you want to call whoever or whatever gone and done it, screwed themselves in the bargain too in the end, which is only what they deserved, even if the marks, including yours truly, sure 'nuff didn't.

When the shit hit the swamp cooler ceiling fan and blew down the inflatable dollar, I found myself shafted up the ass by two mortgages I couldn't even think of carrying under the sudden circumstances and I needed buildings to stay in any business at all.

When in doubt, follow the money, so who made out in the Great Deflation? Or thought they would? Or might still?

Seems to me it had to be the wise guys who blew all the hot air into the balloon that tanked the housing and building market back in the day of the so-called Great Recession and the whole damned real economy with it. The banks wrote mortgages they knew were shit, packaged them into so-called collateralized debt obligations perfumed to smell like shinola, which they fobbed off on the suckers, who repackaged them and sold them off to other suckers, and so on and so forth, until there was so much ring-around-the rosy that they all ended up buying their own crap more times removed than they could follow, and down the whole house of marked cards came.

Or as some smart-ass wrote at the time, "They wrote the biggest rubber check in history and passed it off on themselves."

Well, as some other smart-ass pointed out, you can't allow yourself to get washed away by the same stream of bullshit twice, so this time around, "They," whoever They is, tried something different, unless you're one of those innocents or cynics able to believe the Great Deflation just happened.

What with half the houses and a good share of the business real estate in the good ol' US of A stuck with mortgages that was under water—something we all in New Orleans knew more than we wanted to post-Katrina—and the whole economy holdin' on to the rim of the toilet bowl thanks to the real-estate market collapse threatening to drag it all the way down the willy hole, even tight-assed Republican politicians had the brain cells to realize that something had to be done before they got sucked down with it.

A lot of different somethings as it turned out, all of them designed to put a floor under the mortgage market, all of them various means by which state and mostly federal governments and agencies put iron-glad guarantees under various kinds of no-risk mortgages rendering them no-risk in the process. No less than 20 percent down. Not less than twenty-year amortizations at fixed interest rates of no more than 7 percent annually with balloon payments at the end strictly forbidden.

Sweetheart deals for both the banks and those who could pony up the down payment. Even more so in post-Katrina and late pre–Hurricane Season New Orleans, where there were all sorts of trick deals to get the down payment on the federal cuff as hurricane recovernment money, thanks in no small part to good ol' Brad Pitt, who waved his magic wand and got Ninth Ward Katrina victims brand-new houses with the down payment ponied up as a subsidy.

Sure seemed like a no-brainer to me at the time. While I could hardly get a government subsidy for the down payment on a mortgage to buy a whorehouse even in New Orleans, I *could* wangle a little something extra on the down payment on a mortgage to buy the building in the Quarter containing a cash-cow saloon by enticing my friendly neighborhood bank to fold in enough extra of Uncle Sap's money in a combined deal to cover the down payment on the cathouse in the Garden District too. This was koshered by calling the annual cash flow from the saloons and the bordello whose premises I was renting at the time "capital" to inflate my net worth, and greasing the requisite palm to look the other way. It ain't called the Big Easy for nothing.

But then the Great Deflation hit the fan and the good times, which seemed just about to start rollin' again, got squashed down with a thud that made the Great Recession seem like a replay of Herbert Hoover's and FDR's and Huey Long's golden oldies.

How did it happen? You could pay with your deflated dollar and make your choice of crazy conspiracy theories. The Chinese stood to benefit because they were holding all that paper denominated in dollars. OPEC made out like bandits because oil was priced in dollars and they could jack the price just about as high as they wanted. Ditto the drug cartels. Ditto Mafia loan sharks. Would you believe a conspiracy of all of the above? Would you believe Elvis gone and masterminded it after returning from Mars on his flying saucer?

"Never attribute anything to conspiracy that can be explained by assholery," yet another wise guy suggested, and I'd never discount it as a major factor in human monkey business, and especially not when there were all sorts of fancy computer trading programs helpful in aiding all the players in tripping over each other's dicks at the same time.

However it happened, the dollar somehow went up big-time against everything else. Maybe it started with the Chinese cutting the value of the renminbi for some inscrutable reason like giving lagging exports a shot in the arm, and the Japanese and Europeans and all were forced to play follow the leader. Or maybe it really was the Loan Lizards of Wall Street out to gobble up the land of the free and everything built on it, in conspiracy with other secret masters or not, since they did, after all, have the clout in Washington to keep the Fed from trying to keep the dollar down, especially since both the Republicans and the Democrats were beating their patriotic breasts and competing with one another to take the credit for the glorious comeback of the superbuck.

Was great fun, folks, now wasn't it? Who didn't think the good times were on a roll when the dollar that would've previously bought you one cheap stogie now would buy a whole box of primo cigars? Who didn't want to buy a Chinese entertainment console for the price of a plate of General Tso's Chicken? Who didn't want to take the Grand Tour of Europe for the price of a week in Disney World? No one, or so it seemed at first, when everything cost five times less dollars to buy than the year before. Every man a king, every gal a queen, as good ol' Huey Long promised in order to win elections way back in the day.

But for each dollar that *bought* five times more, someone

had to be *selling* something for five times less. I was selling a bottle's worth of Jack Daniel's for the price I used to get for a shot of bar whiskey. A full nighter with one of my best girls in the royale suite now went for the previous price of a blow job behind a parked car. The same thing, of course, was going on in every business in the country.

Well, those who adapt survive, which was anyone with a brain in his head large enough to figure out that you had to cut what were now ridiculously high wages, which wasn't too hard to do, seeing that the Federal Minimum Wage would now have supported a family of twelve in high style if it wasn't adjusted downward, seeing as how the annual federal and state budget deficits could be eliminated simply by letting the taxes fall slower than the falling budgets in dollar terms.

Seemed for a moment nobody got screwed.

Nobody, that is, who didn't owe debt written in stone in the pre-deflation numbers.

Which, what with mortgages, and credit cards, and corporate and government bonds and the national debt, was just about nobody, the governments of the United States, Louisiana, and New Orleans, and yours truly included.

Genuine riches, like gamblers' luck, have to flow from one place to another if they're moving at all. *Real* wealth is the kind that can't be created or destroyed by the price of bullshit futures on the schlock exchange or the dollar price of pussy. Farmland, factories, sports franchises, boats and trains and planes, real estate. The lion's share of which had debt of one kind or another to the Credit Card Banditos, the Loan Lizards of Wall Street, the Chinese, Ali Blah Blah and the Forty Financial Engineers.

Debt that could neither be carried nor written down to its true worth in current superbuck dollars, and believe me I tried!

During the Great Recession, these bastards had ended up selling Confederate Money derivatives and deadbeat-backed mortgage bonds to themselves in the biggest pyramid scam in history, and when it collapsed, they ended up repossessing a lot of real estate they couldn't unload without all these government mortgage backing programs.

Now the same Loan Shark Lizards were holding mortgages on even more real estate, mortgages whose values were far from under water to say the least in steroid dollar terms, but whose interest payments were now impossible for most of us to meet for the same reason, and were foreclosing on whatever tasty morsels they chose to wrap their reptilian tongues around.

It didn't take a financial engineer to see that when the government sucked the necessary hot air out of the dollar and it fell back to earth, as it had to if the Chinese weren't going to foreclose on the entire United States, those who had run this version of the Great Scam would own the country—real estate, livestock, and factories—and be able to turn it into their plantations like the lords and ladies of the antebellum romances.

That's who wins and who loses, but don't ask *me* whether the winners just staggered into it, the luck of stepping in their own shit as they say, or whether it was a diabolical evil conspiracy. I reckon the historians, and the conspiracy creeps, and the novelists and movie makers, will be playing at figuring *that* out for the next hundred years or so, and living quite well off of trying.

J. B. Lafitte, like millions of other folks not in on the scam, had a more immediate impossible problem. I was deep in foreclosure on the whorehouse in the Garden District and the saloon building in the Quarter, and having by then abandoned the saloons and the whorehouse whose premises I had been renting, if I didn't find some way to weasel out of it shortly, I'd be entirely out on the street.

And at the time, I hadn't a clue.

6

Luke's Alligator Swamp Police did indeed become the acknowledged top gang in their turf, with the local citizenry benefiting by this rude new enforcement of something like order if not law.

The police might still not be loved or even exactly respected by the main beneficiaries thereof, fear and loathing of the cops being all but bred into the gene pool of most of New Orleans, let alone the Alligator Swamp, but there was grudging appreciation of the diminishment of rapes, armed robbries, murder, and general mindless mayhem.

And the gangbangers came to realize that the rules of engagement enforced by the Alligator Swamp Police had certain advantages over the previously darwinian law of this here jungle, like your chances of getting killed were noticeably diminished while the proceeds of the usual monkey business were not.

They came to accept that the police were something you could deal with as long as you played by their rules. Don't give them no trouble, and they won't screw with you.

It worked for as far north, south, and east of the Brad Pitt Houses as the Alligator Swamp Police could make their presence known without airboats or reinforcements, which were not about to be forthcoming.

The Experimental Community Outreach Unit was a success. One would have thought that Luke Martin would have gotten the credit and maybe even a quick promotion to sergeant. One would have thought that similar units would be deployed all over the Alligator Swamp.

One would have been dead wrong.

The main business of the New Orleans Police Department was business, namely keeping trouble out of the Zone and "New Orleans Proper," and there were nowhere near enough cops to do this by maintaining a cordon of cops around the Alligator Swamp. Nor was there enough budget or manpower to set up Experimental Community Outreach Units all over the Swamp, besides which the usual strategy of instilling fear of the police in general in the denizens thereof by unpredictable raids and reliably predictable brutality had been been working well enough on the cheap for a long time.

Luke was given to understand that the Experimental Community Outreach Unit had been an experiment that was supposed to fail, something to shut up the noise emanating from the Brad Pitt Houses and satisfy the politicians playing to this bothersome peanut gallery. Because if it was loudly proclaimed a success, the media pressure to do the financially impossible and clone it all over the Alligator Swamp would be a political no-win situation for City Hall.

So keep your trap shut, kid, Luke was ordered. Who goes along, gets along. And before he could consider protesting even within the department, they gave him a consolation prize, they did him a favor, though he didn't think so at the time.

They pulled him out of the Swamp and made him an ordinary cop in New Orleans Proper, an emotional demotion for a top Alligator Swamp gang honcho, but a far sweeter beat to any true New Orleans cop.

Which step by step was what Luke evolved into.

In the Swamp, he had been happy playing the top gang-banger honcho, but in the Quarter, in the Zone, in New Orleans Proper, the police were part of the System Big Easy style.

The primary job of the police was to prevent murders, robberies, rapes, and muggings to the extent possible and acceptable to those facing election, and to arrest enough murderers, thieves, rapists, and muggers to look competent on the news broadcasts and sites. Corporate swindles were not to be looked into as long as they were incorporated into the approved overall monkey business of New Orleans.

"Vice," namely whorehouses, genteel streetwalking, a certain tolerated level of drug dealing by approved entrepreneurs, back-alley poker and craps, and so forth, was generally not a police problem either. Far from it, since these enterprises had to rent their unofficial licenses from the police with cash in paper bags, small ones for small-fry, larger and larger ones for bigger and bigger fish.

The corruption of public servants by the unofficial powers that be was not a problem for the police either, unless power struggles downtown dragged them into it, in which case the problem was Kingfish-sized, but not to anyone below the level of captain.

Such intricate and complicated machinery could of course hardly run without a sufficient amount of grease at every level. The police had no license to steal, nor were any but soon-to-be terminated rogues fucking around with dealing or pimping, but ordinary cops were not to be denied free drinks and food in saloons, or their fair share of the cash flow.

Luke had no moral problems with any of this—indeed, growing up as a Swamp Alligator, "moral problems" had been an unknown concept—nor did he long object to being ripped from his roots in the swampland and planted in richer higher ground.

His salary supported rent just south of Claiborne as soon as the paychecks started coming in because no one was about to demand security deposits or months in advance or any of that shit from a cop or they'd find themselves hip-deep in code violations.

A patrolman's salary and his ration of grease afforded Luke Martin a lifestyle he had never dreamed of attaining, indeed never really had understood existed. An apartment in a rough-edged corner of the Upper Ninth. He could eat in restaurants. He could buy new clothes. He could hang out in the Blue Meanie.

The Blue Meanie was a cop bar, not officially of course, but the presence of uniforms, badges, and NOPD-issued sidearms did not encourage casual patronage by a general run of bar-flies. It was not the only cop bar in town, but the handful of others tended to be racially segregated too, not officially of course, but blue cloth did not guarantee black skin a warm welcome in a white cop bar and vice versa.

The Blue Meanie, though, was *the* cop bar, and as the name implied, all those wearing the blue tribal colors were truly welcome.

An *upscale* police saloon, where wives, girlfriends, would-be girlfriends, cop groupies, and the younger offspring of police families going into the family business did not feel un-comfortable.

Luke had been made aware of this scene by the cop social network: that in the Blue Meanie, even a newbie recent rookie could feel he belonged, could shoot the shit with anyone en-titled to wear the *blue* colors, even the occasional avuncular sergeant, and that *skin* color was irrelevant.

The married guys were comfortable showing up with their wives and their legally adult sons and daughters. Guys who were seriously hooked up could be more or less assured that no one would hit on their girlfriend. The unattached, such as Luke, could achieve quick hookups with cop groupies, and/or cruise the scene in more genteel style if something more genteel was what they were after.

Luke had turned the cops in the Experimental Community Outreach Unit into a top predator gang, but citywide the New Orleans Police were more like a tribe than a gang, and Luke found that this was the tribe he wanted to get into. And after a couple of months he came to realize he was already in it.

The Alligator Swamp Police had never been a hot news item and indeed their short story had never been spread beyond police circles under stringent unofficial orders from City Hall, but it was hardly the sort of tale that would not eventually spread by word of mouth among the members of the tribe, and no more so than in a cop saloon where the tongue-looseners were freely flowing.

Luke Martin was not a legendary hero, but his single significant exploit inevitably became known in the Blue Meanie to the point where it even got him a free beer or a shot of bar whiskey to brag about it once in a while for, after all, the notion of a handful of cops intimidating a swampfull of Alligator gangs with sheer display of police firepower went down more smoothly in such environs than most of the firewater the bartenders were pouring.

Perhaps it was inevitable destiny that he would meet up with, and hook up with, and eventually marry Luella Johnson. Or perhaps her daddy had set it up. Or perhaps she had caused her daddy to set it up. Or perhaps all of the above. In the months and years that followed, she would never give him a straight answer, nor would Sergeant Bruce Johnson or the rest of the extended Johnson clan, and it would always remain a subject of good-natured family dispute.

Luke was standing in the crowd by the bar on a Saturday

night when he first caught sight of her, making her entrance not quite on the arm of a balding paunchy gray-haired old dude dressed as a sergeant.

"Who dat?" he inquired of the barfly on his right.

"That there fox is *Luella Johnson*," he was told in a tone of voice that in effect added, *a belle of this here barroom, you mean you don't know?*

Maybe half a head shorter than Luke was, hard to tell because she was wearing alligator-skin cowboy boots. Short-sleeved and reasonably tight-fitting forest green pantsuit like something Jane would dish herself out in on a dinner date with Tarzan. One modest gold chain necklace. Matching earrings. Dark brown skin almost black, but sharply quadroon Creole features. Black hair in loosely afro curls. No makeup. Emerald green eyes scanning the room like laser gunsights. Maybe twenty-five. Struttin' into the Blue Meanie like she sure was sure of herself.

"Who dat with her, looks old enough to be her daddy?"

"*Is* her daddy . . ."

"Sergeant Bruce Johnson," added the guy on the left, and between them, they gave Luke the briefing.

The Johnsons were sort of fading police aristocracy, cops at least three or four generations back. Bruce Johnson's father had gotten as far as captain, *his* daddy had made lieutenant, and there were a scattering of lieutenants back a few generations on her mama's side too, and more cops and occasional sergeants and lieutenants back there in the pedigree than Luke's two informants had ever kept track of.

"Don't know him personal-like, but the story you hear is that ol' Bruce coulda been a lieutenant at the least, but for some crazy reason he *likes* stayin' a sergeant—"

"Probably take the promotion for the pension boost just before he retires, no one's *that* crazy, hah, hah, hah—"

"That sweet thang's his oldest daughter, got another one almost as tasty-lookin' but not yet even sweet fifteen yet . . ."

"And they *Catholics* too."

"Meanin' what?"

"Meanin' don't let your pecker get its hopes up too hard, Luke."

Whether or not it was Luke's horny imagination that Luella Johnson was running her laser-sight eyes over him from time to time that night, he was certainly tracking her, but Daddy seemed to be holding her close, and even if he wasn't, Luke had no idea of a workable pickup line, and so they didn't actually meet until two weeks later.

And it was Sergeant Johnson who made the intros.

He and his daughter were already seated at a table when Luke entered the saloon and Luke was on his way to standing room at the bar when Johnson rose and made his way across the room to intercept his trajectory.

"You already know who I am, son, and I already know who you are, so let's forget about that all, an' let me buy you the first round, 'cause my daughter been noticing you, and I been noticing you noticing her, an' she wants to be introduced proper-like, and I ain't got no objections."

And so saying, he ushered Luke to their table, ordered three Abita beers, and performed the informal formalities. "Luella, this here is Patrolman Luke Martin, Mr. Alligator Swamp Police, as if you didn't know, an' Luke, this here is my daughter Luella, as if we ain't both caught you lookin'."

Luke would've been caught blushing had he been white although the color of his face did not conceal his tongue-tied embarrassment. But Luella Johnson just laughed and deflected it to her papa.

"That's my daddy, Luke, politically correct he's not, silver-tongued neither, which is why he's still a sergeant."

"*Cotton-mouthed neither*," Bruce Johnson corrected, "an' no desire to have to be, which is why I'm still a sergeant *by choice*."

"Daddy's a proud card-carrying member of the police proletariat, Luke, no department politics for him, unlike *his* daddy, but don't believe all his aw-shucks shit-kickin', he's—"

"A proud card-carrying member of the police *union,* son. You been to a meeting yet?"

"Uh . . . no. . . ."

"Be happy to introduce you—"

"Daddy's a shop steward—"

"Shop steward *retired*—"

Luke had the feeling that this all was some kind of doin' the family insider dozens, but what it all meant was beyond him, and he had no idea how to respond in a manner that would score him points where he wanted to score them, namely with Luella.

"Uh, you employed, Miz Johnson?" he said lamely, realizing how lame his words sounded even as they emerged from his mouth. "I mean—"

But Luella Johnson favored him with another of her good-natured rescuing laughs. "Call me *Luella,*" she told him, "Miz Johnson is what the kids have to call me, an' you don't."

"You've got kids? You're married? I mean—"

Another of those Luella Johnson laughs. "I *know* what you mean. No, I'm not married, but I've got about thirty kids at last count—"

"Huh?"

Another gentle laugh at his expense. "I'm a schoolteacher."

"Uh, what do you teach?"

"Third grade. And don't say it."

"Say what?"

"Funny you don't look like a third-grade schoolteacher.

And funny, too, Luke Martin, you don't look like an Alligator up from the Swamp."

Luke managed to laugh with her and her daddy at that, but just barely.

And so it went, namely nowhere really seriously the first time, or the second, or the third, always in the Blue Meanie, and always under the eyes of Daddy Johnson, both of them seeming to be leisurely checking Luke out, and in the process seeming to be briefing Luke on the Johnson family story, Luella's place in it according to Sergeant Johnson, the place *she* wanted to have in it, which was not entirely the same thing, and conceivably how he just might figure into it if he passed muster.

The Johnsons were a police family about as far back as such memory could go, which was even before the family name got anglicized from Jareau for vaguely practical reasons soon after the Louisiana Purchase, black Creoles from the very beginnings of New Orleans, meaning so-called free people of color, who had never been slaves even when Louisiana was part of the Confederacy, with some Irish blood in there somewhere, who had gravitated to the New Orleans police force about as soon as there was a police force to gravitate to.

And "the Johnson police family" was not just Johnsons— that was the patrilineal line from way back when, but Johnson men had married into other such police families, and their women had married into the Johnsons, and though it was only backhandedly acknowledged, there was a bit of more recent white blood here and there in the crossbreeding.

All this seemed to matter a great deal to Luella Johnson though not nearly as much to her father, apparently a bone of genteel contention between them, and while all this family police department ancestry seemed a tad ridiculous to a born and bred Swamp Alligator and more than a little pretentious,

Luke could sort of grasp how it might be playing out by translating it to himself in gangbanger terms.

After all, wasn't he the one who had made what mark he had by translating the Experimental Community Outreach Unit into the Alligator Swamp Police?

Think of the Johnsons as a gang with long-standing clout within the larger tribe that was the New Orleans Police Department, what with all those lieutenants and captains givin' 'em bragging rights, and Luella a princess of the main line of the Johnson gang.

Except that *Bruce* Johnson wasn't at all interested in playing that game, and Luke could see why, 'cause both of them saw it as pretentious bullshit and to Luella's daddy as sort of treason to his beat cop homies. Luella's daddy was happy having risen to sergeant, which was about as far as a good true-blue cop could go without involving himself in department politics and worse still the greasy business and paper-bag passing and counting that went with it.

To use a fancy word that Luke had acquired from Luella but still felt queasy about the concept let alone saying it out loud, Bruce Johnson was an *idealist,* which as near as Luke could tell, was someone who upon occasion acted against his own selfish interests because . . . because . . . well, because he believed it was right according to some elusive "higher standard" Luella called "morality."

But Luella seemed to have a less simple attitude toward her father's idealism, admiring it as a personal trait, but not at all pleased that it had prevented him from rising further in the police gang pecker order and therefore herself as the daughter of a captain or at least a lieutenant.

What Luke Martin thought about this silly brand of bullshit, namely that it *was* silly bullshit, was not really the point as far as he was concerned, unconcerned as he was with becoming an "idealist" following a gang code that called itself "morality."

The point as far as he was concerned, was how to slide himself into it. Because Luella Johnson had become someone he definitely wanted to slide himself into in definitely self-interested terms.

Finally Daddy Johnson allowed his darling daughter to enter the Blue Meanie all by her lonesome. But not for long: she made it quickly clear to Luke that having finally gained sufficient approval as a "cop and more or less a gentleman," it was for the purpose of allowing the two of them to arrange to "date."

Luke had some idea of what that was supposed to mean, but little notion of how to go about it, his experience with the ladies having been confined to banging hookers, screwing drunken cop groupies, and the occasional one-night hookups that began in the bar and ended in bed with nothing of significance in-between, so that what was supposed to happen in-between was unknown territory.

Luella, however, was apparently experienced in dancing this game and, teacher that she was, provided the necessary instructions. They spent about two months, which began to seem like two years of the blue balls to Luke, eating in restaurants, drinking modestly in jazz bars, walking hand-in-hand in the moonlight along the French Quarter levee, and otherwise enjoying one another's company without it getting any further than a little kissing and cuddling, with him escorting her home to the family house and returning alone to his own digs afterward, more and more frustrated.

Finally he had had enough, and after an Oysters Bienville and crawfish etoufée dinner washed down with a bottle of white wine and an uncharacteristic couple rounds of margaritas afterward, he was sufficiently lubricated to judge that she was too and summoned up the courage to ease into it in what he was sufficiently lubricated to believe was a "genteel" manner.

"What we doin', Luella?" he more or less demanded.

"What you mean, Luke?"

"You know what I mean."

She favored him with one of those laughs that could disarm a meth-head serial killer with a hard-on. "We are doin' what my daddy would say is *courting*."

"Courting? I don't see no judge hangin' 'round."

"But he's there."

"What do you mean by *that,* Luella?"

"You know what I mean, Luke."

Well, Luke grudgingly supposed he more or less did, having seen birds in the swamp dancing around each other like this before getting down to business, and even the nutria had a few little moves before banging like bunnies. But he was no swamp bird or rat—well, not exactly anymore—and had no time-tested move to proceed from the mating dance to the main event.

"Well, yeah, maybe, like your daddy's watching over your shoulder when he's not even around, Catholic thing or something like that, ain't it, but don't you think it's time for, uh . . . the . . . uh the ah . . ."

"I know what you mean, Luke."

"Well?"

A sly little laugh, a tilt of the head, a teasing tone of voice. "Well, I thought you'd never ask."

"No, you didn't."

And they laughed together, paid the tab, and caught a cab to Luke's apartment. A pigpen it wasn't: Luke didn't eat there much and when he did it was mostly microwave and Mr. Coffee so there was no pile of dirty dishes in the sink, and he kept the place reasonably clean. The bedroom was just that, a room with a bed in it and not much else, unmade but with reasonably clean sheets, a bedside lamp on a table with a dimmer, and no evidence of prior female company.

But for some reason Luella seemed nervous and spooked, not at all her usual style, glancing around at him, the bed, the toilet door. "Uh . . . I have to powder my nose. . . ."

"Sorry, but I got no coke, hah, hah, hah."

The little joke seemed to go over like a fart in a barroom. She spun on her heels, opened the toilet door, dashed inside, and closed it behind her, leaving Luke befuddled as to what had suddenly gone wrong.

Probably just had to take a piss real bad, yeah, that's gotta be it, he told himself, so while she was at it, which began to seem longer than it should be, he undressed, lay back on the bed, and slipped a condom on to his all-too-ready cock like a cop and a gentleman.

When she finally emerged, it seemed she was as ripe and ready as he was since she made her entrance into the bedroom entirely and enticingly naked, and looking even better with her clothes off, which was saying something, Luella being such a sharp and shapely dresser.

But there was something strangely different about her—the confident wiseass sophisticate Luella in control of whatever situation just wasn't there. She stood before the bed, nibbling at her lower lip and staring at his well-packaged pecker as if he had pulled his pistol on her or something.

"What's the matter, Luella?"

"Nothing's the matter," she told him unconvincingly.

"Well then . . ." he crooned, slapping the bed beside him invitingly.

She knelt down on the back end of the bed and crawled hesitantly toward him on her hands and knees. He sat up, took her by the shoulders and, kissing her passionately, pulled her down on top of him, laying back again, and then rolling them over into the customary position.

He nibbled at her titties a bit, kissed her long and deep while massaging her sweet ass, went through it all again several times, without getting much of a response, though it wasn't like she was pushing him away either. So he shrugged to himself, and slipped it in—no problem there, she seemed ready enough.

He went at it long and hard, but pausing when he got to his own edge and pacing himself like a gentleman was supposed to do, waiting for her to catch up. It was hard to tell whether she was or she wasn't—she grunted and came back at him, she moaned and screamed a little, her body started twitching and shaking. Luke had banged enough hos to be familiar with females detached from the fucking in question, but this wasn't like that. She seemed to be trying hard to be there, to finally come and grant him permission to do likewise, but there was something, well, desperate or phony or something else he couldn't understand about it.

But finally she spasmed and screamed loud and collapsed softly beneath him as he allowed himself what by now was more relief than pleasure. He lay there atop her, looking into her eyes and trying to figure out what had been going on behind them. They were shining with contentment, her lips were smiling, and she finally favored him with a long tender kiss, then rolled him off of her, and snuggled up under his shoulder.

All this without a word being spoken.

"Well, at last that's over," she finally told him, but with a happy sigh and a great big smile.

"Well, you're glad that's *over*! What the fuck is that?"

And she laughed that Luella laugh right in his face.

"Don't tell me you haven't guessed."

"Guessed what?"

She slid her hand down his chest, grabbed his dick, and shook it at him.

There was blood on the condom.

"I was a virgin."

7

Mama Legba, the television star, would claim to have been "born on a bayou," why not, the lyrical line rang the musical bell of everyone south of Baton Rouge so it was good for the image, as it had been when she was no more than a street act in the Quarter, and it played even better on the air as the self-styled Voodoo Queen of Louisiana.

And it was technically true. MaryLou Boudreau had been her own self-creation for about as long as she could remember, and she had indeed been born on a bayou in Saint Bernard Parish, or anyway what was left of one, and yes, to a Creole mama and a Cajun papa, and all that jazz, as the official press bio had it. But Mom and Pop hadn't exactly been the offspring of umpteen generations of zydeco musicians keeping the faith in the swampland of beloved folkie lore.

They grew up in bayou country, all right, but as children of a skanky hippie commune inhabited by the addled descendents of the debris of the '60s Summer of Love, growing bad grass and stunted vegetables, collecting food stamps, and whatever else they could scam out of whatever governments, while being stoned to the gills twenty-four seven.

Mom and Pop escaped to the Big Easy soon after MaryLou

was born to a lowlife highlife in the Quarter: bartending, waitressing, singing badly and playing banjo and guitar worse for street change around Jackson Square so they could keep telling themselves they were in show business, dealing a little this and that on the side maybe. MaryLou Boudreau didn't ask and they didn't tell.

They had made her a part of the act once she was old enough to walk and pass a hat, cheaper than hiring a monkey, and cuter anyway. But such innocent cuteness couldn't last forever, and certainly not past grade school, and seeing as how she had trouble carrying a tune and couldn't learn to play a musical instrument beyond the kazoo, in order to emulate her parents and kid herself that she was also in show business, her contribution to the family act consisted of dressing as tightly and skimpily as the loosely enforced law would allow to display her ripening nubility, dance rather clumsily to the music, and pass the hat beneath her wriggling pootie.

After high school she found that any kind of job beyond occasional waitressing or bartending was no more available than it had been for Mom and Pop. She couldn't even dance well enough to land gigs stripping in any but the lowest dive, and even if she were willing to descend to hooking, which she wasn't, even there the competition would be stiff.

So it was a life of waitressing and bartending—and when things got bad, even occasional dishwashing—and the family act around Jefferson Square when the evenings were free from employment, which was more often than not, and more often than not doin' their stuff in weekend Secondary Parades when the weather was good and one was to be found.

Inspired by Mardi Gras, these Secondary Parades were put on all year round except in the Hurricane Season by neighborhood associations or sports fans or whatever else felt like dancing through the streets for the fun of it. People paraded in homemade costumes and sometimes there were silly home-made floats, more often not, but there were always bands hopefully auditioning for paying gigs, and assorted street acts such as the Boudreaus hoping at least to gain enough buzz to enhance their take as street acts around the Quarter.

There were even a few so-called Secondary Parade Queens who aspired to and sometimes even occasionally gained places on actual Mardi Gras Krewe floats, and while MaryLou had not even risen that far, it was the next step up the only ladder available to her.

In the pursuit of which she created a character for herself for the parades and the performances around Jackson Square and other French Quarter venues: MarieLou Laveau.

Although she knew little about voodoo except that there had been several voodoo priestesses who had called them-selves "Marie Laveau," or a singular Marie Laveau who had been reincarnated several times if you wanted to believe such stuff, "MaryLou Laveau" sounded pretty much like Marie Laveau if you slurred it enough.

And if you danced around in a black bikini sprinkled with stardust sequins, an open diaphanous black lace cloak done up likewise, and a fake gold crown, you could at least become known around the Quarter as a street character who called herself "MaryLou Laveau," even though no one really believed you were the latest reincarnation of the fabled Voodoo Queen of New Orleans.

"MaryLou Laveau the Voodoo Queen" might be a semi-comic character but she was generally received good-naturedly since she didn't go so far as to take herself seriously, and at least it was an identity and a modest measure of very local fame.

MaryLou had partaken of the herb in the spaghetti sauce or brownies, the occasional mushroom in the tea on special occasions, for as long as she could remember—didn't every mama's child and wasn't it always around the house?— though being righteously anti-tobacco her parents wouldn't let her actually *smoke* anything, so even as an adult, she didn't favor hash pipes or blunts or joints.

But one magic evening, the three of them ventured to Jackson Square to do the act, which as usual was drawing more mosquitoes than coins tossed in the hat, when a tottery and feeble old black man in threadbare tails and a comic opera top hat stopped for a moment to listen.

A patheticoid old rummy in top hat and tails wasn't exactly outré in these environs, and of course he would be carrying an ivory-headed cane, though the dreadlocks didn't exactly match the rest of the costume. What he was smoking looked like a fancy cigar, but the smoke smelled more like the herb.

He took a deep drag on his spliff, if that was really what it was, meeting her eyes with a rheumy and bloodshot glance as he did, and completely *changed* on the exhale.

His posture was abruptly transformed from that of a feeble old drunk into that of a lithely upright ballet dancer, and those eyes lit up like icy green lasers boring into her soul with irresistible power and terrifying precision.

"You and me are gonna be like husband and wife," he told her. "Erzuli wants a ticket to ride, and the horse she's betting on is gonna be you. You're gonna be a one-trick pony, chile, but it's gonna be the best trick there is."

MaryLou found herself opening her mouth to receive the cigar or spliff or whatever it was between her lips, and taking a long drag and—

—and the next thing she knew was the fading memory of having been dancing like a fiend on fire, with Mom banging out the same intoxicating drumbeat on a garbage can as Pop was on the body of his banjo, as the crowd around them was doing with their feet on the pavement, with the rhythmic clapping of their hands.

How long had she been there, how long had she been dancing like that? No way of telling, she hadn't exactly been there, wherever *there* was, she had never danced like that before or even imagined it, and *she* hadn't exactly been dancing; something or someone else had been *dancing her body* like a hand up a puppet.

But now it was gone, it was over, her knees were rubber, her lungs were panting, and Pop had to catch her in the act of falling down in total exhaustion.

The old man in top and tails was still there, but what he had become with a deep breath of whatever he had been smoking was gone with the wind, and he looked as dumbfounded and poleaxed as MaryLou felt as he turned and staggered away through the crowd.

There *was* a crowd, by far the biggest one the act had ever drawn, and the hat was fuller than it had ever been before, and for the first time ever, there were more bills than coins. And maybe a dozen of the audience were crossing themselves as they slunk away as if they had been caught watching a fuck video while a dozen more smiled knowing smiles and exited with little phantom bows, whatever all that meant.

MaryLou might not know what it meant, but Pop thought he did. "Voodoo," he told Mom on the way out of Jackson Square. "Some loa was riding her—"

"You believe in that stuff?"

"Does it matter? Half this city does, and that's what the act looked like and that's good enough."

"Good enough for what?"

"Good enough for this!" Pop declared, shaking the hat stuffed with money and shoving it under Mom's nose.

"But how did it happen?" Mom's hungry eyes became more

suspiciously guarded. "And why? They say those loas have their own reasons."

"Doesn't matter. What matters is figurin' out how to make it keep happening."

They tried their best. The magical performance proved to be repeatable once in a while and enhanced proceeds but it was hit and mostly miss. Mr. Top Hat and Tails never showed up again, a drag on a spliff or a puff on a cigar didn't necessarily call anything forth. It happened or it didn't. Whatever it was took charge when it felt like it and had a mind of its own.

All MaryLou could remember was what Mr. Top Hat and Tails had been wearing, so she googled that. It wasn't easy or exactly definitive, but what the old drunk had been wearing seemed to look like the Mardi Gras costume of a voodoo spirit, a demon, who called himself Papa Legba, a sort of ringmaster of the supernatural loa krewe, a gatekeeper or doorman at the velvet rope to their magical realm.

And that clue to the *who* keyed her memory of the *what* he had said before she had blacked out, and therefore the who or what that had taken over.

"Erzuli wants a ticket to ride and the horse she's betting on is gonna be you. You're gonna be a one-trick pony but it's gonna be the best trick there is."

Now she had the name of who supposedly danced her body around when she felt like it, so she googled "Erzuli," and learned that Erzuli was the most powerful female spirit in the pantheon of voodoo loas, powerful enough to have Papa Legba himself by the balls when she wanted to, the power of the female spirit itself—muse and seductress, nurturing and ambitious, earth mother and vamp, loved and admired, but too complex and capricious to be entirely trusted.

Did MaryLou believe in this voodoo stuff? Mom and Pop professed to believe in it and encouraged her to do likewise, since when it happened it was great for business and when it didn't the act stunk as usual. And something *did* take her body over from time to time, something that gave her dancing powers that she never remembered having, something that would seem to be having a high old time at her conscious expense.

So she googled "Voodoo" and "Vudu" and "Voudon," for there were many ways of spelling it, and more versions of what it was supposed to be about than you could read in a lifetime, and more disagreement on the details of the loa krewe than that. But she was able to boil it all down into what seemed to be agreed on, the Voodoo for Dummies version.

Voodoo was an ancient religion brought over by slaves from Africa. Nothing to do with Jesus or Mohammed or Moses and their singular honkie God. Spirits, whole carload lots of them, with powers of this or that, and it could get pretty specific, and they didn't care about sin all that much, in fact they mostly like to boogie, and if you did the ceremonies right and were lucky, you might be able to ask for their assistance and get it, though maybe not always exactly as you had intended.

So she bought her way into a voodoo act in a fancy back alley cellar off Bourbon Street that tourists could pay to get into as spectators but whose cast might just have been the real thing.

They cut the head off a chicken and let it run around headless and spread the blood around with a whisk. They spit rum on a fire, they beat on drums and then they danced to it, and a few of them commenced to twitch and jerk, to roll their eyes back into their heads.

But none of it summoned forth Erzuli as far as MaryLou was concerned. Seemed like she needed to connect up with the real deal to find out if there really *was* a real deal, and if so, what to do about it.

Having a rep around the Square and the Quarter as "Mary-Lou Laveau" the street character "Voodoo Queen" got her into any number of phony conversations with phonies, but wasn't any help in tracking down a serious not-for-tourists voodoo ceremony, and while actually dancing while possessed from unpredictable time to time might fill the hat and even get her a second identity as "White Girl Who Dances With Loas," getting to be allowed to *actively participate* in a serious voodoo ritual was not so easy for a white girl, chosen as a horse by a loa from time to time or not.

But all kinds of people *did* bear witness to these possessions, so the word *did* get around, so getting it around to someone who took them seriously and might be sympathetic to a White Girl Who Dances With Loas and was a *who* who mattered was the luck of the dice.

Well, roll the bones often enough long enough, and sooner or later they come up seven instead of snake eyes, and the time finally came when MaryLou came down from where she could never remember not being with a middle-aged black woman in a kind of white robe cinched at her ample waist and a candy-striped kerchief artfully wrapped around her head like a turban studying her speculatively or knowingly or maybe both.

"Who's the loa been riding you, White Girl Dances With Loas?"

"I believe it's Erzuli—"

"What gives you the right to believe that?"

"Well, uh, Papa Legba told me that—"

The woman in the white robe rolled her eyes and shook her head, and managed to do both sarcastically. *"Papa Legba told you, did he?"*

"Well I googled her, but—"

"You googled her, did you?"

"I mean, I never exactly met her, but—"

"Of course you ain't, riders don't go around swappin' idle chitchat with their horses! Who you think you are, girl?"

"Well, uh, maybe that's what I'm trying to find out, I mean—"

"I know what you mean, White Girl Dances With Loas, and maybe we all might like to find out what they up to if we can," the woman in the white robe said, handing her some kind of business card. "Tomorrow at midnight, I'd tell you don't be late, but this is New Orleans, so don't be too early."

"Where N. Villiere crosses Congress" was all MaryLou saw written on it when she looked down, and the woman was gone when she looked up.

When she got there at more or less the appointed hour by electro-rickshaw, N. Villiere crossed Congress in a neighborhood that was not quite ominous at midnight, but not someplace where it seemed prudent for a white girl or any girl to hang around looking lost for very long. Rickety shotgun houses and bungalows and suchlike up on stilts, earthen sidewalks that had long given up on post–Hurricane Season repaving, working streetlights and lights in the windows, but nobody on the streets.

Fortunately, or more likely by design, a middle-aged black man in clean blue jeans and a Saints T-shirt emerged from an alley and beckoned. "This way, White Girl Dances With Loas," he said to reassure her when MaryLou hesitated, and she followed him up the alley into what had no doubt once been a garage.

No cars, of course, about a dozen people, all of them black, standing around, none of them under forty to look at them, all of them plainly dressed as if for a day of hand labor, except for the woman in white. Strange African-looking masks, Indonesian shadow puppets, colorful flags of unknown and

maybe nonexistent countries on the gray walls. A round barbecue grill turned into a brazier with a wood fire flaming in
it. Something that looked like a homemade Hindu altar to
something that looked vaguely like a cross between Shiva and
a vampire Buddha.

Three guys squatting on the floor, in fact an act she had seen
around Jackson Square, an African bass drum, ancient hippie
bongos, and a nameless instrument that was a vacuum cleaner
hose you whirled around while playing the thing with a saxo-
phone mouthpiece.

Everyone stared at her but nobody said anything.

The woman in white threw a big handful of herbs mixed
with incense on the fire, and billows of white smoke smelled like
a mix of pot, jasmine, and patchouli perfumed the room. The
band began to play, a heavy regular beat on the big drum,
something strange at nearly tap-dancing speed on the bongos,
something even stranger coming out of the whirling vacuum
cleaner hose as if a jazz sax were being played through an Aus-
sie didgeridoo, which in fact it more or less was.

A bottle of rum was passed around, just enough for everyone to have a single swallow, including MaryLou. Cheap cigars were passed around, not everyone took one, and MaryLou
passed.

People started dancing. No one danced with anyone, free-
form old hippie style and nothing particularly special about
it, and after hesitating for a bit, MaryLou joined in. The woman
in white finished the rum and spat a mouthful into the fire.

The bongo beat quickened, the dancing got somewhat frenzied, but nothing more than what you'd see in a crowded
Bourbon Street disco. A few eyes began to roll. The bass drum
became insistent and dominant.

The bongo beat faded into the background. The whirling
sax-hose became a deep bone-tingling mantric hum. More

eyes began to roll. A few of the dancers began to groan, and moan, and twitch.

Someone produced a chicken from somewhere and slit its throat before the altar, showering it with blood, and the chicken ran around for a few bars as the music got louder and louder, as three or four of the dancers went into full spastic like the chicken, shouting and hollering in what might have been speaking in tongues.

MaryLou felt herself swept up in it, but there was nothing supernatural about it, the only difference between this and the family act during the usual performance was that what would have been the skeptical audience was dancing with her, and she was sure nobody was going to pass the hat.

A gray-haired man who must have been in his sixties jerked and twitched up to her with his eyes rolled back in their sockets and the whites showing, waving a lit cigar. He took a big puff, maybe even a lungful drag, and blew a huge cloud of smoke in MaryLou's face. As he did, the eyes rolled back to where they belonged, but were red and glowing as they stared right through her from—

—the next thing MaryLou knew, she was lying on her back on the dirty concrete floor, panting to catch her breath, her legs achingly sore, her face dripping sweat, and a circle of people staring down at her with little knowing smiles and looks of dreamy satisfaction. Or maybe stupefaction. Or maybe both.

The woman in white glided through the circle, reached down, and helped MaryLou to her feet. "Well?" MaryLou demanded in a hoarsely breathless whisper.

"Well, White Girl Who Dances With Loas got a new name for herself. You her horse, all right . . . White Girl Who Dances With Erzuli."

That was the exit line, but after that, MaryLou became an

occasional participant and she was ridden by Erzuli maybe half the time. But no one except the woman in white would deign to tell her anything of significance—it seemed partly a race thing, and maybe envy too.

But from her, over time, MaryLou got a little beyond the short course in voodoo. Yes, brought from Africa, come to America, along with the slave trade, settled in New Orleans and vicinity for reasons no one human knows, and seems like the loas maybe don't know either.

What *are* the loas?

Spirits, you might call them, spirits with powers or the spir its *of* powers, not demons or angels, nothing to do with something called Satan, not the sons and daughters of some singular honkie God, not exactly gods themselves, not like in the super-hero films, don't look like anything, 'cause they ain't got no bodies. Whole boatloads of 'em, somewhere which is nowhere, with all sorts of powers, they don't care about sin, they ain't good or bad 'cause they don't even understand what that is 'cause they ain't got no morality neither.

What do they want from us?

Same sort of thing we want from them. We don't have their powers so we want them to use them for all sorts of our own purposes. They don't have bodies, and they like to boogie in the flesh, so they borrow ours. Sometimes you might get a favor if you asked for it, but it might not be exactly what you wanted, they got what some folks might call wicked senses of humor.

How can you . . . summon . . . invite . . . ?

You can't, White Girl Who Dances With Erzuli. You the horse, she's the rider. A loa don't ask, and you can't tell.

Well, how can I . . . talk to her . . . ?

Well, sometimes a loa might ride a horse to use his or her lips to speak to a human, but they talk first and you usually just listen.

I mean, while she's . . . riding me . . . so I can tell her I want to experience what's happening.

You can't, chile, nobody can. It just don't work that way.

Why not?

Because they rule what they want to and that's the way they want it.

This was not sufficient for a street dancer who needed to tell Erzuli to show up for performances when called upon and allow her her own awareness when being ridden. MaryLou was far from being satisfied being ridden by Erzuli; she wanted to *be* Erzuli—what red-blooded American girl wouldn't, or at least be there *with* Erzuli to enjoy the experience and the memories.

She went to more and more ceremonies. She even tried Santeria a few times but that didn't work either. Erzuli rode her when she felt like it, and that was it, tough tittie, White Girl Who Dances With Me.

The quest got really obsessional and her parents were of mixed mind about it. Pop wanted her to give it up, it wasn't improving the act any further, and it was in danger of driving his daughter crazy. But Mom, being a mama, had a less jaundiced attitude to her daughter's determination to strike some sort of karmic deal with Erzuli, and it was she who suggested the acid.

"Time to give white man's medicine a try, MaryLou. Turn on, tune out, drop in."

So MaryLou dropped 500 mikes half an hour or so before entering the garage for her next attempted séance with the loa, timing it so that she would peak if and when Erzuli chose to ride her.

By now, MaryLou was familiar with the ritual, the drums, the rum, the incense on the fire, the garage filling with the sweetly pungent smoke, the sacrifice of the chicken, the sprinkling of the blood, the beginning of the dance, the rolling back of eyes, the twitching and jerking.

But on acid it was the same on one level, but quite different on another. The clouds of incense pulsed to the beating heart rhythm of the bass drum, strobed up and down a rainbow spectrum of colors to the flicker-flacker of the bongos, and the whirring mantric drone of the sax-hose entered her, whirling and swirling her around as she began to dance, and MaryLou began to lose contact with the borders of her body, if loss it was, or rather the gaining of their opening up, opening out, opening wide, to a space that was not a space—

—to a here that was not exactly here nor there, and she was dancing in it, dancing through it, it was dancing through her, there was something inside of her like a second set of bones, like her nervous system gone neon electric with a will of its own. . . .

And she sensed that *this* was somehow Erzuli, and then she was sure it was, because there was a part of MaryLou that remained in her body this time, that could feel that body dancing like a demon on the floor, dancing as she had never experienced dancing before. . . .

Who dat come knock-knock-knocking on my heaven's door supposed to be a horse and nothing more? said a voice in her head. Only it wasn't exactly a voice and where it came from wasn't exactly inside her head, more like an invisible childhood companion talking into her thoughts.

So MaryLou talked back in the same manner as any human chile, any conscious manifestation of whatever might be behind the masks of the dance, might converse with what was now dancing unmasked with and within her.

About time, the horse told her rider. *About time you let me be here now. You and me gotta have a little girl-to-girl talk.*

Let you? What makes you think I'm letting you do anything,

White Girl Who Eruzli Chooses For The Dance? I can choose who I dance through where and when, hon', but this is the first time a horse ever talked back to her rider. We got the power over most everything that's not what y'all call matter or maya or atomic particles or whatever, but we ain't got no bodies, we ain't made of matter, so we ain't got no power over matter, we can't even touch it, 'cause we got nothin' t'touch it with. We wanna dance, we gotta do it through you, hey girl, we want to fuck, we want to come, we want to get stoned, we need your flesh to do it through. So what's happening now is human magic, not ours. And we been waiting for you to work it for a long, long time.*

You have?

Oh yeah, hon', we been waiting for a Talking Horse like y'all been waiting for the return of Jesus or Elvis, so's we can save our mutual asses material and otherwise. We're not where y'all would call anywhere, but let's just say we're connected to New Orleans and environs because we love it like maybe you would say this would be our homeland in America if a homeland we could have, an' you people here are our chosen horses, in case you haven't noticed.

I don't understand. MaryLou tried to think back, but she didn't, because she did. She understood that these loas were souls without bodies, consciousnesses floating in the quantum flux, avatars of the Atman, as zombies or most fictional versions of the Living Dead were bodies without souls. Whether that would make sense to Albert Einstein and the Pope or not, it was a no-brainer in her current state of consciousness.

An' I'm sure y'all have noticed you have royally screwed up the matter of our mutual homeland, and it ain't gonna be happy days for us either if you don't get your material shit together before there's nothing left of Louisiana but Alligator Swamp and rednecks. We do have good taste in pickin' our horses, as it now no doubt pleases you to believe. So me and Papa Legba, or just me, between you and me, girl, we ain't a democracy, and I'd have him by the balls if he had them any time I wanted, decided to lead us loas out of the closet to get you horses some horse sense so's y'all can handle the material end of the bargain better than you been doing.

What bargain? MaryLou demanded. *You do whatever you want to do with us, and we don't even get to enjoy being there! What kind of a bargain is that?*

Well, you got a point there, hon' and we been waiting quite a while for human material magic to deliver us a talking horse we can make a deal with. Because we need a willing horse we can talk to who knows more about where we wanna ride in your material world than we do, and this is gonna be a bargain you gonna love too much to refuse—

I'll be the judge of that, thank you very much, and before you go any further, your end of the deal has to at least be that I'm there with you when you ride me or else—

Or else what?

Or else there's no deal, Erzuli. You just told me you need a willing horse to get where you want to ride, now didn't you?

Well, I gotta admit you got me there, hon'—

And if you get to call me up when you need to ride, I get to to call you up when I need you, that's only just—

Don't push your luck too far, girl, I don't know what this just might mean, and I don't really want to—

That's a deal-breaker, MaryLou told the loa. After all, wasn't that what she had been after in the first place?

Well. . . .

Well, what?

Well, bargaining with each other to get what we want is something we all have to do all too often, material girls or not. . . . So . . .

So?

So the deal is you can call, but whether we come when you do is our choice each time.

Not good enough.

That's our deal-breaker, girl. . . .

Well . . . I guess I could live with that, Erzuli, but then, I've got to agree to let you when you want to ride too.

"No way, White Girl Who Erzuli Chooses To Ride, your cowboys don't take that from their horseflesh, and we ain't never gonna take it from you!

Well, then, I don't know—

You haven't even asked where we're gonna be goin', hon', which is why we need you to make this deal, and which is why you're gonna love it too much to be able to turn it down.

And why are you so sure of that?

Because where we're goin' is where any girl who finds herself stuck dancing around Jackson Square for spare change wants to be more than anyplace else in her material world, where what is matter and what is not ride to into the bright lights of show business, hon', Erzuli told her.

Say what?

That's where we're goin', MaryLou Boudreau Who's Gonna Become Mama Legba. That's where we're gonna ride together, girl, think you can say no to that? We all are gonna be stars, sister! We are gonna be on television! Think just might even sell what you might call your soul for that?

8

After a couple of months or so of "courting," which consisted of "dating" without overnighters, during which the sex got progressively better for the otherwise sophisticated ex-virgin who took to avid study of the Kama Sutra and the ex–Swamp Alligator whose previous concept of sexual sophistication was paying a mediocre hooker for a blow job, Luke and Luella proceeded to "engagement."

Since Luke had no family he cared to speak to, this became a Johnson family affair. "A family affair" was something Luke Martin had never experienced, let alone the gang rules of Catholic New Orleans cops.

He was required to invest a month's wages in a diamond "engagement ring," with the understanding that Sergeant Daddy would spring for the wedding band. There would be a church wedding. The children would be raised as Catholics.

That was the Catholic of it, expensive, pointless as far as Luke was concerned, but otherwise no problem, especially since Sergeant Daddy assured him that the couple would make out like bandits on the wedding presents.

The cop of it was that while there would be a stuffy banquet in a middling "Creole" restaurant after the ceremony, the real party would take place afterward in the Blue Meanie.

The New Orleans of it was that Luke and Luella could enjoy

all-nighters together before the wedding, preferably in the Johnson house, and though Luke had hardly yet put in enough years to make sergeant, when he had, the skids would be greased as part of the "dowry."

Plus a house to live in.

A family of cops was not likely to have the wherewithal to buy Luke and Luella a house or even front a down payment sufficient to secure a mortgage with monthlies affordable on the salaries of a cop and a schoolteacher. But this was the New Orleans of the Hurricane Seasons, and if the federal subsidy games were not as easy to play as they had been immediately Post-Katrina, this *was* New Orleans, this *was* a family of New Orleans cops, there *was* a sufficiently powerful and more than sufficiently economically streetwise union, Luke was a member, and Bruce Johnson would remain a union poobah even after his retirement.

There were several species of federal down payment subsidies for "distressed areas of New Orleans," and any number of ways to manipulate the paperwork known to the union legal eagles by which to expand the definition of "distressed area" to include a two-bedroom shotgun house in good repair and high up enough on piles to park a car under, or a boat if worse came to worse, well away from the lowlands and low-life of the Alligator Swamp, not really that far east of Esplanade, well north of Claiborne, and nowhere near what had once been the Industrial Canal. Whaddya say, Officer Martin, we got a deal?

The deal worked backward from the monthly payments that a cop and a teacher could afford to a $170,000 fixed rate fifteen-year mortgage with $25,000 down courtesy of Uncle Sap in Washington.

And so it came to pass in the days before the Great Deflation. Things got a little dicey when Luella got pregnant with little Bruce and had to take a leave of half-pay absence, and kind of tight when they told her her job had been axed in the usual general belt-tightening for whatever didn't fatten the belt-sizes of the politicians and she couldn't get it back.

But hey, being a housewife with one kid twenty-four seven wasn't that different from being a schoolteacher with thirty of them thirty-five hours a week if you looked at the math right, and the just-retired but still well-connected Bruce Johnson was promising Luke that promotion to sergeant and the pay raise that came with it real soon. They could make it through.

Then the shit hit the fan. It hit a lot of people's fans.

All too soon enough it was being called the Great Deflation.

No one would admit to knowing what had really happened because it was angrily assumed that only those who had made their usual trillions off this latest disaster for the American would-be middle class really knew how it had been done. Therefore since only those in on it knew what the full truth really was, anyone who opened their mouths too wide would be lynched by popular demand of all races, creeds, genders, and religions.

About all that Luke knew for sure was that the value of the dollar started to rapidly rise, something that never had happened before. This was greeted with all-around hurrahs for anyone like the Martins living on a fixed income, for of course, that meant that the prices of things went down while Luke's salary was fixed by union contract.

But neither the city government nor those in Baton Rouge and Washington, stuck with salaries for those they employed denominated in drastically deflated dollars locked in by union contracts, thought it was very funny.

The feds kept dropping the minimum wage in keeping with the fall of the poverty line in superbuck numbers, and as Bruce Johnson explained to Luke when it became the New Orleans

Police Department's inevitable turn, as contracts expired, the unions were in no position to fight the indexing of the salary cuts, since, after all, as long as salaries were not being cut faster than the superbuck was rising, no one's buying power was being reduced.

No one, that is, not holding the bag with a fixed rate mortgage whose numbers had been written in stone in pre-superbuck dollars. No one except millions of suckers nationwide and tens of thousands in New Orleans who now found themselves constrained to eat nothing but hot dogs, po'boys, and red beans and rice like Luke and Luella and Little Bruce in order to keep paying the monthlies.

Not that they were able to fork over the mortgage payments regularly; every other month or so after the warning notices was the best they and folks in the same pickle barrel could manage.

But the banks and secondary and tertiary mortgage-holders were flexible about it at first, since even that was making out like the bandits they were in current superbuck terms, and the only alternative, foreclosing on millions of houses and tanking the real estate market again, would have made the so-called Great Recession way back when seem like the Good Old Days.

Hard times for sure and with no end in sight, but at least it was bare-bones survival, at least the Martin family, like millions of others, wasn't being kicked out into the street.

But they were all dependent on the kindness of strangers. And the strangers in question were the Loan Lizards of Wall Street, never noted for their philanthropic impulses.

And then, for whatever darkly inscrutable reason, they did start foreclosing from shore to shining shore. The victims were in a rage, but what could they do except invent more and more paranoid conspiracy theories?

Well, they *could* hold off contract repo men at gunpoint, they *could* fire in the air over the heads of sheriffs, which they started doing, but such half-assed and solitary armed resistance could only served to get the dirty work turned over to the cops.

So Luke found himself one of the many cops wielding the sharp end of the shitty stick. But the New Orleans Police Association was a hard-ass union, and Big Joe Roody's threat that trying to force its members to evict *each other* would result in a total police strike was taken very seriously in City Hall.

But after a while, there were threats from Baton Rouge to send in the State Police or the National Guard to do it if the New Orleans Police wouldn't, and it seemed like a game of chicken in which everyone would lose big time if the cars collided. So some kind of slimy under-the-table deal was made between City Hall and the union president, which had cops starting to gingerly foreclose on houses owned by other cops serving in far-off precincts so that brothers would hopefully at least never actually have to face each other in the line of duty.

This might stink like rat shit and be a violation of the union rules, but this was New Orleans, and the union realized that the least awful thing to do was see no evil. So Luke could hardly claim that he hadn't expected to be some day served with a final eviction notice by some cop he had never met.

And here it was, the full legal form of his name on a final eviction notice. But he could hardly have imagined that even Sergeant Slaughter would hand it to him and tell him to serve it on himself.

Nor had Larabee himself, it seemed. Even he had limits.

"What the fuck am I supposed to do now?" he moaned. "Pass it on to another precinct? I'd have to go through the lieutenant to do that, and he'd have to go through the captain, and—"

"Shit flows downhill," Luke suggested helpfully.

"So, Martin?"

Luke could only shrug.

But then Sergeant Slaughter's piggy little eyes bugged like a lightbulb went on over his head, and the mofo showed his teeth in an alligator smile.

"Hey, Bruce Johnson's your father-in-law, now isn't he?" he said, sliding the eviction notice into a desk drawer. "He can take this straight to Big Joe Roody, now can't he? So you know what, Martin, I'm gonna do exactly nothing until I hear from the union."

Luke had seen Big Joe in the distance a few times at barbecues and such like, but he had never met Joe Roody, and knew the president of the Police Association of New Orleans only by reputation, which was formidable to the point of legendary.

Roody had been a captain when he was first elected PANO president, and the first thing he had done after taking office was resign as a police officer, so he could "devote his attention full-time to running the union and avoid any conflicts of interest."

This had not been done before, and there had been a certain uproar, but when it became clear a successful police strike later that it meant the union president was now no longer answerable to the department chain of command and the police superintendent as a cop, the cunning wisdom of it became quite apparent.

That was about the time Roody had started to be known as Big Joe, approvingly by the union membership, and not without a certain dread by whoever was police superintendent, as a tough union leader capable of giving him and even the mayor more than enough shit to keep them from giving the same to him, with enough political street smarts and willingness to do whatever deals benefited his membership to keep them from wanting to try.

Bruce Johnson knew Big Joe well enough to get him on the phone in person about five minutes after Luke told his father-in-law the sad and outrageous tale, and later that very afternoon, they were in his office at union headquarters on Esplanade.

By tailor's measurement Big Joe Roody wasn't all that huge, maybe six-four in height, pushing fifty inches across the shoulders, and something beyond forty inches around the waist, and his office was not exactly a broom closet, but somehow Joe Roody made it seem cramped with him in it.

He looked fifty or so, his ambiguously tan head was shaved, his white business shirt was worn tieless with the sleeves rolled up past the elbows to show off impressive arm muscles, his racial pedigree could not be figured as one thing or another from his facial features, and he affected chomping on a cigar he never seemed to light. His voice was a dominating duet of mellow bellow and hard-edge rasp.

He radiated his Big Joeness in a magical manner that instantly convinced Luke that this was a dude you wanted on your side in a back-alley brawl or the political equivalent down there in City Hall.

"Well, Joe, what are we gonna do about it?" Bruce Johnson demanded after about thirty seconds of introductions and not much more wasted in repeating what he had already told Roody on the phone.

"What are *we* gonna do, Bruce? You mean what am *I* gonna do about it, don't you?"

"What's the union gonna do? We both know it's the same thing!"

Big Joe Roody laughed a rumbly belly laugh. "Come on, Bruce, you know I just carry out the will of my membership."

"That and telling them what that is."

"That's called *leadership*," Big Joe growled sarcastically.

"Bottom line, Joe," said Bruce Johnson. "Cut the bullshit, this is serious."

"Oh really? What I'm gonna to about it is call a general membership meeting like a good union leader should do, and put the situation to a democratic vote—"

"Please—"

Big Joe held up a big ham-hand halfway through Bruce Johnson's groan. "—right there in Duncan Plaza in front of City Hall. Every brother who's not on shift, and if you can divide by three, which even the mayor and the police superintendent can probably manage, that means two-thirds of the entire force."

"They're gonna let us do that?" Luke found himself exclaiming.

"Well, kid, I suppose they could order the cops to arrest us for trespassing. . . . Oh, I forgot, *we're* the cops. They might be pea-brained enough down there to order a cop to evict himself, but I know damn well they're not dumb-ass crazy enough to order the entire police force to arrest itself and then sue the city for police brutality."

"What's this meeting supposed to do for Luke?"

"Ask not what the union can do for Luke, Bruce, let me tell you what he's going to do for the union. He's gonna get up there on that big round stage in the middle of Duncan Plaza and tell the brotherhood and the news media just what he told you."

"To do what, Joe?"

"What I've been trying to figure out how to do for a while now." Big Joe Roody's eyes seemed to harden and he waved his cigar around for emphasis. "Which is get a resolution passed that no cop anywhere in New Orleans is to evict another cop from his house anywhere in New Orleans. A resolution with teeth."

"It's already in the latest contract, Joe," Bruce Johnson reminded him.

"Yeah, it's in the contract, but the union's had to look the other way when pressure from City Hall comes down on Superintendent Mulligan to force cops to evict cops in far away precincts when ordered—"

"How can they get away with that?" Luke demanded angrily.

"Because we're *the cops*," Big Joe told him. "People always hate the cops until they need them because all we are otherwise is a pain in their asses, givin' 'em tickets, busting them for dope, or pimping, or their latest armed robbery, what's to like when you meet a cop enforcing the law on *you*? So we never have popular support in this town or anywhere else in the history of the world, the good folk don't have nothing to do with us most of the time, and it's our job to be enemies of everyone else. So we been having to look the other way on some precinct captains following orders from City Hall to evict some cops in other precincts, in return for City Hall keeping the media from goin' on loudly about how many other voters we've really been evicting, which wouldn't exactly smell like political roses. So we've had each other by the testicles."

Big Joe's full lips open in a big sardonic grin. "Until now. Now your son-in-law's sad and funny story's gonna be the wedge I've needed, Bruce."

"To do what?"

"To force those fuckers to make a choice. Luke here stands up there on that stage, wavin' that eviction notice like Neville Chamberlain at Munich as he delivers the punchline."

"Force them to make a choice, Joe? I don't get it."

"Between delivering what the banks and smart money and all are paying them for at the cost of being slaughtered on the air by every comedian in the State of Louisiana and maybe even Mama Legba too and a police strike lettin' the Alligators out of the Swamp, or lettin' the union enforce the letter of the contract forbidding *any* cop to evict *any* brother, and telling the smart-money boys, hey, we're the best government your money can buy, but what can we do, Big Joe Roody's got us by the balls this time, and y'all know for sure that if we don't go along on this one, we ain't going to get reelected to do you any more good later."

"You expect me to get up and make a speech to all those people?" Luke protested, but the words rang kind of false even as they emerged from his mouth.

And he certainly didn't fool Joe Ruddy.

"Spare me the shit-kicker act, Luke," Big Joe told him. "You think I don't know all about the Alligator Swamp Police?"

He beamed at Luke as only he could beam, cocked his head, and winked at him knowingly. "Takes one to know one, kid, you *enjoyed* it then, now didn't you? And you're really gonna enjoy it now."

9

I*t's Mama Legba and her Supernatural Krewe!*"

The announcement was canned and so was the accompanying fanfare, the rented venue for today was a high-school basketball arena still smelling vaguely of sneaker sweat and Lysol, and the stage was a rickety temporary one at mid-court.

The studio audience was no more than a few hundred people, but that didn't matter. What mattered was on the other side of the el cheapo two-camera live hookup, namely the numbers out there in ratings land, on the top local broadcast TV channels in New Orleans, Baton Rouge, and Shreveport, syndicated live on various secondary channels on most cable hookups in Louisiana, and streamed on its own Web site and smartphone apps for devotees in the rest of the universe.

Nor was it exactly "Mama Legba" who pranced up the makeshift stairs up onto the makeshift stage in black jumpsuit spangled with stardust, a long white high-collared cape draped over her shoulders, and an outsized tiara of iridescent green peacock tail feathers crowning her with glory, and brandishing a shotgun mike wrapped in gold foil as a scepter.

At this stage of the show, before Erzuli or any other of the Supernatural Krewe took over, it was just MaryLou Boudreau in a Mama Legba Mardis Gras costume under whiteish face makeup and heavy dark eye shadow to age her a decade or so for the camera.

Some unbooked, uncontrolled, and uncontrollable appearances in minor talk-show audiences by MaryLou ridden by Erzuli or another of the Supernatural Krewe, and they were booking her on the same sort of stuff as an unpaid guest. And then, when Papa Legba demanded just recompense live on the air a few times and finally with Baron Samedi and Ogoun doing guest-star shots to back him up, they started paying.

This had been enough to get her picked up by Harry Klein, then a rather down-at-the-heels agent, but good enough to come up with the format for Mama Legba and Her Supernatural Krewe and sell it to the kind of second-level net and cable channels that featured local and regional televangelists and chef shows, umpteenth runs of series that were famous a long, long time ago, and pitchmen for kitchen tools, lawn furniture, and snake-oil cures. From that to the current more elevated distribution was simply a matter of outlets reading the rising ratings and jumping aboard.

It had been the consensus of the entities who had agreed to it behind MaryLou's conscious back that the stage name should be "Mama Legba." After all, Erzuli was "mama" to Legba's "papa," the brains behind Pa, and/or who had him by the balls when she felt like it.

But what went up on stage was not pure Erzuli either, rather a kind of composite entity. MaryLou's was Mama Legba's material body full-time and her "soul" or "personality" part-time as less than authentic human ringmaster supposedly in control of the loa acts, and upon occasion Erzuli's foil in a double-voiced act.

Mama Legba and Her Supernatural Krewe now had a major fan base in the Big Easy, excellent penetration in the Delta and Cajun country, dwindling slowly as it proceeded up the

Mississippi past Baton Rouge, regarded as the work of Satan in upstate Bible Belt Country, where there was nevertheless a Born-Again audience that couldn't resist tuning in for a guilt-ridden peek at what Jesus was up against.

"Who among you has need of intercession by Mama Legba and my Supernatural Krewe?" MaryLou demanded as the unvarying, opening line.

"Who has a problem that Jesus can't fix? Who is living in a gypsy camp under Interstate Ten? Who is about to be kicked out onto the street? Who is about to lose their lover? Who is sick with something the doctors can't cure? Who wants to *lose* a lousy lover they can't get rid of themselves? Who needs to meet the love of their life? Who wants to pay back the boss that fired them? Who needs Mama Legba and Her Supernatural Krewe?"

The studio audience would have roared out "We all do!" in unison if they weren't individually all screaming "Me!"

That was the sort of live audience that always showed up on the broadcast, screened for it by now, competing with each other for the doorman's attention in camera-candy costumes more than fit for a secondary parade, colorfully broadcasting the woes of their tales.

Matrons in hospital gowns hooked up to phony rolling IV stands. Dickensian beggar families in filthed-up rags. Evicted folks with pushcarts of their worldly goods. Giant nutria. Hookers in teenage leatherpunk gear. Tough-guy thieves in Robin Hood drag handcuffed to phony cops brandishing baseball bats.

All fighting for the attention of Mama Legba, the aid of the loas, and their fifteen minutes of fame on television.

MaryLou always delivered the standard opening, and it was still MaryLou who did the picking and choosing with the shotgun mike, since Erzuli and the guest stars from the

Supernatural Krewe decided whether or not the sob stories she chose won the brass ring and therefore had to hear them before they deigned to ride the composite entity and become "Mama Legba."

MaryLou pointed her scepter-mike at the likely looking black man in the saffron Hari Krishna robe holding up an empty beggar bowl with the appropriate pathetically whining expression.

"I been living unner da Eye-Ten since the last Hurricane Season, tryin' ta work da Quarter, but no luck an' da cops makin' my poor miserable life even more, an' I need some a da magic to fill this here bowl. . . ."

The loa Linto upon occasion took pity on the beggar trade, turning the inept into the cute and cuddly, but not all that often, and not this time either.

MaryLou tried the woman in the homemade nutria costume, which obviously had taken an impressive amount of inexpert work, but nevertheless made the food-chain scourge of the marshlands look like the giant rapacious rat of its odious reputation, no doubt hoping that Loco, more or less loa of the biosphere, might just come up with some kind of plague to rid the bayou country of this voracious varmint.

"I call upon Mama Legba and Her Supernatural Krewe to save the nutria!"

MaryLou groaned and cut her off as the audience booed and screamed, the nutria being about as popular in lower Louisiana as pythons in Florida or rabbits in Australia, and unsurprisingly no fave rave with Loco either.

"I worked thirteen years in the sales and I've still got my job," said a well-groomed white man in a standard-issue black business suit, with a wife and two kiddies flanking him behind two purloined shopping carts overflowing with the usual street-survival gear. "I bought us a house back in the day before the superbuck, and last month the cops came and kicked us out into the street at gunpoint after the mortgage payments already sucked us dry. What are we supposed to do, Mama Legba? I've been googling, and so I call you to send us Erzuli, she's the loa of good fortune, is she not?"

Are you not? MaryLou demanded to the default loa inside her head. *Can't you give this guy a break?*

MaryLou had no say in who what loa might choose to have Mama Legba favor or what might be said through her lips, but she and Erzuli could converse inside their mutual head and MaryLou could initiate the back and forth and cajole, whine, and complain as much as she liked, and Erzuli seemed to rather enjoy the backtalk.

No way, hon', this honkie inna money suit be a dark horse of the honkie god Mammon, who usually goes by Brigitte here in the Krewe, he ain't poor by Babalu's accounting, and like I keep tellin' you, girl, we don't do no business with business, money, or monkey. If I did, you'd be filthy rich.

And that was that. Erzuli couldn't be bullied, indeed was quite capable of bullying most other members of the Supernatural Krewe, though Papa Legba seemed to overrule her occasionally and let MaryLou talk back to her on the air.

He claims it's because he thinks the act is better if we do a Punch and Judy inside of Mama Legba once in a while for comic relief, Erzuli had told her skeptically, *and he is the loa of crossroads and fortune, so I suppose show biz too, but between you and me, hon', he's mainly trying to show me who really wears the immaterial pants.*

So MaryLou was even granted a certain amount of duet airtime with Erzuli in control of Mama Legba, but she was never consciously there when another loa was riding, and it was always Erzuli who took over solo when it was time to summon other spirits from the vasty deep.

"My boyfriend done run off with a *faggot* an' I want his johnson to get stuck up his butt an' fall off!"

"The cops who kicked me out inna street went inside stole my TV and tablet an' I need 'em back!"

"My no-good son's gone and turned into a junkie, an' I think he's dealin' onna street to pay for it, an' I want the cops to arrest him anna judge to give him like six months just to teach him a lesson."

None of this crap roused an answer, and who could blame the loas? Not MaryLou, who knew she was having a bad show with the scepter-mike so far, or there was just nothing interesting enough to any of them out there to provoke a guest-star appearance.

There seemed to be a loa for just about anything, some like Erzuli and Papa Legba major players, others, like Bade, Agwe, Dumballah, specializing in various forms of luck, or knowledge, or performance, and not very reliable, and apparently even more minor spirits back there below the line, as they would say in show biz.

In that respect, the magic of show biz, major and minor, was not that far removed from voodoo.

"My pimp, he beat me, he got no job, he make me work the streets, he screw around, he tell me I'm no good at it, he won't even make no love to me no more. You gotta get me outa this, Mama Legba!"

This from a black woman not quite entering middle age and not a bad looker, in severe el cheapo miniskirt, a bra straight off the racks at Kmart smeared with black paint and glitter, and high black plastic boots.

Well, Erzuli? This good enough for you?

"Let me at the bastard!"

This was not just inside MaryLou's head. MaryLou heard the words come out of her own mouth, out of Mama Legba's mouth, but in the voice Erzuli used when she was working it, made otherworldly by some kind of natural, if that was the word, reverb effect.

"I give you a spell to put on him, sister, you go get yourself some rose water, mix in with your own spit, an' grease his rovin' rod when he asleep, an' he ain't gonna get it up for nobody else, no way, no how."

"I call this spell the pussy whip," MaryLou felt moved to add herself, and Erzuli, laughing inside her head, let her do it in her own voice to the laughter and cheers from most of the female part of the audience.

Pussy whip? Now what in the material world or ours be that, hon'?

Allow me?

This I gotta hear! And even Papa Legba be laughing."

"Your no-good won't just get it up for no one but you, you gonna control when and if he gets it up at all!" MaryLou's voice said through Mama Legba's snarling lips. "And I'll bet you watching this on TV right now, you pathetic piece of crap, you give it a try and see!"

Who-ee, girl! That give him what for! But that give me an idea—

"That bad boy gonna change his ways!" the voice of Erzuli proclaimed, "you hear me out there in TV land, peckerhead? He's gonna fall in love with you for real, now ain't that a bitch, he gonna worship that pussy of yours like it was the Gates of Eden! He gonna do anything to get inside!"

"And you have the power," MaryLou added. "That poor thang of his is gonna be up for you all the time but—"

"—it's gonna go limp as a dead eel every time he tries unless he gets down on his knees an' prays to it—"

"—and you have to give him leave—"

"—an' I don't advise you spoil him by doing that too often—"

"—and he's gonna want to take you off the street so bad that if he can't work or steal enough he'll . . . he'll . . ."

MaryLou found herself embarrassingly at a loss. *Over to You, Erzuli.*

Sorry about this, hon', but Guede wants the punchline, on this one, an' he got a real good one!

And the next thing that MaryLou knew, she was standing there in front of an audience in a total and totally satisfying uproar. Seemed like every woman was clapping and laughing and cheering at the same time, Erzuli was laughing uproariously inside her head and even a goodly number of the men, sweet-and-sour faced, couldn't quite contain themselves.

"You over there, with the dog and the shopping cart—"

No business like show business! MaryLou sang wordlessly to Erzuli. *And we're the stars!*

With special appearances by guest stars from Mama Legba's Supernatural Krewe—

Which I never get to hear! What did I miss this time, what did Guede say, Erzuli?

Got off a real good one, hon'.

Erzuli cackled like the wicked witch of West Hollywood.

Just tell him to, and he'll go out and peddle his butt inna gay bars!

10

While it wasn't quite true that Luke Martin hadn't been accustomed to public speaking, having made what mark he had as the mouthpiece and honcho of the Alligator Swamp Police, he had certainly never faced something like *this*.

There he sat, in full uniform, on a folding chair atop the stage of the roofed rotunda in the center of Duncan Square, facing City Hall, flanked by Big Joe Roody and Terry O'Day, the union's public relations spokesman, and waiting to go on as the park filled to its boundaries with brother police officers.

Big Joe had told Luke and his father-in-law to spread the word of Luke's crazy assignment to enforce a final eviction notice on himself in the Blue Meanie, and on the advice of O'Day had kept Luke away from the press for a week while word of mouth defused throughout the force.

Meanwhile, coordinated by O'Day, half a dozen cops facing eviction made appearances in the studio audience of Mama Legba and Her Supernatural Krewe, and one of them even got to plead for supernatural help, though it was greeted with boos and hisses from the audience and stonewalled by Mama Legba's "loas," whatever they really were.

So the press was well primed when O'Day announced that Big Joe Roody was calling an unprecedented outdoor official meeting of the Police Association of New Orleans right square in the face of City Hall, where Patrolman Martin Luther Martin would introduce a formal resolution to be voted on by the membership.

The cameras were there. The microphones were there. The upload trucks with their dish antennas were parked on the street right in front of City Hall and now the park was blue with cops and the shooting lights went on.

O'Day stood up and walked to the eastern part of the stage, where a forest of microphones and cameras had been positioned, so that the big sleazy sign announcing CITY HALL atop the otherwise pallid pastel-gray-and-green building would be clearly visible in the main shot throughout the coverage.

He nodded down at the press crouched at the foot of the rotunda with a thin-lipped little smile, then looked out over the lake of blue uniforms. "Y'all are not here to hear me, brothers," he proclaimed, "and Joe Roody needs no introduction, so he's not gonna get any from me!"

A modest ripple of laughter.

"So, over to you, Joe."

Big Joe Roody rose from his chair and strode past O'Day returning to his seat, not exactly ponderously, but like a Saints lineman loping up to the line of scrimmage, and nodded to acknowledge the applause.

"For once I don't think you're here to listen to me make a speech, and so for once I'm not gonna make one," Big Joe announced to more applause mixed with laughter. "And most of you probably know Officer Martin's story, but for those who don't, he's gonna tell you. And since I'm technically not a voting member of the Police Association of New Orleans, he's gonna read you the motion to do something about it, but just between me and y'all, I think you'll know who wrote it. So, over to *you*, Officer Luke Martin!"

On cue, Luke gave Big Joe enough time to cross his path on the way to sitting down so that they could exchange high fives on his way to the microphones and cameras, and then there he was, in front of a couple of thousand fellow cops.

Smack dab in front of City Hall, and live on the Internet and radio and television.

The motion had been written out for him and he had the paper in his hand, and O'Day had written some bullshit script for him too, but Luke had given up trying to memorize it, besides which it had seemed about as dead to him as a deep-fried catfish.

He was on his own.

Or was he?

For as he stood there frozen for a long uncomfortable moment, hands began to rhythmically clap, feet began to stamp, like a baseball crowd calling for a grand slam from the clean-up hitter with the bases loaded, as his brother officers told him that they were with him. And maybe, just maybe, as pissed off as he was.

A damn victim for sure, but as he stood up there like a fuckin' hero, like a tent-show preacher, like Mama fuckin' Legba *live on television,* in front of an audience of his brothers, the thunder of pounding feet and the clap of demanding hands rolling over him and moving through him, Luke Martin felt a high unlike any he had ever imagined.

He felt the Power!

There sure wasn't anything like *this* being peddled on the low down streets or the high-class coke dens either! He was more righteously pissed off than he had ever been in his life, he was more alive than he had ever been, this was was *his* moment in the spotlight, and *he had the Power.*

So he just rode it and let it carry him away.

"Well, a lotta y'all heard the first part a my story, just like yours, right, you buy a house on a police officer's salary with some kinda help on a down payment and mortgage monthlies you figure no problem at the time. Seemed like they were giving it away, right, like the first hit from a street dealer, y'all know just what I mean, doncha? Sound familiar to you guys, now don't it?"

Shouts and growls and right-ons.

"But when the dollar turns into the superbuck, when this Great Deflation shit hit the fan, we find the fuckin' mortgage payment eats up just about our whole new salary, we can't keep up the monthlies even if we starved our families to death. And who gets ordered to kick us out onna street, brothers? *We do*, that's who!"

More shouts and growls, more ominous this time, no right-ons, and a loud chorus of boos. Luke took out a blank piece of paper and waved it like a battle flag.

"An' then I get THIS FUCKIN' THING!" he roared. "Go evict yourself, Luke Martin! Some son of a bitch maybe thought it was funny! Any a you think it's funny?"

Dead silence.

"So I say, *you go fuck yourselves, whoever you are!* City Hall, Loan Lizards, Fat Cats and Polecats, I say up their asses, whoever, and however, and wherever, or whatever they are, who want to dump us out of our houses and into the shit laughing all the way to the banks they own themselves! I say there ain't nothing lower crawling in the Mississippi mud than these motherfucking bloodsuckers, y'all know just what I mean, now doncha, except maybe a cop who would evict another cop for being one of their victims!"

The cheers were deafening, fit this time to maybe knock out some of the windows on City Hall, or for sure to be heard loud and clear through them. As instructed, Luke just stood there waiting for the signal from Terry O'Day to make the motion.

O'Day didn't nod for what seemed to Luke like a glorious forever. When he finally did and Luke tossed away the phony eviction notice and whipped out the other piece of paper, the one with the formal motion written on it, and held it up for silence, he got it.

"I move that no officer of any rank in the New Orleans Police Department serve or enforce any eviction notice on any officer of any rank in the New Orleans Police Department," he bellowed at the top of his lungs sound system or not, "or issue any order to do so, or take any punitive action against any officer of any rank in the New Orleans Police Department for refusing to obey any such order from any source whatsoever."

Big Joe Roody strode to the microphones and shouted even louder above the tumult.

"Might I possible hear any seconds?" he inquired.

This was greeted by a unanimous uproar.

"Somehow I think we got a second or two," said Big Joe. "So unless I hear any objections, I call the vote. Opposed?"

No one was crazy or brave enough or both to utter a word.

"I declare the motion passed by voice vote," Big Joe declared. He paused, turned to face City Hall, raised his right arm and gave it a full upright middle finger salute. "Unanimously."

Well, the big news was good news for cops facing eviction at police gunpoint, but not exactly for J. B. Lafitte or anyone else in the same bucket of shit with me who wasn't a member of Big Joe Roody's union.

The media, and the mayor, and the various local chapters of the local Loan Lizards leaning on them, were calling it a "police strike," but it wasn't really a strike at all, since the cops were still doing everything they usually did, arresting the usual suspects, collecting the usual paper bags, keeping the Swamp Alligators out of the Quarter and New Orleans Proper, and so forth—everything except evicting each other.

Including still doing the dirty work when it came to evicting anyone else. If you were a cop, no cop would evict you; if you weren't, tough titty, they were still throwing everyone else being foreclosed on out into the street, at gunpoint if need be.

Unsurprisingly enough to everyone except the New Orleans Police Department, which had always had about as much political street smarts as a Holy Roller preaching teetotalism on Bourbon Street, this did not exactly gain them popular support from John Q. Sucker, and the cops were not exactly gaining public support for their selfish little "strike."

Though of course the banks and even more shysterly shady financial entities who were demanding that the mayor, or the governor, or *somebody* do something to collect their legal property were about as popular as the same Holy Roller preacher in a whorehouse.

So for the Democratic mayor to ask the Republican governor to send in the State Police to evict armed cops, even if the Powers That Be *did* own him too, would have been political suicide, even if it didn't result in gunfights, which, given the bad blood between the New Orleans Police and the State Troopers, it probably would.

The governor, likewise of course in thrall to the local krewe of the Lizards of Wall Street, wasn't running for reelection and might have done it if asked, but he was the lamest of ducks now in this this election year, and was planning to run for the next available Senate seat.

Lafitte's Landing was no cop bar, but as in any such Bourbon Street establishment, the local cops enjoyed free hospitality in and out of uniform and the traditional monthly paper bags, only good public relations, so some of the regulars were cops and some of the cops were regulars, a cozy situation for the saloon business. So I got tipped off when the final foreclosure and eviction notice was about to be served.

Now ol' J. B. had never been involved in party politics. Democratic and Republican hacks got free fucks in my Garden District whorehouse and free drinks in my Quarter bar within reason as insurance payment on the necessary favors when it came to liquor licenses, nonenforcement of closing times, whorehouse protection, and so forth, but that's as deep as it got until I got into shit that these so-called political connections couldn't or wouldn't get me out of, namely the imminent loss of my saloon and my bordello, the very establishments that had been laying the freebies on these ingrate bastards all these years.

Wouldn't you have been pissed off? Wouldn't you have wanted to get even?

Wouldn't you have considered it not only voodoo justice but a pure hoot to save your own enlightened self-interest doing it?

I had been doing a lot of thinking about this beforehand, as you might have imagined, and I had come up with a plan, a Hail Mary maybe, but I didn't have a better idea. And anyway, I owed my friendly local policemen for the tip-off, now didn't I?

It can get to be a pain and a little expensive because reporters, especially second- and third-rate ones, can drink like fish or state legislators as long as it's free, but it's a useful expense to keep little items about your Bourbon Street tourist attraction in the local media, and it's for sure cheaper than buying advertising, which you can't afford anyway.

And while I had no direct connection to Terry O'Day, I did have enough connections to the press folks who *could* get the PANO press maven to answer their calls and could therefore get him to answer mine.

"Now listen up, Brother O'Day," I told him when I got him on the horn, "those who go along get along, and I got a deal for you that's gonna be good for both ballclubs—"

"In plain English, if you can manage it, Mr. Lafitte, and I'm not your brother."

"You will be, *Mr.* O'Day," I told him patiently.

Even as just a voice on the phone, this guy rubbed me the wrong way and judging by how stupidly the union was handling their so-called strike, he didn't exactly impress me as a public relations genius, but running saloons and bordellos in the Big Easy does teach you when to hold your nose and be diplomatic, so I laid it out as gently as I could so that his little pea brain could handle it.

"The word from the bird is that I'm shortly to be served the final eviction notice on my Bourbon Street saloon," I told him.

"So?" O'Day said coldly.

"So I want your Poster Boy, Patrolman Luke Martin, sent to do the dirty work, in return for which I will arrange live press coverage."

"You're not making any sense, Lafitte, why would either of us want a thing like that?"

"Because I don't want the eviction notice to be served, and he's not gonna serve it."

"What the hell are you talking about? You got about thirty seconds to give me a reason not to hang up on you."

"Y'all been screwing up the *relations* of the New Orleans Police with the *public* big-time, O'Day, you're getting your boys about as much popular support for this so-called police strike as Sherman got from the good old boys on his march through Georgia and I know how to turn it around."

"Oh you do, do you?"

"Yeah, I do. I know how to turn the New Orleans Police into heroes of the people."

"After which you'll do what, walk on water?"

"Look, O'Day, whoever thought up that pissant strike motion in front of City Hall didn't get it."

"Was *Joe Roody* who thought it up, Lafitte. You wanna try to tell Big Joe how he got it wrong?"

"I'm gonna tell *you*, Brother O'Day, so you can tell him and get some of the credit, which I can imagine you just might need with your boss right now. Namely that the police protecting only cops from eviction while doing the evil bidding of the bloodsucking bankers when it comes to kicking ordinary citizens out into the street is an I'm all right jack attitude not exactly winning your union members any popularity contests."

"I need you to tell me that . . . ?" O'Day grunted sourly.

"Maybe not, but it seems you need ol' J. B. to tell you how to fix it."

A long silence.

"I'm still listening," O'Day told me with quite a different attitude.

"The police refuse to evict *anyone*," I told him. "Including, of course, yours truly, and you go public with it."

"Holy shit!"

"That's holy shit, of course, now ain't it, Terry?"

"Maybe . . . but the politics . . . I don't know . . . you have no idea. . . ."

"Oh, I think I do. Why don't you have a little talk with Joe Roody about it? And I tell you what, you can tell him we sort of cooked this up together, and when talks to me, and he will want to, I won't contradict you"

"I do appreciate that . . . Brother Lafitte."

"Those who go along, get along, Brother O'Day."

11

Luke Martin had had his share of Bourbon Street duty, but never at a time like this: before noon, with the bars and strip joints and sex shows all closed, and the mobs of drunken tourists sleeping it off, and the balconies overhanging the mostly deserted sidewalks empty except for a few bleary hookers sipping coffee and clearing their heads in the open air.

Joe Roody had not exactly ordered him to this meeting in Lafitte's Landing, since he was a union leader not a police officer, and Luke had been instructed to show up out of uniform, but in practice it amounted to the same thing: a cop did not say no to Big Joe Roody.

Nor would Roody tell him what in hell this was about. All Luke could get out of him when he asked was "Continuing to save your ass, maybe, kid, among our own collective behinds."

Lafitte's Landing's street front was some kind of phony old wooden sailboat thing, though the wood at least was real and really weathered by who knew how many Hurricane Seasons, with western movie swinging doors, crossed swords above them, and skull and crossbones flags over the the name sign flanking some old dude wearing a pirate hat, though no parrot was in evidence.

Inside it was much longer that it was wide, with a bar with stools along one wall, a food-service counter and the toilets along the other, and a presently empty stage in back. The rest of the big room was filled with tables and chairs, over which hung phony rough-hewn candelabras and disco balls.

The only person in the room was a guy maybe in his late fifties or early sixties, clean-shaven, but with a mess of just short of collar-length curly salt-and-pepper hair, hard brown eyes, shaggy brows, a permanent-looking little smart-ass grin, and wearing a black silk jacket over a white ruffled shirt and green string-tie, looking more like a movie riverboat gambler than any bartender.

Nevertheless, he had produced two steins and drawn the beers by the time Luke made his way over. "I'm Jean-Baptiste Lafitte, and the drinks are on the house this morning, Officer Martin," he drawled in a rapid-fire rap, "and don't say you don't need one this early, you will, Luke, and you might as start callin' me J. B. like everyone else 'cause you and me are gonna get real familiar."

And before Luke could do much more than get his mouth open, Big Joe Roody, trailed by Terry O'Day, barged into the saloon like a tugboat charging up the Mississippi and up to the bar.

"Have a beer on the house, Joe. You too, of course, Terry."

"Don't mind if I do, and as long as it's on the house, I'll have a shot of straight malt too, Laphroaig if you've got it."

"Pass," said O'Day. "I get the feeling one of us better stay sober."

Those who had them took their drinks over to a table, and O'Day, who didn't, spoke first, but hardly got a word in before Joe Roody took over.

"I told Joe what you told me and—"

"I'm interested enough to be here," Big Joe interrupted, "but skeptical enough to want this discussion over by lunchtime, unless of course your kitchen is open for lunch, and this joint serves seafood gumbo or crawfish étouffée or something else decent, and that's on the house too."

Lafitte laughed. "Short and sweet, Joe, and anyway I don't pay the cook to hang around here when there are no customers. The idea is that the police refuse to serve eviction notices on anyone and—"

"And thereby clean the crap of arrogant selfishness off our boot heels and change our image to the heroes of the people. And keep you from losing this joint and the whorehouse you got in the Garden District."

"You got it."

"You insult me, Lafitte, you really think I got where I am by being so thick I couldn't figure that out myself? You so naïve you need me to tell you why I can't order my members to do that?"

"You can call me J. B., and you got me wrong, Joe, I wasn't born last Fat Tuesday, and I know damn well you weren't either. In the first place, you're the union leader not the police superintendent, so you can't order your membership not to follow official orders—"

"Not quite . . . J. B. . . . I just did, remember? Or there wouldn't be this so-called police strike the Fat Cats and Loan Lizards are trying to get the mayor or the governor or the fuckin' president to break with the State Police or the National Guard or the 82nd Airborne Division."

"But it's not a *real* strike, now is it? I mean you're just getting away with it because, after all, there's not that much money involved in seizing the real estate of at most a few hundred cops compared to what would be at stake *if nothing could be repossessed in all of New Orleans.*"

"You sure got that much right, J. B.," Big Joe said, regarding

Lafitte with what seemed to Luke to be much more interest. Luke too was becoming more and more interested, and particularly in why on Earth *he* was sitting here while the two of them went at each other. But he figured the best thing, at least for now, was to keep his trap shut, live and learn. Hopefully. . . .

"If you called for another vote, one which advised your members not to—"

"—serve eviction notices on anyone? No way, José. Yeah, it probably would pass, but what we're not doing now is technically covered in the contract, and my membership is just following the letters like a slowdown, no one can say it isn't *legal*. But refusing to follow orders when it's *not* protected by the contract, that would be illegal, and the powers that be got enough at stake and enough on the judges in this town to get me and who the hell knows how many cops thrown in Angola. You got any idea how popular we'd be in prison?"

"You got any idea how popular anyone running for governor in this election year would be if they were in favor of sending in the state troopers or the Guard to break a police strike that was protecting *all of the people* from being thrown out on the street?"

"About the same . . ." muttered Big Joe Roody. "Except maybe *they* wouldn't have to pack their own Vaseline. . . . Okay, you got my attention, J. B. And I guess I wouldn't be here if you didn't think you had a way I could call for such a thing and get away with it. . . ."

"*You* don't, *he* does," J. B. Lafitte said, nodding in Luke's direction.

Luke had been sitting there quietly like a fly on the wall, trying to make sense of all this political bullshit, and trying to figure out what part he was supposed to play in it all, but now all three sets of eyes were on him, he was beginning to get the drift of it, and it was time he spoke up for himself before this went any further.

"You want me to do something like I did in front of City Hall, right?" he said, not sure whether he was addressing this to Lafitte, or Roody, or both. "Make some speech you give me telling the whole force to refuse to obey an official order on my own hook, so it looks like my own idea, not yours."

"Smart boy," said Big Joe Roody.

"I don't like it, Mr. Roody. I mean, you just said you didn't think *you* could get away with that, and you're Big Joe Roody, an' I'm just Officer Nobody you want to play Officer Fall Guy."

"You're already Officer Somebody, Luke Martin," Lafitte reminded him.

"As you just said, Martin," O'Day pointed out, "you did something similar in front of City Hall and the whole city saw you do it on television."

"But like you said, Joe, *you* stood up and did it yourself, you'd have like as not ended up in Angola. And *you're* Big Joe Roody."

"But *you're* not the head of the police union, kid, you're not legally responsible for ordering anything because you don't have the legal authority to do it. But you *do* have First Amendment rights to voice your own opinion."

"But if I don't have the authority, what's the point of—"

"You don't *need* any *authority*, 'cause you got the *power*!" Lafitte purred at him like a dope dealer making his pitch for your first hit of heroin. "You're already the hero of your brother officers, and this is is gonna make you *the hero of the people* faster than you can repeat the Kingfish's tried-and-true political platform, Soak the Fat Cats and Spread It Out Thin!

Nobody ever lost an election in Louisiana running on *that* one!"

"Running for office? Who said I want to run for office?"

"No one, Luke, but every local politician is going to be so afraid that you *might* run against them that they'll see to it that you make lieutenant to keep you from doing it. It's a royal flush in spades, Luke, a hand that can't be beaten."

"*Lieutenant?* I haven't even made sergeant yet. And it seems like you're asking me to make an example of myself by refusing to follow an order. I could be fired for cause or worse. Maybe much worse."

Lafitte turned to Roody. "Can you protect him?"

It was Terry O'Day who answered. "We stage this right, and we arrange the right coverage, and he won't need any union protection, the media will do the job for us, might even be able to get him on Mama Legba, why not, not a one-shot of the event, we keep him in front of the cameras for as long as we need to."

"What do you say to that, Luke?" asked Joe Roody.

Luke thought about it hard, but not very long. If he said no, he'd be saying it to Big Joe Roody, not just this J. B. Lafitte or O'Day. Big Joe would be pissed off and he might never make sergeant, let alone lieutenant. Luella's daddy would be pissed off.

Luella would be *very* pissed off. Very, very pissed off.

Put that way, what choice did he really have?

This was, after all, the Big Easy, where if you wanted to get along, you had fuckin' well better go along.

But that should cut both ways, now shouldn't it?

"*Lieutenant?*" he asked, or more like it, demanded, looking straight into Big Joe Roody's eyes without blinking. "You can guarantee that?"

"Maybe. I'm the head of the union, not the police department, so I can't *promise* you lieutenant, but . . ."

"But what?"

"But I can *promise* you sergeant. I've sure got enough grease to lubricate the machinery into coming up with that."

12

O'Day did his job and I did mine, and by the time of the appointed hour, namely 6:00 P.M., prime time for local news coverage, there was a good enough media mob in front of Lafitte's Landing; half a dozen camera crews, a couple of upload trucks with big round satellite dishes on the roofs, a dozen or so traditional print reporters.

The appearance of cameras and microphones on Bourbon Street always attracted a good crowd of rubberneckers hoping to catch sight of some third-rate celebrity, or if they were really lucky, a movie star on a location shoot in New Orleans' famous French Quarter, and of course I did not exactly discourage them from quenching their thirsts in my saloon while waiting for whatever they thought they were waiting for.

But this time they were going to get their full fifteen minutes of airtime as extras out on the street, since I had closed down the saloon right in the middle of the happy hour, which had them jabbering like magpies and buzzing like bees.

We had agreed not to tell the press exactly what it was they were going to cover except that Luke Martin would make an appearance, but they would have had to have had a lot more than the usual free drinks on the house not to have figured out that it would have something to do with an eviction notice, seeing as how Lafitte's Landing was closed at a time when every saloon in town that was able was open for happy-hour business.

There was no cheering when a squad car pulled up and Martin—in full body armor and toting an ominous M35 assault rifle—climbed out with the fatal piece of paper in his hands, only a general disappointed and confused muttering from the rubberneckers, since most of these flash crowds were usually composed largely of tourists who didn't realize that this was indeed a local celebrity.

But the press crowded in and those who had them turned on their shooting lights as he marched up to the swinging doors where I had been waiting. O'Day and I had had a little disagreement on the script, but those who go along, get along, and I let him have his way with this cornball piece of business.

"You are Jean-Baptist Lafitte, proprietor of this place of business?" Martin said loudly as I emerged into the press coverage.

"I'm J. B. Lafitte, *owner* of Lafitte's Landing."

"I am Officer Martin Luther Martin of the New Orleans Police Department, and this is a final eviction notice," he said, shoving the thing dramatically under my nose, "and I am ordered to evict you from these premises."

Now came what I believed was the corny part, but which Terry O'Day had insisted would build dramatic tension that would prolong and enhance the coverage and make it look more like Luke was acting spontaneously. So I delivered my line, and don't blame me for it, I didn't write it.

"Why don't we come inside and discuss this over a beer or two like Southern gentlemen?"

At which point, I did not quite bow, but bent slightly at the waist, and ushered him through the swinging doors like the maître d' of my own saloon, which of course didn't have one.

There was no one inside except Terry O'Day, sitting at the

bar without a drink, who commenced staring at his watch as we entered. "Five minutes," he said, "should be just long enough to be credible, not long enough to lose the coverage."

"Just long enough to really have a beer," Luke Martin suggested. "And since it's on the house, ain't it, how about a shot of tequila with it?"

I shrugged, went behind the bar, and served up the drinks. O'Day, as usual, wasn't having any; I, as was not usual, had a beer and a shot in my own bar too.

We sat there saying nothing for the full five minutes—what was there to say?—until O'Day looked up at Luke, and nodded.

"Break a leg, Martin."

Luke stared at him in befuddlement, so I shoved him in the general direction of the door, trotting along two steps behind him as he emerged into shooting lights and still camera flashes alone, and stood there blinking and blinded for a moment.

"I can't do this anymore," he shouted a little too loudly. "How can I? How can I evict *anyone* from their houses or businesses for the same Loan Lizards who wanted me to kick *myself* and my family out into the street so they could steal our home? How can any cop kick another cop out of his home? We can't! We won't! An' now we don't!"

This much was more or less according to O'Day's script and Martin sounded like he was reading it off a teleprompter, and I had the feeling he knew it, and maybe that's why he went off on his own.

"So screw this!" he roared, tearing the eviction notice into small pieces and tossing them like Mardi Gras confetti toward the crowd and right at the cameras. "Screw the bastards tryin' to turn *your police force* into *their* rent-a-cop pigs!"

Unanimous loud cheers from the crowd, fist shakes, and right-ons, not only from the locals, but the tourists too, who after all, were going through much the same sort of shit all over the poor ol' US of A.

"That's what I'm saying to the people of New Orleans, and that's what I'm saying to my brothers in blue! Whose side are we on? The mofos out to stealin' our homes an' businesses an' whatever else they can lay their dirty paws on, or the people pay the taxes that pay our salaries? Screw *who*? Screw *them*! Screw unto others before they screw us first! Any cop who serves an eviction notice here inna Big Easy is pissing on his own badge! Any cop lets himself be turned into a pig like that don't deserve to wear one! And any cop who does ain't no blue brother a mine!"

Whoo-ee! Shouts and rebel yells, fists waving in the air, flashes goin' off, and even *reporters* joining in, would you believe it! Whatever *It* was this boy had it!

Boy? Just maybe a couple of minutes ago, but while ol' J. B. had only seen something like this fewer times than he needed the fingers of one hand to count, I knew it when I saw it, who really wouldn't, that moment when you see a boy cross over and become a man.

"My full name is Martin Luther Martin, my daddy ain't much, bein' still inna joint and deserving it, but I guess he knew enough to know what it was supposed to mean long before I did, which is only now. Was a silly name, I thought, was a burden no one shoulda dropped on the back of some poor kid in the Alligator Swamp, but I gotta tell y'all, for the first time since I crawled my way up out of the Alligator Swamp I'm proud to carry it forward as far as I can! I'm proud to be standing here telling you that your police are on *your* side! I'm proud to be proud to be *Officer* Martin Luther Martin! Power to y'all! Power to y'all from *your* Police! Power to the People! Power to the People's Police!"

13

Luke had made himself a hero with his brother cops all right, with anyone in New Orleans facing eviction, with PANO and Big Joe Roody, but certainly not with Mayor Douglas Bradford, a Democrat under heavy pressure from the Loan Lizards to demand that the lame duck Republican governor send in the State Police as strike breakers, or Police Superintendent Dick Mulligan, who found himself caught between City Hall and the union.

"Sergeant was the best I could do for you right now, kid," Joe told him. "Mulligan is shitting in his pants and Bradford is looking for a hole to disappear down into, and I had to play some real hardball just to get you that, not to mention just saving your ass. I had to make it clear to both of them that if the State Police showed their peckerwood pusses inside New Orleans to evict the good citizens or any shit came down on you, there would be a *real* police strike, and it would be a wildcat, and just as Mardi Gras was about to begin."

"What's a wildcat?"

"A spontaneous strike by union members not the result of an official strike vote that I'm not legally responsible for because I didn't call for it, and I couldn't stop it if I wanted to, which of course I don't, something a bit like what you called for, kiddo."

"But then isn't that a real wildcat strike already?"

"That's what Bradford said. You call *that* a strike? I told him. Any attempt to use the State Troopers to break it, and you'll see what a *real* police strike is."

"Which is?"

"Which is no cops show up for work at all. No traffic control. No arrests. No crowd control. The Alligators coming up from the Swamp into the Zone and the Quarter as much as they please. *During Mardi Gras.*" Big Joe laughed. "You should have seen his face, Luke; he woulda turned white if he wasn't white already."

So Big Joe Roody got Luke promoted to sergeant, but Luke learned that the New Orleans Police Department really had two honchos—Joe Roody, who commanded PANO at the pleasure of the union membership and Superintendent Mulligan, who sat at the top of the department chain of command.

Roody had the power of threatening a strike, which was enough to protect Luke from any overt retaliation by Mulligan and get him his promotion, but Mulligan controlled duty assignments. So Sergeant Martin Luther Martin was assigned a desk in the police public relations department where his duties were to sit behind a desk doing nothing, and his orders, not to be disobeyed, were to keep his big mouth shut unless and until official words were put into it. Or else.

While this might be boring, it was the softest duty Luke had ever had or even imagined, being paid for doing nothing, and with a raise too, and it sure beat chasing down perps, handing out traffic tickets, and dealing with crazed junkies, and drunks who just might be packing, or worse still being called to deal with domestic violence.

Those who go along, get along, and Sergeant Martin Luther Martin was getting along just fine, and lazing around listening to music, reading newspapers and magazines, watching TV on his phone screen, and sneaking sips of beer from the six-pack in his desk drawer and the occasional doobie in the alley, did not exactly seem a hard way to go along.

At first.

But Terry O'Day was doing his job, not that he really had to. Keeping the Poster Boy for the limited media-called "police strike" and what was beginning to really call itself the People's Police away from the press might be within the powers of the police superintendent, but keeping the press from attacking the department and City Hall for "muzzling him" was not.

Especially when Big Joe Roody was readily available and willing to bitch about it in interviews in order to keep the "wildcat" going and the State Police upstate where they belonged.

So Luke found himself the baseball bat with which Roody was beating the mayor and the superintendent into submission and the hostage of the police department chain of command, in the news as a topic of contention, but unable to speak for himself.

"So what, Luke?" Luella told him. "You've made sergeant, you've got the raise, you're a public hero with a cushy desk job. What are you complaining about? What would you want to say anyway?"

Luke couldn't come up with an answer to that. What *would* he say? What *could* he say that he hadn't said already? And why the fuck did he want to stand up there and say it in public? Although he could admit to himself that he *did* want to play hero of the people in front of the cameras and mikes again, he couldn't figure out why.

Finally, O'Day, or more more likely, Joe Roody, cut some kind of political deal that Luke could barely understand, and wasn't so sure he wanted to.

"City Hall's kept you under raps, Martin," O'Day told him, "but no one can keep Big Joe Roody's mouth shut, and no one can keep the strike out of the news leads or keep everyone and his cousin from badgering me for interviews with you. So we made a deal. Joe eases up on the pressure, and the superintendent eases up on you. You can do appearances approved by the department as long as you praise Bradford."

"Praise him for what?" Luke demanded in total befuddlement. "He's pissed off at me, isn't he?"

"Yeah, but His Dishonor the Mayor wants to run for the Senate two years from now, and he wants a pat on the back from you for resisting the Republican bastards in Baton Rouge who are leaning on him to call in the State Troopers or even the National Guard as strike breakers because the Fat Cats that own their asses are coming down on *them* to get it done."

"I guess he deserves it, doesn't he?"

"Who gives a shit?" O'Day told him. "It's a good horse trade. Bradford keeps the strike-breakers out of New Orleans and you beatify the cynical bastard who's going to have to go to the same Fat Cats for campaign funding two years from now and try to convince them that it would have been political suicide to have played their game of ball after he became a hero of the people. Your job in this piece of political theater is to play the devil that made him do it to the Loan Lizards."

"I don't get it," Luke told O'Day, but he was beginning to smell the stink coming off it, something like goose-grease and a fish stand been out in the hot sun way too long.

"Don't worry about it, Martin, you don't have to. I'll give you a script, all you gotta do is stick to it when you go on next Friday."

"Go on? Go on what?"

Terry O'Day smiled at him with all the warmth of a real

yawning alligator. "What I promised you, Martin, remember? I got you on Mama Legba."

I don't I like this, Harry," MaryLou had told Mama Legba's agent.

"What's not to like, babes?" Harry Klein had told her. "It's a sweetheart deal, sweetheart."

"It just doesn't seem, well, kosher."

"What's not kosher about it? O'Day gets his boy some prime regional airtime, and we get some national coverage that I think will give us a chance to take the show national: Discovery, Showtime, HBO, who knows, maybe even a major broadcast network."

Klein had done good work moving Mama Legba and Her Supernatural Krewe from third-rate local cable channels up to major distribution in New Orleans, most of Louisiana, and the Gulf Coast as far away as Tampa, and even Houston and Galveston, and MaryLou *could* see where he was coming from and it *did* make cold show-biz sense.

The Police Department PR people, or this Terry O'Day, had kept Luke Martin off the air ever since his "People's Police" speech, but he and the so-called New Orleans Police Strike were still lead-story news in the Big Easy and a juicy enough feature nationally so that O'Day's promise to get Luke his first TV appearance since then some national coverage had credence, and it made sense that Harry had a reasonable chance to use that to market the show nationally.

But there was still something wrong to the whole setup.

Because it *was* a setup.

"It violates the format, Harry. Everyone in the audience is supposed to have the same chance at being called on."

"Bullshit, MaryLou! You choose who to point the mike at,

and you do it because you think the costumes are gonna make for good TV. Everyone *doesn't* have the same chance!"

"We don't do celebrities."

"Jesus Christ, girl, Martin isn't some second-tier talk-show celebrity, he's front man for a legitimate *news story*."

"Whatever. We can't announce that someone is going to be on the show in advance."

"For shit's sake, we can't *not* announce it. How the hell else am I supposed to get national coverage? Besides which, O'Day has made it a deal breaker."

"I'll have to sleep on it," MaryLou had told him, meaning discuss it with Erzuli, though of course she couldn't tell Harry Klein that, who could not and probably should not, be convinced that the show was anything more than a clever format for an actress who was the Second Coming of Rich Little when it came to doing voices.

"Great! You sleep on it, and I'll spend the night tearing my hair out and chewing my fingernails to the bone."

I don't see why not, hon', had been Erzuli's take on it. *So you give this dude some airtime to say his piece. It's not like you're promising that me or anyone one else in the Krewe is gonna come when he calls.*

And then there had been a laugh inside her head as silent as Erzuli's words but somehow a lot louder and more than a little sardonic. And what spoke within her next was clearly a chorus.

But it would make for a good show, now wouldn't it?

So there they were, backstage in a thousand-seat television studio rented for the occasion to accommodate the additional TV crews, watching the studio audience filing in; MaryLou, Erzuli, and the rest of the Supernatural Krewe lurking behind her in the composite entity that was Mama Legba.

This being the week before the beginning of Mardi Gras,

the costumes were more elaborate than usual, more expensive too by the look of the tailoring, the glitter, the peacock feathers, the bling, the elaborate and elaborately bejewelled hairdos, the boobs in fancy bustiers, the abundance of bare and painted skin male and female, more like what you would see throwing beads off a float than the usual hard-luck stories and supplicants.

Making the entrance of Officer Martin Luther Martin in a simple blue police uniform quite dramatic in contrast, and of course all the more so as TV crews not her own pinned him in shoot spotlights as he made his prearranged front-row seat.

"It's Mama Legba and Her Supernatural Krewe!"

14

L uke had seen this circus act on TV often enough, all too often in fact, since Luella thought it hilarious and Little Bruce thought it was cool, but as far as he was concerned it was about as funny as a loudmouth drunk he had to drag off the streetlight he was hugging and as cool as high noon in a New Orleans August, and he sure never imagined he would find himself part of the show or had ever wanted to.

But here he was, waiting to go on, sitting through preliminary tear-jerking and booty-shaking stories that seemed to be boring the audience and the so-called loas who "Mama Legba" wasn't bothering to fake as much as they were boring him. Which was probably the point, like a stripper cock-teasing the johns what was supposed to seem like forever before showing her tits and just maybe her pussy.

What that made *him,* Luke didn't want to think about.

But now he was about to find out because the spotlight swung his way as Mama Legba finally pointed her microphone at him.

TV show appearance or not, O'Day hadn't actually given him a script to memorize, he knew better than that, Luke doubted he could even do it if he wanted to, which he didn't, but if Terry O'Day hadn't told him how to do it, he had told Luke what he was supposed to get done.

"Don't worry about this loa crap, Martin, we don't give a swamp rat's ass if MaryLou Boudreau decides to favor you with that part of the act or not, that's her call, not our problem. We just need you to stand up there and praise His Dishonor for keeping the State Trooper strike-breakers out of New Orleans in such a manner as to make it seem like you're threatening dire retribution if he caves to Baton Rouge and changes his mind. You can handle that, can't you, Sergeant Alligator Swamp Police?"

MaryLou did not have a good feeling about this even though Luke Martin was greeted with cheers and waving fists and outright applause by the studio audience. He looked spiffy in his well-tailored and freshly pressed uniform and his well-formed features were suitably heroic, but spiffy and heroic were not exactly what she was supposed to select for when picking and choosing from the studio audience, let alone a spiffy hero of the People's Police in a cop costume. And Martin, who had delivered a star performance outside Lafitte's Landing, looked as if he felt he was about to bomb now.

"I think y'all know why I'm here," he began, looking around, left, right, at the studio audience, not at her or the camera. "I'm here to speak for my brother officers and the people of New Orleans to thank His Dis . . . His Honor Mayor Douglas Bradford for his . . . courage in supporting our refusal to . . . ah . . . enforce eviction notices and keeping the . . . mofos in Baton Rouge from sending in no-good scabbing State Trooper strike-breakers. . . ."

Shit!

Better give this flannel-mouth dork the quick hook, hon', Erzuli told her.

As if she had to.

"But what are you asking of Mama Legba and her Supernatural Krewe?" MaryLou broke in.

"What am I asking of Mama Legba and her Supernatural Krewe . . . ?" Martin repeated like a dazed parrot, blinking and frozen like a deer blinded by the klieg lights.

What *am* I asking? Luke found himself asking himself. What the fuck am I supposed to say now?

He shrugged to himself, or maybe the camera actually caught it, nothing for it but to stop his brain thinking about it, and let his mouth do the thinking for him.

"What I'm asking from Mama Legba an' your whatever is what I'm asking of Mayor Bradford and everyone else, natural, supernatural, or otherwise who gives a hoot in hell about what happens to this city! Your police are doin' their part, your mayor is doin' his part, and we all are asking you all to do your part, which is whatever you can to save New Orleans and your own asses, natural, supernatural, or otherwise from the Loan Sharks an' Lizards of Wall Street and their flunkies in Baton Rouge!"

Loud cheers and foot-stomping applause from the live audience, but up on the stage, Mama Legba was sweeping her microphone away from him to point it hastily elsewhere, and then—

—and then she froze.

"What do you offer?"

The voice that emerged from her lips was as male as it gets, deep, powerful, lofty, fit to having Luke's bones quivering.

"What do I offer . . . ?" he muttered as whatever was doing the talking pointed the microphone back at him like some king with a scepter.

"WHAT . . . DO . . . YOU . . . OFFER?"

Another male voice, this one even louder, harsher, and more than a little scary.

"Hey, honey-buns, relax, doncha get it, we're willing to deal?" A female voice, soft, seductive, and, well, sexy.

"What do you want?" Luke managed to ask.

Yet another voice, this one male, but with a laughing attitude behind it, like a good-time Charlie. "Music, wine, beer, rum, dancing naked in the streets! Kick out the jams! Slaughter the lambs! Don't give any damns! Be the great I ams!"

"Say what?" was about all Luke could manage.

"Guede's talkin' about Mardi Gras, hon'," the seductive female voice explained. "He don't talk so clear 'cause he's high most of the time. What we want from y'all is Mardi Gras as it's supposed to be."

"Which is . . . ?"

"The real deal! No rules! Drink in the streets! Fuck on the balconies! Smoke the herb! Dance with the snakes! Down with the fakes! Come as you like, be what you are, every man a king, every gal a star! We want to party hearty in the flesh, an' since we ain't got no bodies, if you don't, we can't. So let the good times roll, and get yo uptight tight blue asses outa the way!"

Whatever was going on, whatever or whoevers he was dickering with, Luke was beginning to get it. These loas, or whatever they were, *were* dickering, and while these were no Swamp Alligator gangbanger honchos, and he sure wasn't in the catbird seat as the honcho of the Alligator Swamp Police this time around, it seemed to him that he had sung them pretty much the same song.

"Who goes along, gets along, you want the cops not to need you, and expect the same, is that it?"

"Let Mardi Gras be Mardi Gras!" declared the voice called Guede. "Give us happy horses to ride!"

"He means no rules except the famous four golden rules, hon'."

"Which are?"

"No violence, no robbin', no rapin', and y'all don't bother anyone who ain't breaking any of the other three, anything else your *People's Police* see the *People* doin', you just smile and step aside!"

"I think I can go with that," Luke found himself saying. After all, how different was it from the rules he had laid down to the gangbangers in the Alligator Swamp? "But delivering it is something else again. . . ."

He laughed to himself even as he said it. "So what do *you* offer? I'm not the mayor, I'm not the police superintendent, I'm not even a lieutenant. You gotta come up with something they'll sign off on."

And there was a voice like mighty waves roaring through the reeds of a marshland, like a whirlwind blowing through the streets, like the soggy battering of a driving rain, like trees falling and electric wires snapping, and walls cracking, and flood waters surging up under the pilings of houses.

"We will hold back the Hurricane Season this year. New Orleans will be spared."

"*You can do that?*"

"Well, sort of, hon'. It's sort of matter which we can't rule, and it's sort of power which we can, so we can sort of kick it around a little. What he means is New Orleans will be spared the *worst of it,* but we're not perfect, and we're not talkin' about Mobile or Galveston and maybe not even Baton Rouge."

"Do we have a pact?" demanded the voice from the storm.

"Screw Baton Rouge!" Luke found himself saying, and the studio audience, which has been deathly silent during all this, cheered and laughed. "Power to the People from the People's Police! Let the good times rock and roll!"

15

Mardi Gras had been more or less going slowly south, if y'all pardon the expression, ever since Katrina, some even say ever since they moved the parades off Bourbon Street because the gutters had gotten too jammed by the crowds for the major floats to get through.

But that was before my time as a Bourbon Street saloon keeper, before the advent of the Hurricane Season, which, though it never came close to hitting the Gulf Coast for months after Fat Tuesday, did not exactly give what it left of New Orleans a tourist attraction lift.

What the Bourbon Street Casino Hotel in Vegas did to the Mardi Gras trade, however, was a boot in the butt recent enough to be personal. Everyone living off the Quarter tourist trade could see it coming the moment they announced they were going to build a replica of Bourbon Street inside a mall-world-casino with iron-lace balconies overlooking the nightly parades featuring the current headliners playing in the phony Preservation Hall. Replicas of New Orleans restaurants serving up fast-foody replicas of famous Cajun and Creole dishes. All as family-friendly as a Disney World and no Alligator Swamp surrounding it.

How was the real thing supposed to compete with that?

And it got even worse when the Great Deflation beat the Bejesus out of what was left of the American middle class, Mardi Gras was pulling in less and less of the vanishing late winter tourist trade and becoming more and more what it had originally been way back when, a citywide party New Orleans threw for itself.

And while that may have pleased a certain Spanish moss and magnolia self-appointed cultural elite in the Garden District congratulating themselves for not having to make a living off the déclassé tourist trade, it did not sit well with those of us such as yours truly who did, nor the pragmatic economic powers that be, who paid enough dues to the Chamber of Commerce and the Tourist Board to overpower the local Loan Lizards when it came to whose self-interest was going to buy City Hall.

Meaning that while the demands the Loan Sharks were making in Baton Rouge to send in the Troopers or the Guard to break the police strike were enhanced by what the upstate Holy Rollers were calling called the People's Police's "Pact With the Devil," negotiated on television by Luke Martin, in New Orleans it was a Godsend, if you'll pardon the expression, His Dishonor Mayor Bradford could hardly want to refuse.

Since it was good for the Big Easy's most important remaining source of dwindling revenue, how could any New Orleans politician not ready for the funny farm in a straitjacket come out against what was the town's motto, namely "Let the Good Times Roll?"

They couldn't and it did.

It had been a long, long time, and probably never, since New Orleans had seen a Mardi Gras like this. And as a Bourbon Street saloon keeper with an apartment over the bar with a balcony, I had a front-row seat, though I hardly had the time to sit down in it with a Hurricane or Mint Julep to toss throws of beads and plastic doubloons to the permanent crowds of revelers below.

Still, no way the big floats of the major krewes like Baccus, and Rex, and Endymion, and Zulu, could be dragged down Bourbon Street with the second-rate celebrities tossing throws and doubloons to the frenzied masses, so the main parades were still only along wide avenues like St. Charles, Canal, Decatur, Rampart, and Esplanade.

I never had a moment to see any of them live, but on the replays after Fat Tuesday, I saw that, amazingly enough, they were pretty much what was happening on Bourbon Street writ large and high-budget, and Bourbon Street was for sure something else, something that neither New Orleans or anywhere else had seen ever before, and I was right in the middle of it.

As usual, every saloon, strip joint, porn palace, and restaurant on both sides of the street that had frontage room had a band out there, and as usual the competition from all of them, instead of turning it into an ear-killing noise, somehow managed to turn into the familiar boogying beat of New Orleans Mardi Gras. As usual, there were plenty of street acts in fantasy ball costumes inching and dancing their way through the solid wall of tourists and locals jamming the street. As usual, every bar was permanently filled, every seat had a drunk in it still buying booze, Lafitte's Landing well included. As usual, people who had rented chairs or standing room on the balconies were tossing throws to the crowds below, which were in the usual frenzy to snag them before someone else did.

But that was all was usual.

They weren't just tossing cheap beads and plastic tokens, they were tossing condoms, amyl nitrate sniffers, balloons of nitrous oxide, spliffs. It wasn't only ladies showing their tits for applause, there were people of both sexes and many genders up there on the balconies stripping down to exactly nothing and performing acts free in full view fit to kill off the business of the strip joints and porn shows and then some.

Down on the street it was more of the same only much more so. Inside a fog of pot smoke that did nothing to hide what was going on from the eyeballs. Half of the crowd was in half-naked costume, and half of those who weren't were doing the full Monty. Couples, threesomes, even the occasional foursome, were screwing up against walls in full view at any given time, and the crowd itself danced up the street like an endless Chinese New Year's dragon made out of flesh and feathers, glitter and bling, twisting and twirling to the crazy music, twitching and jerking like snake-handling speakers in tongues, and from the look of it, no few of them kicking that gong around.

And what cops there were, some of them looking morally outraged, some of them trying to make like they were and failing, others accepting the joints and drinks they were forever being handed with a nod and a smile, just moseyed up and down the street making sure there were no fights or pickpocketing in the crowds, a few here and there even tossing plastic doubloons themselves.

When I managed to get ahold of one, I saw that it was stamped out of styrofoam with a cookie cutter and painted blue. On one side there was just the silhouette of a badge in yellow. On the other side in crudely lettered yellow was just "The People's Police."

Sergeant Luke Martin had found it impossible to pay for his own drinks in the Blue Meanie since Mardi Gras began and the hero of the People's Police, at least in the eyes of his fellow officers who were enjoying popularity with the wildly partying citizenry and the tourists for the first time, not only escaped any of the rotating bummer duty keeping the Swamp Alligators away from it, but was given nothing but the most coveted tours of duty "controlling," but in reality mostly enjoying, the scenes around the major parades.

Baccus, Rex, Endymion, Proteus, the grand tour of the major krewes and their elaborate major floats along the major parade routes; if Luke hadn't seen them all, he had certainly seen more of them than anyone else on the police force. As a sergeant, Luke commanded a squad of "crowd control" officers spread out along each parade route. But this terminology was quite obsolete, since the crowds were for the most part just having a drunken stoned-out dancing and fucking in the street good time, none of which could be controlled except by massive arrests by the riot squads, and no one was trying.

So the "duty," such as it was, consisted mostly of snakedancing and sashaying through the crowds more or less at the speed of the most amusingly flamboyant floats to the chaotic jazz of the mixed music, smiling, nodding, dancing a bit himself when the spirit and the free drinks and joints thrust upon him moved him, and trying to stay sober and keep his fly from being unzipped.

And now here he was on Rampart Street and here came the Krewe of Zulu down it on its way to Canal along the northern border of the Quarter.

Zulu was an all-black parade, had been when that got the krewe called uppity niggers and then Toms, and then Black Power Panthers, and now maybe the number-one stars of Mardi Gras. Part of the old mystique was that Zulu supposedly never announced its route beforehand, but part of the Big Easy was that most anyone who cared to find out knew it anyway.

Rampart being a wide main drag without wide sidewalks

or overhanging balconies, the crowds poured out into the gutter and the floats glided through them like ships through the sea, and indeed there was even a slaver sailship taken over by its cargo, a retro jazz band done up like African warriors in broken chains.

Behind that came an enormous glowing pink elephant from the top of which mostly naked ladies in feathers and bling and grandees in ringmaster hats and tuxes whirled light sabers and tossed beads and doubloons to the crowds.

And there, making its way toward him, riding a wave of enhanced cheering and brass fanfares came the Zulu King's float, a huge many-tiered tower done in multicolored neon, arising out of a palm tree forest and decked out with balconies from which members of the krewe tossed Zulu doubloons and throws of beads.

Luke glided through the crowd towards it, thanks to his suddenly beloved blue uniform. Whether this was because he was recognized personally or just because the People's Police were the fave raves of this Mardi Gras, with their T-shirts selling almost as well as those of the New Orleans Saints bearing the 66 of their star quarterback Brady Butterworth, was hard to tell, if for no other reason than because no one in the crowd seemed capable of recognizing much more detail than a blue blur and a shiny brass badge.

Number 66 was the King of Zulu this year, and the Saints quarterback sat on a gilded throne that looked vaguely like a stadium seat for God Himself, wearing his football uniform with the standard crown replacing the helmet and an ermine-ringed green superhero cloak.

In his left hand he held a scepter in the form of a spear, which he thrust aloft now and again, and in his right, a gilded coconut. The Gold Coconut was the single most coveted item in any Mardi Gras and supposedly only one got tossed into a crowd each year although no one could really be sure of that, and Butterworth drove the crowd into a feeding frenzy every time he teased them by raising it above his shoulder as if to throw a touchdown pass.

Luke found something a bit disgusting about it, but on the other hand, if he could actually hand Little Bruce *the* Gold Coconut tossed by *Brady Butterworth,* his son would be the prince of the schoolyard. . . .

So . . . might as well give it a try.

His uniform was enough to allow Luke to slide through the screaming mob to the front rank as the King's float glided up to where he was standing.

Chance? Good luck? Mama Legba magic? As the float came abreast of him, Butterworth's gaze seemed to fall upon him, and then they locked eyes for a long moment as it went by.

Something passed between them, as Butterworth nodded without looking away, and without looking away, the Saints quarterback rose, half turned, raised the Gold Coconut, pumped it once, twice, and as Luke raised his hands to receive it, threw him a touchdown pass.

Which Luke fumbled as the heavy coconut smacked his outstretched hand and fell to the ground.

Well, not really to the ground because a forest of hands like a zillion octopus tentacles grabbed and yanked at it before it could fall that far, until a big brawny brute wearing the 66 T-shirt got his mitts on it, hugged it to his chest, and used his elbows to clear his way.

And then he noticed Luke.

And his eyes lit up.

"Martin fuckin' Luther Martin!"

He battered his way through to Luke.

"Hey, bro'," he said, giving Luke the high-five, "y'know thanks to you an' Mama Legba, me and mine ain't livin inna cardboard box city under the I-10. We still got our house what's rightfully ours."

And he handed Luke the Gold Coconut.

"And this is rightfully yours," he told him, and walked away.

*B*etter put on the mask, and while you're at it, the costume too, Erzuli had told MaryLou.

Masquerade as myself?

Mama Legba isn't exactly yourself, now is she, girl? And since there's hundreds or maybe thousand of women out there wearing Mama Legba masks and costumes, it's the best disguise there is, hiding in plain sight.

Erzuli wanted to mingle with the Mardi Gras crowds and MaryLou couldn't really deny that she did too. Who wasn't at least curious about what was now being called Mama Legba's Mad Mardi Gras in the press and promotions, least of all the human half of Mama Legba herself?

But actually renting a half-assed Mama Legba costume instead of just putting on the real thing and buying a cheap stylized mask of her own face didn't make any sense to MaryLou until she arrived in Jackson Square.

Jackson Square was bordered on three sides by the pedestrian streets which MaryLou and her parents had worked back in the day and on the fourth by Decatur, which was open to traffic and especially the mule-drawn carriages. But Jackson Square Park was enclosed by a fence all the way around and could be entered only by two gates, supposedly to protect the foliage from an excess of the street life but really, as anyone who had ever worked the square knew, to keep the street acts out.

Now, however, the gates were wide open, and the pedestrian streets were so packed to the gills that the bands and other street acts had retreated inside the park through the wide open gates, and past the smiling cops. The park was jam-packed with revelers too, as well as dealers openly peddling loose joints, hookers showing off their wares, X-rated costumes, here and there where they could find room couples and threesome of variegated gender and plumage having at it.

Half the people in the crowds were costumed too, roughly half of them were women, and at least 10 percent of *those* were wearing store-bought or homemade Mama Legba costumes just like MaryLou and the same cheap papier-mâché mask.

If MaryLou had showed up unmasked, her own face, that is the face of the real Mama Legba the television star, would have been immediately recognized, and what would have happened to her then in this drunken stoned-out dancing frenzy, however good-natured, was something she didn't care to contemplate let alone experience, and she could now well understand why Erzuli didn't want to either.

So, hiding in plain sight, the real Mama Legba was able to party hearty with the revelers as just another copycat, buying a spliff and a Sazerac, drinking, smoking, dancing along to the musics like MaryLou when MaryLou felt like it, not even drawing an audience when the more adroit Erzuli took possession.

Indeed, while none of the wearers of the Mama Legba costumes seemed to be among them, there were any number of people in the crowd, costumed and otherwise, who were puffing on spliffs as if channeling the ghost of Bob Marley, gulping down booze as if to summon up whole herds of phantom pink elephants, mating in and out of the shrubbery and dancing like they never danced before.

And rather than moving through the dance, it was the frenzied supercharged dance itself that seemed to be moving through *them,* moving from person to person, flitting here and there, gawky dorks suddenly rolling their eyes back and dancing with the energy and grace and demonic energy with which MaryLou was well familiar from serving as Erzuli's horse and then falling abruptly back into the material world when the loa dismounted.

Well, sure, hon', Erzuli told her when MaryLou pinned her on it. *We immaterial girls and boys just wanna have fun too! An' since we ain't got no bodies, we gotta ride yours to boogie in the material world. Don't you get it? That's why we made our deal with the cops, we want to party like what we are, and that ain't anything gonna get no Family Friendly ratings from no Holy Rollers or enforcers of tight-assed moral rectumtude!*

16

Well, it sure was the most successful Mardi Gras in years as far as the tourist business was concerned, and yours truly was certainly feeling no pain countin' up the profit total after Fat Tuesday. But what goes up, must come down, we've all heard said, though I never heard anyone explain why, and you probably haven't either, and it wasn't just the beginning of Lent. Nor was it immediate fear of the Hurricane Season, which wasn't due to hit for months either.

Admittedly the tourist business always dropped like a stone after Mardi Gras, although of course it didn't take nearly as big a dive as it did around the middle of June when the Hurricane Season started.

But there was an election for governor of Louisiana this year, and every Republican candidate for the nomination was on the run for the upstate vote, and every two-bit preacher up there in Louisiana's Bible Belt was goin' on about how wicked New Orleans had gone all the way this time and made an open deal with the Devil on television for everyone to see.

In New Orleans, it had come to be known as Mama Legba's Mad Mardi Gras.

Upstate, it was generally regarded as Satan's.

It was the usual Republican smoke screen to hide *their* usual dirty deal with *Mammon*, but on steroids. Rile up the rednecks, peckerwoods, and general Holy Rollers with righteous rage against Godless Atheistic New Orleans, and maybe they'll be riled up enough not to notice that the economic Powers That Be foreclosing on *their* farms and homes too own your asses and you can once more flim-flam the yokels into voting Republican against their own obvious self-interest.

This time around the stakes were even higher because there were local police forces up there copy-catting the People's Police of New Orleans at least to the point where most of them were at least refusing to evict their fellow cops, and a growing number of them were refusing to evict *anybody*.

Well, of course, the Powers That Be didn't feel they could afford to let this communist un-American evil to spread, so the pressure from the Loan Lizards and Company on those vying for the Republican nomination to promise to send in the Troopers or the Guard to New Orleans and enforce "the laws of God, Man, and the State of Louisiana" was intense enough to have all of them swearing to send in one or the other or both or maybe demand the Pentagon send in the U.S. Marines.

So the usual anxious anticipation of the Hurricane Season started earlier this year because of the beginning of the Louisiana political season, which was even crazier than usual. Which is saying something in a state where Governor Fast Eddie Edwards got approval of casino gambling by swearing to keep his business in New Orleans and never go to Vegas to roll the bones again, where Huey Long built a new governor's mansion in the form of a half-scale version of the White House because he wanted to feel at home in the real thing when he moved in, and where Earl Long, Huey's nutcase brother, pissed on the legislature and was governor while in the state loony bin and sprung himself by firing hospital head after hospital head until he finally appointed one willing to certify that he was not insane.

Both New Orleans and the upstate Republicans were waiting for the Hurricane Season, the Big Easy with baited breath hoping against hope that Mama Legba's Supernatural Krewe really *could* protect the city, while and the Republicans breathing fire and brimstone and fixin' to turn up the heat even higher if they did.

That's right, the deciding political question this turn around the merry-go-round was whether or not Satan was going to protect New Orleans from the Hurricane Season!

And if you think *that's* crazy, let ol' J. B. tell you what's *really* crazy. Namely that if no major hurricane whacked New Orleans, whichever hack won the Republican primary would probably be elected governor by running against the Devil and his henchman, the Democratic candidate, and send in the Guard as promised, but if the usual disasters hit, meaning that Satan hadn't delivered on his bargain or hadn't been involved in the first place, the Republican would most likely lose.

So New Orleans needed a major storm during the season to protect it from the National Guard and the Republicans had to be praying for Sin City to be spared to prove that Luke Martin and the "People's Police" really had sold the city's soul to the Devil.

Well, the way the election schedule had been bent around to accommodate the Hurricane Season a while back, the primary votes came in May to avoid its beginning, and the election itself had been pushed forward to the Tuesday before Thanksgiving, well after its usual end.

Harlan W. Brown, a state senator from Born Again redneck country, won the Republican primary, and Elvis Gleason Montrose, likewise a state senator but from New Orleans, won the Democratic primary.

The smart money, not that you had to be Albert Einstein to do the math, was that Montrose had his balls in a nutcracker. His only chance depended on turning out an even more overwhelming Democratic vote out of New Orleans and environs than usual, which meant there was no way he could promise to send in the State Police or the National Guard to break the wildly popular strike by the popular People's Police.

But even if Montrose got every last vote, it wouldn't be a winning hand unless he could do it without getting a bigger upstate vote than any Democrat had gotten since Eddie Edwards and then some.

Brown might not be a mental giant, but he wasn't dim enough to suppose that a candidate promising to send in the State Troopers or the National Guard or the Marines to occupy the city so that evictions could resume and law and order as the Bible intended could be enforced wasn't going to come out of New Orleans with more than a handful of votes, so he had nothing to lose and everything to gain by running against un-Godly un-American Satanic Sin City and would've put on a sheet and a pillowcase mask if he didn't have the Klan vote already locked up.

Montrose would screw himself as a traitor in New Orleans if he went anywhere near sending in the National Guard, but he would screw himself big-time upstate if he defended the People's Police, as a servant of the servants of Satan at best and the Devil's right hand at worst, a club which Brown was already righteously and gleefully banging him over the head with.

So he tried to mush-mouth his way out of it, fobbing the issue off on Joe Roody, who had made it clear that there would be a total police strike if the State Police or the National Guard set foot in New Orleans, and the Troopers certainly didn't have the manpower to police even a small city, and using the National Guard raised both state and federal Constitutional questions, so it would be irresponsible to promise something the elected governor might not even be able to deliver, blah, blah, blah. . . .

Like every Democratic candidate for anything these dire economic days, Montrose tried to shift attention to where Republicans were the ones up against the wall. It wasn't just homeowners in New Orleans who were being squeezed out of their homes by the Loan Lizards before the police strike, they were gobbling up houses upstate too and all the farmland that had been leveraged to the max and, as it turned out, well beyond, in order to plant every acre during the worldwide grain and corn shortage. And of course by promising to send the Guard into New Orleans to enforce evictions, Brown was making it clear that he would do the same thing to break the copycat police strikes upstate.

This of course was nothing but the truth, but telling the truth, especially when it was more down and dirty than simple, did not necessarily win you elections anywhere in the US of A, let alone the great state of Louisiana, so Brown was certainly getting the best of this one-sided political freestyle fight as Hurricane Season time approached.

The first tropical storm of the Season turned into a Category 3 hurricane named Albert, which whacked Cuba pretty good but veered up the Atlantic Coast and pretty much turned into a pussycat by the time it hit Cape Hatteras. Barry made it to Category 4 and whirled up the Gulf of Mexico in the very general direction of the Louisiana Delta, but made landfall on the Florida Panhandle, and New Orleans got nothing worse than wind and rain and high water, turning the eastern Alligator Swamp into the usual Season-long bayou-veined marshland.

Nothing to really talk about, and Montrose didn't, sticking to his economic guns, but that didn't stop Brown from preaching about it anyway, and keeping his own flannel mouth shut about the farm foreclosures goin' on upstate, so as far as the polls went, nothing much was really happening, with Brown maintaining a lead over Montrose 41 to 31 with a bigger undecided than usual this early on in both the political season and the Hurricane Season. But with Carlo, as more or less expected by all sides, they started to turn into the same thing.

Carlo was another Category 4, but this one seemed to be making a beeline track for what was left of the main bird-foot mouth of the Mississippi Delta, from which, even if it didn't shove a major league Gulf flood tide up the river and turn Lake Pontchartrain into a seawater bay fit to overflow the northern Alligator Swamp into New Orleans Proper, would give the downriver levees a run for their money.

But Carlo hung a left turn before that and came ashore between New Orleans and Shreveport, and closer to Shreveport, much of which ended up evacuated and underwater, while the Big Easy got nothing worse than fifty-mile-an-hour winds and a driving rain that made traffic impossible for a few days on the flooded streets and avenues, and didn't even cut electricity at all.

Well, of course, this wasn't the first time a Category 4 had spared New Orleans, and during the usual Hurricane Season's out of a dozen or score hurricanes stirred up, only a half dozen or so hit the city with direct haymakers. But this wasn't the usual Hurricane Season, this was the *Political* Hurricane Season, and Brown played it for all it was worth.

Which wasn't as much as he had probably counted on when he denounced Sin City's good fortune as the Devil delivering his part of the deal with his hell-spawned demons. This might have increased his upstate lead over Montrose, but it did not play very well in Shreveport and environs, especially when Shreveport's mayor got airtime on Mama Legba denouncing Brown for making political whoopee out of his city's disaster and half-seriously asking his Satanic Majesty to make the same deal with his constituency too. Montrose gained ground in the western Gulf Coast without having to say anything at all.

David, though, worked its way up past Category 5, winds up to 150 mph, a wide son of a bitch too, turning Cuba and Puerto Rico into island-wide swamplands, turning westward to take out Merida and Vera Cruz with tidal bores before turning more northerly, and predicted to make landfall somewhere between Mobile and New Orleans wide enough to flood them both over the levees and into the towns.

Mobile was small enough to more or less send its population making temporary tracks inland. But New Orleans wasn't and couldn't, and so didn't, and all Mayor Bradford could do was Activate Plan A: close the schools, government offices, public transit, parks; close the streets to civilian traffic and so forth; pull the storm shutters down over the windows on all city buildings that had them; advise everyone who could to do likewise, stay indoors and pray without specifying to who or to what.

Churches had the option to stay open as refuges. This being the Big Easy, where half the population at least could be relied upon to prefer facing a Category 5 hurricane lifting glasses to Bacchus as fast as we could fill them to praying to Jesus in the pews, so were the saloons.

Plan A in New Orleans.

A Plan B, the city didn't have.

17

After Category 5 David and Category 4 Edward danced around New Orleans too, the online and print press in New Orleans starting doing positive features *praising* Mama Legba and her Supernatural Krewe of "loas," while the Bible Belt press upstate continued to foam at the mouth against them.

The police department, with no argument from Terry O'Day or Joe Roody, had thus far kept Luke under wraps, not wanting him to say anything to any form of the press unless and until they could figure out what that should be, and Luke who had no idea either certainly had no objection. But neither the department, nor O'Day, nor even Roody, could forever hold the press pack away from the guy who was either the hero of the People's Police or the villain who sold what soul the Big Easy might ever have had to Lucifer.

"So we better find out more about loas than what's on TV and the blogsites, because that's what they're gonna throw at you first, last, and always," Luella told him, and Luke could hardly disagree with that.

Luke wasn't very much for reading or researching on the Internet, but Luella, being an ex-schoolteacher, was, and she did the heavy lifting while he followed behind. There were tons of books, Web pages, blogsites, and whatever about loas, but they really didn't agree on much of anything, except that voodoo, or voudou, or vudu—there wasn't even any agreement on the spelling—was an ancient African religion or belief or superstition that came to America and particularly Louisiana, with the slave trade.

That much Luella the schoolteacher could declare historical fact.

"There are supposed to be these godlings or spirits for everything from the birds and the bees to to sex, drugs, and rock-and-roll, like Roman and Greeks polytheism."

That much Luella could declare "comparative anthropology."

But while Luella wasn't exactly the most hard-core Catholic in New Orleans and New Orleans Catholicism was far from the most tight-assed in the world, she was enough of a Catholic to consider the idea that such supernatural spirits actually existed, superstition or psychosis or both and just maybe blasphemy too.

"But I thought you believed in supernatural spirits, Luella."

"*Say what?*"

"The, what do you call it, the Trinity? God the father spirit, Jesus the son spirit, and a third spirit even called the *Holy Ghost.*"

"That's different!"

"How?"

"Uh . . . because they're manifestations of the One God. . . ."

Luke had never thought about God or religion at all as a Swamp Alligator, not many people in the Swamp did, least of all his jailbird father and junkie mother, and even though he had been married in a Catholic ceremony, he hadn't taken the religious part seriously, not even as seriously as Luella, which wasn't all that much either. But now the question of whether supernatural spirits, good or evil, could or did exist had not

only become political, not only become police business, but
had become quite personal.

So he had to think about such stuff now. And if there could
be supernatural spirits like God and Jesus, let alone a Ghost,
Holy or otherwise, why not loas?

"But aren't those preachers goin' on about the loas being
demons from Hell and the Devil an' all? So how can they be
saying I made a deal with evil spirits that they don't believe
exist?"

"You saying you believe they really exist, Martin Luther
Martin? You saying you really made a deal with supernatural
spirits?"

Luke sighed, shrugged, and sighed again.

"I'm confused, Luella. The more I hear the Holy Rollers
going on about my so-called deal with the demons of Hell an'
all to spare New Orleans from the worst of the Hurricane Season in return for the People's Police going along to get along
during Mardi Gras, it seems like just about the same deal I had
the Alligator Swamp Police make with the gangbangers."

"*Mama Legba's loas are the same thing as gangbangers in
the Alligator Swamp?*"

"No! Yes . . . I mean, the People's Police's part of the deal
could just as well have been my own idea, and Mama Legba
just a real good actress playing me along because she liked the
idea of a Mad Mardi Gras too. She was a street act to begin
with, wasn't she? And it sure has helped her show-business
career!"

"Speaking as a Catholic, I must admit I sort of have to be
believe that, don't I?" Luella told him. "But. . . ."

"But?"

"But as you may have noticed, Luke, no hurricane has
really hit New Orleans so far this whole Hurricane Season."

"So?"

"So speaking as a Catholic, I don't like believing it at all, but I have to admit that these nonexistent spirits, evil or otherwise, seem to have lived up to their end of the bargain, now haven't they?"

Like the Father, the Son, and the Holy Ghost, Luke suddenly realized. Whether they're real or not out there up in heaven or some other place other than this world, might not even matter if you were a Catholic who really believed in them. Because then they were real inside your own head, real enough to like make you stay a virgin, or pray to a wooden cross, or give up meat for Lent.

This, he knew, was a thought he damn well had better keep to himself. Thus far in their marriage he had avoided any arguments about religion, Jesus, God, or the Catholic Church by going along with whatever Luella and the Johnson family wanted him to go along with. And since he had never had a serious opinion about anything religious before, no problem, no sweat.

So no point in getting into it now. But there was one crazy notion on a voodoo Web site that Luella had shown him that he couldn't quite understand but couldn't keep from rattling around in his brain, maybe just *because* he couldn't understand it. Some scientists had discovered, or claimed they had discovered, or believed they had discovered, something they called "dark matter," which couldn't be seen, couldn't be felt, had no weight, but still was there.

But really real, *not* "supernatural."

Like the loas?

Not "spirits" but creatures made of such stuff?

He was still trying to get some kind of grasp on how something or someone could be real and not real at the same time, maybe like a part an actress was playing in a movie on TV, the part itself, not the actress, like Mama Legba and her loas maybe, when he was brought right back down to the heart-pounding down and dirty by a call from Terry O'Day.

"You're invited to a meeting tomorrow at eleven, Martin. This is not an invitation you can refuse."

"With whom?"

"Can't tell you that. You might slip and tell your wife. And she might slip and tell someone else."

"What's with the fuckin' spy-movie crap?"

"You'll find out when you get there."

"Where there?"

"A taxi will pick you up. No gun. No uniform."

And O'Day hung up.

Even though there was pelting wind-driven rain the next morning from the fringes of the latest hurricane to miss New Orleans, the taxi was on time, and took Luke on a spooky and scary ride through the nearly empty streets.

When he asked the cabbie where they were going, the dude gave him a dirty laugh. "Hey, bro', you don't have to play the game with me, I ain't about to tell your wife. You must either not be gettin' any lately at home or be hornier than a barrel a monkeys onna Spanish Fly to be goin' to a cathouse at eleven in the A.M. inna backwash of a Category 3!"

"Say what?"

But the cabbie just laughed and laughed, and when they got there, Luke saw why, there being a fancy three-story white house in the Garden District, overhung by tall wind-whipped trees, a covered porch all around the ground floor, balconies up top, filigree, phony columns an' all.

An upscale whorehouse known to everyone on the police force for the quality of its girls, its reputation for discretion, and for prices no cop under the rank of captain could think of affording.

"Have a good time!" the cabbie told him.

Somehow Luke doubted that he would.

He was greeted at the door with a handshake and a big sincere-looking smile by none other than the owner of Lafitte's Landing, J. B. Lafitte. "Welcome to my other, not at all humble, establishment, Sergeant Martin, in fact there are those who say it's the best little whorehouse in New Orleans, and who am I to argue with them?"

There was no one working the cloak room, so Lafitte did the honors himself with Luke's rain gear. "I wouldn't still be the impresario of this house of pleasure if not for you, so I owe you big-time, and anything and everything here is on the house any time you want."

Luke knew what he would have said to that before Luella, but he had resisted temptation ever since, though not on this level, and didn't trust himself to say anything just now, so he smiled, nodded, and kept his mouth shut as Lafitte led him into the big ground-floor main salon.

Lafitte laughed as Luke's jaw dropped. "I know, I know, you don't have to say it, it looks just like the Hollywood version of what a first-class bordello in the Big Easy is supposed to be. Well, that's because that's what it is. Even the rich, famous, powerful, and connected have fantasies of what a place like this is supposed to be created for them by show biz, so the real thing had better mimic the Hollywood version or they're gonna be disappointed."

The walls were all red velvet flocking and gilded framing. The floor was some kind of deep red wood. There was a stage at the far end with a full jazz band setup and enough room left for scores of strippers or porn queens or whatever to strut their stuff. Subtly curved brass bars with black marble tops embraced the room like hookers' welcoming arms. Couches, easy chairs, and tables were placed around the room, but leaving plenty of space in the middle for a dance floor.

The salon was the full three stories high and two tiers of interior balconies with cafe tables mirrored the ones outside, reachable by two dramatic spiral staircases. The ceiling featured a vast Roman orgy scene whose participants did not quite resemble movie stars living and dead closely enough to risk lawsuits.

Poleaxed by the setting for a long moment, Luke's first take was that it was empty. But then he saw that it wasn't. Then he saw that there were five men sitting at a round table toward the back of the room. Then as Lafitte led him toward them and he saw who they were, his next take was awe.

Terry O'Day.

Big Joe Roody.

Police Superintendent Dick Mulligan,

Mayor Douglas Bradford.

Elvis Gleason Montrose.

What the fuck is going on?

Two heavyweight politicians, the top cop, the head of the union, his media man, and an empty seat at the table that could only be his.

Whatever it was, Luke had the feeling that a fancy whorehouse was going to turn out to be just where a meeting like this belonged.

Montrose glanced briefly at Lafitte, who nodded and disappeared up the nearest spiral staircase. It was easy enough to see who was running things, and after all he *was* the rooster atop this political pecker order, but it was Superintendent Mulligan who spoke first while Luke was still sitting down, as if to remind the rest of them that Luke was under *his* command.

"I suppose you're wondering why I ordered you here, Sergeant Martin."

"I sure am!" Luke blurted. But Mulligan wasn't in uniform

and neither was he, and the order or invitation, or whatever it was, had come from O'Day, meaning the union, not the Department. "You did?"

"No, he didn't," said Elvis Gleason Montrose.

Luke glanced at Roody. Big Joe shrugged and nodded no.

"*I* did, Sergeant. Martin," said the Democratic candidate for governor of Louisiana. Everyone in Louisiana had probably seen him on various screens more than they cared to by now, Luke included, but he had never seen anyone that high up the political ladder in the flesh before.

As a media image, Elvis Gleason Montrose was an immaculately clad suit with somewhat longish hair over a high forehead, piercing blue eyes, and a confident expression frozen on a smoothly unwrinkled face. In the flesh on this gray stormy morning in a deserted whorehouse, he wore dark blue sweats, his eyes were watery, he looked ten years older and twenty pounds heavier, the high forehead was revealed as a receding hairline, and the confident expression seemed plastic and phony.

"So I'll get right to the point," Montrose said. "I need your help."

The way the man looked and the way that he said it convinced Luke that he meant it, but he couldn't imagine how, so he didn't react at all.

This did not seem to faze Montrose. As your usual long-winded mush-mouthed New Orleans politician, he probably didn't care to be interupted once he had your attention and went into a campaign speech or the long-winded answer to an interviewer's question even when it was supposed to be yes or no. *Especially* when it was supposed to be yes or no.

"Now, you are probably asking yourself what can a mere police sergeant do to help a candidate for governor of the great state of Louisiana—"

"I wouldn't quite put it that way," Luke blurted. "I mean, I'm not asking myself anything at all, sir. I'm asking *you* why you're asking *me* for help."

Big Joe choked back a laugh. Montrose seemed to make a difficult but successful attempt to choke down a comeback, obviously pissed-off, but not wanting to get into the dozens with someone he was asking for help, whatever the fuck that might be. Luke imagined that this was probably a skill a politician had to have to get anywhere in his line of work.

"As you may have noticed, I'm not winning this election," he said. "The polls say I'm running fifteen to twenty points behind Brown, and even in an ordinary election for governor, whatever that may mean in this state, any Democratic candidate starts in a hole even though no Republican could be elected nutria catcher down here if he were Jesus H. Christ on a Harley because upstate outvotes New Orleans and downstate and redneck land is solidly Republican, ordinarily sixty-five to thirty-five or something like that. You following me, Sergeant Martin? *Luke,* if I may?"

Luke nodded, rather than saying "Gotcha, Elvis," though he required a certain amount of applied self-discipline himself as his initial awe in the presence of such a political celebrity began to fade. This guy, after all, had opened by admitting that he was asking him for help and now had admitted that he was in deep shit.

"So right now my chances for being elected governor are slim and none," Montrose admitted to Luke's astonishment. "Thanks in significant part to you, Sergeant Martin."

Uh-oh! "What did I do?"

"Oh nothing much, *Sergeant* Martin," Superintendent Mulligan broke in without even a sour look from Montrose. "All you did was make a deal with the Devil to protect New Orleans from the Hurricane Season in return for turning Mardi Gras into Sodom and Gomorrah on behalf of the New Orleans Police Department on your own without any authority. If the Department were the Army, you'd be in the stockade, *Officer Martin*."

"Come off it, Dick, you can't demote him," said Big Joe Roody.

"Oh, *can't* I?"

"Well, I suppose you can, Dick, if you don't mind having a little total strike on your hands until you reinstate him and promote him to lieutenant."

Mulligan shot a poisonous look at Mayor Bradford.

"For once, I'm with Joe."

Montrose took over smoothly. "The point is, Luke, that my chances were slim before, and now, thanks to you, they are none."

Luke was beginning to get the idea, or perhaps the certainty, that his whole thing was some kind of put-up job. "Then why did you run in the first place?" he ventured to ask.

"Would you believe because I believe that this whole Great Deflation is a scam by the vultures of Wall Street and the hedge funds and the investment banks and the rest of the virtual economy that owns this great nation of ours in the form of trillions of dollars in uncollectable debt to convert it into owning the *real* wealth of our state and our country, farmland, mines, commercial real estate, housing, and factories?"

"Well, seeing as I believe it too, and seeing as everyone in Louisiana has heard you say it a thousand times, I guess I can believe that you believe it, but . . ."

"But you find it hard to believe that any politician in Louisiana would run for office in an election he figured to lose without any ulterior motive just because of something he believed in?"

"You said it, not me, Mr. Montrose."

Montrose broke in a twisted kind of grin, the first expression that Luke had seen on his face that seemed entirely sincere.

"Well, you're right, Luke," he said. "I've dipped my wick into my fair share of the honey-pots—who hasn't?—but I'm not independently wealthy, I'm a professional politician; holding office is my job and I can't afford to join the army of the unemployed, I need the salary and the perks, and my ambition is to climb up the ladder. If I managed to get elected governor of Louisiana, I win. But if I don't, I've got a good plan B."

"Plan B?"

"I'm not going to run for reelection, there's going to be an open United States Senate seat two years from now, and I'm going to run for it," Mayor Bradford said. "So if Elvis loses this election, he'll run for mayor of New Orleans and be a lock to win."

"So you see Luke, I really am free to run for governor on principle, I can try to do what I believe is right just because I believe it's right because my ass is well covered. And you believe what I believe, now don't you? And you and everyone else in this state knows that if Harlan Brown is elected governor, he'll send in the National Guard to foreclose on everything legally forcloseable, including your own house, because he's sworn on a mile high stack of Bibles to do it. And no one in this room wants that to happen, now do we?"

"So what do you want from me, to endorse you?" Luke asked. "I guess I can do that if you want." This guy was beginning to look a little better to him, certainly at the very least more than good enough to at least vote for, considering the alternative.

"No way," said Terry O'Day. "He's already got a lock on the vote down here because a vote for Brown is a vote for sending in the Guard, and if you say anything good about him at all, it'll make things even worse than they already are. You don't even mention the name of Elvis Gleason Montrose."

"I don't get it. . . ."

"You attack Harlan Brown and the Republicans on the narrow issue that you own—"

"*Making a deal with the Devil to save New Orleans from the Hurricane Season?*"

"Shit no!" said O'Day. "You own that issue in New Orleans, but upstate *it* owns *you.*"

"Upstate, the Republicans are running to send the National Guard down here to take control of Sin City away from your People's Police in the name of Jesus, law and order, and motherhood," Montrose told Luke. "It's a smoke screen to keep from reminding those folk that voting for Brown would be voting to use the Guard or the State Police to foreclose on them too when push comes to shove. I keep saying that, but it's not getting through."

"And I can? But they hate my guts up there, don't they?"

"Doesn't matter, Luke, because your real upstate audience is going to be the small-town cops and sheriffs and whatever," Big Joe told him. "There's already a growing movement up there by various jurisdictions of our unorganized brothers not to foreclose on brother cops or even anyone else. Turn them into little bitty People's Police forces too. You just keep hitting that over the head with a mallet. Divide and conquer."

"And *you* use it to organize police statewide," Superintendent Mulligan said sourly.

Big Joe Roody laughed. "Why, that's a great idea, why didn't I think of it myself?" he said sarcastically. "Thanks a whole bundle, Dick."

"What's in it for me?" Luke said sharply. Now that he knew what they wanted for him, it was time to dicker. After all, could cutting a deal with Louisiana politicians be more presumptuous than cutting one with Mama Legba's Supernatural Krewe?

"Whatever happens, you're guaranteed your promotion to lieutenant, isn't that right, Doug?"

The mayor nodded his approval. The police superintendent pursed his lips as if he were biting into a turd.

"If he welshes, there'll be a strike that will cost him the Democratic nomination for senator, I can promise you that," said Big Joe Roody.

"And if by some chance I should win, it'll be captain immediately," promised Montrose. "If I lose, it'll take two years longer until I'm mayor. Have we got a deal?"

Luke knew damn well that it was golden. Luella would fry his ass with eggs for breakfast if he didn't take it. He was going to take it. But there was a certain power in that, or anyway enough for a decent bluff from which he could back down if he had to. He was beginning to get the hang of this politics game. And he too had a right and maybe a responsibility to push back a little for what he believed in.

"I want two more things," he said. "I want the Mardi Gras police rules to be made permanent in New Orleans. If you're not killing, robbing, raping, or stealing, if nobody else is hurt by what you're doing personally, you don't get arrested."

"No way!" shouted the police superintendent.

"Shut up, Dick!" the mayor and Big Joe said simultaneously.

"I have no problem with that," said Elvis Gleason Montrose.

"And I want to be able to encourage all those upstate cops to do likewise."

"Icing on the cake," said Elvis Gleason Montrose.

"Hey, Lafitte!" Big Joe Roody roared. "Time to come down and bring out that champagne we ordered!"

18

Well, there was good news and bad news at the September meeting of the French Quarter Pissing and Moaning Society, but then there always was, given that the society was a bunch of owners of saloons, strip joints, restaurants, sex shows, porn parlors and the like, a dozen or so of us usually, whose meetings were held in the establishment of one of us, generally Sunday brunch when it could be closed for a few hours, and generally consisting of the aforementioned well-lubricated pissing and moaning.

This month it was my turn to hold it in Lafitte's Landing and pony up the champagne, Mimosas, Sazeracs, Mint Juleps, and straight shots, but since I got to drink my share of free-bies when it wasn't, I was feeling no pain.

Well, sort of. The good news was that the Hurricane Season was coming to an end and we all had been spared any real damage. The bad news was that business was deep in the usual early post–Hurricane Season slump.

The good news was that Elvis Montrose was rising in the polls against Harlan Brown. They were only 5 or so percent apart, within what is laughingly called the margin for error in a state where error is normal and margin for it is a joke, and Montrose had what the sportscasters call the "Big M," so the chances of Brown not being elected and sending in the National Guard to kick half of us out into the street were getting to be a little better.

This was being achieved by the deal that had Luke Martin fomenting local copycat refusals by upstate police forces to evict anyone from anything, and hammering Brown for the promise he had rope-a-doped himself into to send the Guard into New Orleans to do the foreclosure dirty work, and pointing out that if Brown got elected, no way he would not use the Guard upstate in the same deeply unpopular manner too, while ol' Elvis swore quite convincingly that he would never ever do such a dastardly deed in the service of the bastards bankrolling Brown.

So Montrose had succeeded in using Martin to shift the main issue with the upstate voters away from New Orleans making a deal with Satan to save Sin City from the Hurricane Season, where Brown was the champion of Jesus, Virtue, and Law and Order with a Broomstick Up Its Ass and he was the protector of Evil Big Easy Sleaze to whether or not the Guard would be used to enforce foreclosures upstate too, on which he was their champion and Brown the villain.

But as his end of the deal, Martin got to champion the weird suggestion to Holy Roller Land cops that they also emulate the so-called People's Police and turn their jurisdictions into what the double-dome citizens' rights shysters called "victimless crime free zones" and we all just called letting the good times roll, and this went over north of Baton Rouge like a fuck film festival in Oral Roberts University.

Anyone who had spent any time upstate at all had to know this would happen, let alone a professional politician like Elvis Gleason Montrose, who had cynically used Martin to gain just these results. Good news for him maybe, but at the expense of bad news for the tourist trade, and therefore for the unofficial members of the unofficial French Quarter Pissing and Moaning Society.

The tourist trade had been given a mighty boost by Mama Legba's Mad Mardi Gras, getting New Orleans enticing national publicity as America's most sinful city fit to turn Vegas green with envy, and which everyone here dependent on the tourist economy hoped would carry over through the Hurricane Season and into a profitable fall and winter between then and the next Mardi Gras.

It was bad news for us, meaning bad news for the economy of the whole city, because that wasn't happening. Mama Legba and Her Supernatural Krewe was sliding in the national ratings because the Voodoo Queen of the Mad Mardi Gras versus the Bible Belt Holy Rollers was no longer the hot topic out of Louisiana, the so-called police strikes and the election that would decide whether or not the National Guard would be used to break them was, as Montrose had intended.

Street-smart New Orleans homeboy, good old Elvis, knew just what you needed to be to survive, let alone succeed, as governor of the great state of Louisiana, those lacking the required cynicism better not apply.

You seriously ask how I know the details of this deal? You are really so naïve as to believe that there is a whorehouse in the Garden District not thoroughly wired for video and sound? Let us not insult each other, okay? I will not insult your intelligence, and you do not think of such a thing as "gathering blackmail material."

This time around the biggest pisser and moaner was Charlie Devereau, which was unusual since Charlie was the biggest success story among us and therefore usually had the least to piss and moan about.

Charlie had started out with a single saloon in the Quarter, added a strip joint, another saloon, a restaurant, a third bar, a jazz disco, and so forth, working his way up to where he was today, part owner of several Central Business District hotels, full owner of a casino, and who knew what else. So successful that he was the only one of us who was actually a dues-paying member of the New Orleans Chamber of Commerce and even admitted to having voted Republican upon occasion.

But we didn't hold that against him, because good ol' Charlie didn't attend these brunches for the free drinks or to lord it over us, but because he had a nostalgic fondness and even respect for his French Quarter roots and had never sold any of his various properties down here.

After a number of us had complained about how the tourist trade was just not rebounding with the end of the Hurricane Season here in the Quarter, it was Charlie's turn to piss and moan.

"It looks like the fall season is going to be even worse than it's looking to y'all now, thanks to the damn election. Hotel bookings are way down instead of rising as they should after the Hurricane Season. The family tourist trade is afraid to come down because the so-called police strike is being hyped by the Republicans and the out-of-state media as turning New Orleans into Satan's playpen with the cops supposedly not even keeping the Swamp Alligators out of the Quarter, and Brown screaming that if Montrose wins it's gonna stay that way. But the good-time, uh, *Charlies* aren't booking ahead because if Brown wins, the Big Easy ain't gonna be so easy 'cause it'll be occupied by the National Guard and maybe even under martial law."

Charlie paused to finish his Mimosa and fill his empty glass directly from the bourbon bottle, and I switched over to hard liquor myself upon hearing this *really* bad news from our only big-time Central Business District connection, and I sure wasn't the only one.

"You should hear what's going on in the Chamber of Commerce!" Charlie went on after chug-a-lugging a big slug. "Everybody's hurting right now, and those of us looking at advance bookings would short New Orleans tourist trade futures on Wall Street if there was a way to do it, or bet against it in Vegas if we knew how."

"So what do your Fat Cats plan to do about it?" someone demanded, speaking for all of us.

"Are you kidding? All they see to do about it is what they're doing right now, namely when in trouble, when in doubt, scream and shout, wave your arms, and run about like a chicken with its head cut off."

"They all askin' you to to pick our brains?"

"They'd listen to Earl Long in his straitjacket in the bug house if he wasn't dead like Huey if they thought he'd come up with something, and some of the very Fat Cats he wanted to squeeze and spread the results out thin are probably even praying to the Kingfish's ghost to tell them what to do."

Charlie downed the rest of his bourbon.

"So anyone here got a bright idea?"

The only sound was that of glasses being drained, refilled, drained again, the glasses being the only thing not coming up empty.

Charlie poured himself more bourbon, only half a glass this time, and he only took a sip. "Well, I *do* have wild and crazy idea, and since no one else has any idea at all, I think I am now drunk enough to say it. Let's get Mama Legba to run for governor."

"*WHAT?*"

"She can't win, but who cares? She won't even get enough votes to affect the election."

More dead silence. But I thought that maybe I was beginning to get Charlie's drift.

"It's about *publicity,* guys," Charlie said. "New Orleans was good big news all over the country because of the Mad Mardi Gras, but now the big news out of the Big Easy and the Great State of Louisiana is the election, and the only reasons it's a big ongoing national story is the police strike and the threat of martial law, which are not exactly talking points for the tourist board. So how do we fight that?"

"With a better story!" someone shouted.

"Which is?"

Bingo! I got it. Or I thought I did. After all, you'd need to do more than take off your shoes so you could use your fingers and toes to count how many local TV personalities in the US of A had used their shows to run for office, so why couldn't one use running for office to pump nitrous oxide into her deflating national ratings? Especially when she and everyone else knew and admitted that that was exactly what she was doing.

"An election with the Voodoo Queen of New Orleans running for governor! A Voodoo Queen with a national TV audience! Now there's a story that the blabbarazzi will pick up and run with like hogs after swill!"

"You got it, J. B.," said Charlie. "She'll draw free national and international press coverage like horseshit draws flies, fun coverage, with Brown and Montrose both getting whatever attention they can manage as spear-carriers, and have the tourists forgetting about police strikes and threats of martial law and all that political crap and have 'em flockin' back to the Voodoo Capital of the World like ants to a puddle of blackstrap molasses."

"Can we really do that?"

"Can we not?"

"Is it legal?"

"Would the show get kicked off the air if she ran?"

"Plenty of comedians have run for office like this!"

"You mean the real ones who didn't mean it seriously or the ones got elected?"

A nice little round of laughter at that one.

"But how do we get her to do it, J. B.?"

"How do we persuade the slowly fading TV star of a show going south from its formerly hot ratings to take back the lime-light?" I said. "Well, I suppose we could horsewhip her into doing it with a wet noodle if we had to."

Relieved belly laughs that time.

"So no sweat, right, J. B.?" Charlie purred. "Seems like you're the one to sell this to Mama Legba, like you say, about as hard as, uh, peddling pussy to a shipload of horny sailors. And you're an expert at that, now ain'tcha?"

Charlie Devereau, the bastard, did have a way with words, now didn't he? I swallowed it like . . . uh, a big-mouthed bass taking the tackle baited with a nice fresh little crawdad, hook, line, and sinker. Wouldn't you?

19

re you crazy, babes, you've gotta do it!" Harry Klein told MaryLou, and of course by so doing was telling Erzuli too, and Erzuli was also all for it, and then some.

He's right, hon', what do we have to lose, what's not to like, just about the whole krewe is for it, and that's as close to being unanimous as we ever get.

But MaryLou still didn't like it. She really didn't think it was because running for governor was crazy, after all a girl with a whole passel of ectoplasmic loas in her head working her body and her mouth whenever they felt like it could hardly complain that *anything* was too crazy. Nor was it that she was totally unqualified to be governor and didn't even have an idea of what the job entailed, since she wasn't going to be elected anyway, besides which, this was, after all, *Louisiana,* where incompetence had never exactly disqualified anyone for high office.

Still, there was a swampy whiff about it beyond the usual show biz sleaze even for an ex-street busker, something vaguely, well, actually *immoral,* that MaryLou couldn't quite get a handle on.

"I don't know, Mr. Lafitte," MaryLou said hesitantly, "there's just something about the whole idea that doesn't seem right. . . ."

"Oh for Chrissakes, MaryLou—"

But J. B. Lafitte cut Harry off. "That's understandable, Miz Boudreau," he said calmly. "Truth be told it sounded kinda over the top at first to me too."

"It did?"

"Well, sure it did," Lafitte told her with a little shrug, which she couldn't tell was sincere or show-biz bullshit, just as she had been unable to decide whether Lafitte himself was really the charming rogue he seemed to be the moment he sashayed into Harry Klein's office or whether he was just perfect at playing the part. Or whether there was really a difference.

"But then I started asking myself who wins and who loses, which, after all is always the right question to ask if you want to do what's right too, not just what's gonna do your own sweet self good, and what's right is what you feel good after, don't you agree, Miz Boudreau?"

"I suppose so. . . ."

"So who wins is you, big-time, your ratings recover, your show gets subsidized by the Chamber of Commerce and the Tourist Board. And New Orleans wins, okay maybe not as big-time as you do, but the tourist industry, upon which you as a former street act should know this city depends, gets a sorely needed lift. Now ain'tcha gonna feel good after that?"

Lafitte looked at her strangely while she had it out with Erzuli inside her head, or rather, she supposed, he was looking at her staring at *him* strangely for what must have seemed like a long time, as Harry Klein drummed his fingers impatiently on his desktop.

Come on, MaryLou, what's your problem? Erzuli demanded crossly and perhaps even a little threateningly, an attitude she had never turned on her before.

It's phony! MaryLou blurted, finally realizing what was bothering her.

It's show biz, hon', it's all an act, so how can it be more phony than for instance our show itself? Ain't Mama Legba the biggest phony of all seein' as how what people see on TV don't exactly exist at all? How can it be more phony than Mama Legba herself . . . itself . . . we all?

It's . . . it's unpatriotic!

It's WHAT?

It's . . . it's unpatriotic!

Unpatriotic? You'll pardon me for having to ask what that word means.

It's turning a democratic election into a farce!

Lafitte rose dramatically from his chair with a fixed smile on his face. "Tell you what, Miz Boudreau," he said. "You tell me one person who loses and I'll walk right out of here and never come back."

You tryin' to tell us it isn't a farce already?

The next thing MaryLou knew, Harry Klein was smiling at her in relief and she was smiling at a satisfied-looking J. B. Lafitte on his way out the door.

Did I really believe in loas before I closed a deal with them in Harry Klein's office?

I suppose it depends on what you mean by *believe*. Everybody in New Orleans, in the Delta, as far west as Lafayette, as far north as Baton Rouge, certainly knows that there's a voodoo tradition in southern Louisiana that goes all the way back to the African slave trade. You hear it in the music, you can smell it in the air, see it all over the tourist souvenir shops, even if you've never heard a thing about Marie Laveau, loas, chicken sacrifices, and trance dances, and most folks here, including yours truly certainly have. And that was before Mama Legba and Her Supernatural Krewe went on the air.

Do I believe in Jesus? Do I believe in Mohammed? Do I believe in Buddha? Do I believe in Krishna?

Not in the sense that the various flavors of Holy Rollers believe, after all, they can't all be right about the way Big Daddy in the Sky set up the game, since some of them don't even believe there's only one of Him and some of them do.

But I have to believe that Christianity, Islam, Buddhism, and all, exist, now don't I? So if *they* exist, so does voodoo. It must exist because you see it on television.

Loas? Split personalities like the shrinks would call it? What the theater folks call Method Acting?

If Harry Klein had power of attorney, no sweat, done deal as soon as I walk in the door. But Mama Legba, I mean this former busker, MaryLou Boudreau, has her doubts. So I make with the sweet reason.

". . . who wins is you, big-time, your ratings recover, your show gets subsidized by the Chamber of Commerce and the Tourist Board. And New Orleans wins, okay maybe not as big-time as you do, but the tourist industry, upon which you as a former street act should know this city depends, gets a sorely needed lift. Now ain'tcha gonna feel good after that . . . ?"

And she freezes. She goes blank. Like a wax museum dummy of herself. I'm looking her in the eyes and I'm not seeing anything looking back.

I can hear Klein drumming on the desktop and by the beat of it I can tell that it only lasted a minute or two but let me tell you it felt like forever at the time. What am I supposed to do with this poster girl for a poker face staring at me with dead eyes like a corpse?

Well, it *is* a poker face. Maybe she's hiding her hand behind that mask, and if this was a poker game, what I'd have to do, like it or not, is call.

"Tell you what, Miz Boudreau," I tell her, getting up out of my chair real slowly. "You tell me one person who loses and I'll walk right out of here and never come back." And even more slowly, I turn to leave.

And that's when it happens.

"Come on, hon', sit your sweet ass back down, we just gotta a few little details to work out," she tells me, not only soft and warm as a wet pussy, but with another voice so sexy I want to hire her to answer the phone in my Garden District bordello. And even her eyes are lookin' back at me with the cock-teasing come-hither smile of a top-dollar whore.

I sit back down trying to hide the hard-on in my pants. "Such as . . . ?"

"Such as the format," she tells me.

I glance at Klein who looks like he's shitting pickles. "That's y'all's end of the deal, not mine," I tell her. "The folks who I represent just want you to run for governor, is all their askin', they're not sponsors trying to grab some creative control."

"They have the power," says a male voice that sounds like he's got a lot more of it than the New Orleans Chamber of Commerce, Montrose, and Brown put together.

"What power?"

"The power to keep the Mama Legba show on the air while we run for governor," purrs Mama Legba. It's the voice of Miz Pussy Cat again, but I gotta think of her as Mama Legba because this is what happens on the show all the time, and while I didn't watch it much then, I was beginning to recognize this voice from hearing it on television.

No way around it, if loas existed, I was talking to them. Whether I was talking to their ventriloquist's dummy, or a schizo or a real good vaudeville act didn't matter. I was talking to Mama Legba, and my mission, which I had accepted, was to close this deal.

"No problem," I say, remembering I was the guy who said

the same thing to Charlie and the rest of the Bitching and Moaning Society in my own saloon.

"No matter what?" says another male voice, this one kinda fruity and insinuating, like a star interior decorator to whom the customer is *never* right. "Anything goes?"

"Complete control?" demands the voice that sounds like he's got it already and always has.

Well, maybe I don't like the sound of that, like what would happen if Mama Legba does a geek act on the air or starts speaking in four-letter tongues or turning the show triple X, but I'm there to close the deal, so I do.

"Complete creative control," I more or less agree, but the more or less is good enough.

"The compact is sealed," says Mr. Complete Control, and Mama Legba shakes my hand.

"A pleasure dealin' with ya, hon'," says Mama Legba, blowing me a kiss as I get up to leave. And she's MaryLou Boudreau again before I'm out the door.

So if you ask ol' J. B. whether I believed in loas *after* I closed a deal with them in Harry Klein's office, all I can really say is that I sure closed a deal with something or some *things* inside the head of MaryLou—loas, schizos, Method Acting characters, whatever, just call she, it, or them Mama Legba.

Now, I was never a fan of Mama Legba and Her Supernatural Krewe, I don't believe in being a fan of anything, but now I not only had a business interest in watching every episode as someone making the best part of his living off the tourist trade, but it had become kinda personal.

So yes, I was watching when Mama Legba or whatever was talking through MaryLou Boudreau at the time threw her hat in the ring, live and unexpected on television.

MaryLou Boudreau usually stayed in Mama Legba's catbird seat and did the talking through the introduction, and the call for sad stories from the studio audience, none of the whining stories they told had seemed to be scripted except Luke Martin's now famous "People's Police" speech and Mary-Lou would stick around till Mama Legba's choice of who would get to meet their fairy godmother loa was made.

But this time the audience was obviously full of ringers and all of them seemed scripted. Many of them were just about commercials for the Supernatural Krewe, praise for saving New Orleans from the Hurricane Season in the form of man-in-the-street stories of how by so doing the loas had saved their personal asses, others were pleas to make the supernatural salvation permanent, or to make Mama Legba's Mad Mardi Gras the eternal format for the annual carnal carnival, or both.

And this time around MaryLou picked one after the other for the whole damn show, one after the other without any guest appearance by a loa, boring television on the one hand, but building and building anticipatory tension on the other, until the capper.

With the show close to the end, Mama Legba tossed away her shotgun mike dramatically, and cake-walked closer to the camera and Miz Pussy Cat did the talking.

"We have an announcement to make, and y'all gonna *love* it! You love the Mad Mardi Gras and so do we. And we all love you all! We love New Orleans! We love Louisiana! We proved it during the Hurricane Season, and now we're gonna prove it again! And you . . . are . . . gonna . . . *love it!*"

On came a male voice, sly and smart-ass sounding. "We somehow got dragooned here with slaves from Africa and we've been here ever since. We've answered your calls for help when we liked your style, and you've been our faithful horses when we felt like a ride, and together we've had a great time boogying together through the Mad Mardi Gras—"

And then there was a sudden voice change, and what came on was a booming male opera singer bass with a scat-man edge, and Mama Legba's face turned into a mask of power, and it was hard to convince yourself that the eyes burning into the camera were, well, merely human.

"And we're not gonna let anyone take all that away now are we!" it roared, sounding a lot more like a command than a question. "We're not gonna let anyone or anything bring back the Hurricane Season and take away the Mad Mardi Gras! I am Baron Samedi and I am running for governor of Louisiana and you all are going to vote for me, now aren't you?"

"I'm Erzuli," said the voice of Miz Pussy Cat, "and I'm running for governor of Louisiana."

"I'm Agau and I'm running for governor of Louisiana."

"I'm Bade and I'm running for governor of Louisiana."

On and on through the changes, bang, bang, bang, one after the other.

"I'm Sogbo and I'm running for governor of Louisiana."

"I'm Dumballah and I'm running for governor of Louisiana!"

And then came a voice I knew, a voice I had dickered with, a voice that made it sound like he was final. "I'm Papa Legba, and I'm running for governor of Louisiana."

Well, not exactly, because what spoke next was like Mama Legba and Her Supernatural Krewe doing the Mormon Tabernacle Choir.

"I'm Mama Legba and I'm running for governor of Louisiana."

"For a long time now this state has been laid low by someone once dared to call voodoo economics," said Papa Legba. "Well, that's not us. That's not voodoo anything. We are the real thing. We are voodoo. We have the power. We've used it for you before and we'll use it for you again when you elect

Mama Legba governor of the state of Louisiana. I am Papa Legba, I am the guardian of crossroads, the gatekeeper of luck and destiny, and Mama Legba is the doorway I'm opening for you to walk through. The choice is yours. Voodoo economics or the real deal."

"I'm not from Hollywood, so I'm not telling you to trust us," drawled Miz Pussy Cat, Erzuli as she had called herself.

"We're from Louisiana just like you," said Papa Legba, and Mama Legba wrist-flipped a pair of phantom dice across an invisible table. "And all we're telling you all is you gotta roll the bones, or the bones roll you. Vote for Mama Legba for governor!"

And with a tip of a phantom hat, a little bow, and a big fat smile for the camera, Mama Legba turned and waltzed offstage just as time ran out.

20

It had gotten to the point where MaryLou Boudreau only knew what happened on her own show by looking at the recordings of it afterward.

Her own show? Had Mama Legba and Her Supernatural Krewe ever really been her show? If it ever had been, it certainly wasn't now. It was Mama Legba's show now, and likewise, if "Mama Legba" had ever been primarily her, "she" certainly wasn't now.

The loas had taken over most of the airtime, and MaryLou wasn't even consciously aware of what they were doing except when Erzuli was the one riding her. And what they were doing behind the back of her head when she wasn't there was turning Mama Legba into a puppet show parody of a phony politician.

MaryLou herself was reduced to being the impotent ringmaster at this one-ring circus, pointing the shotgun mike here and there, listening to the praises of the Mad Mardi Gras and the loas who had "saved New Orleans," and pleas for salvation from everything from hurricanes to herpes, from eviction notices and foreclosures to unlovable spouses and diarrhea. To which Mama Legba always promised she would grant when she was elected governor and set everything right.

Was this satire of an election campaign funny? Was it even supposed to be funny? If so, it wasn't to MaryLou Boudreau, it didn't seem to be to the live audiences, and the latest polls were showing that 17 percent of the voters in Louisiana who were being projected as actually *voting* for Mama Legba would seem to be taking it seriously.

What was the Supernatural Krewe really trying to do? Or for that matter did they even know, let alone understand, what they were doing?

MaryLou knew plenty about voodoo even before there was a Mama Legba and had probably been ridden by loas more than anyone else ever, and knew more about the experience than any other "horse," since other "horses" never actually *experienced* the ride at all.

But just what were loas anyway? MaryLou found it hard to buy Africans gods or supernatural spirits, evil or otherwise, and Erzuli claimed neither was what they really were. She did some reading and googling and came up with any number of crackpot theories and theological mumbo-jumbos, most of which didn't make any sense to her.

One that seemed to make a little sense was on a flying saucer site that featured plenty of fuzzy photos and videos of the cavorting lights in the sky, but claimed that they were "natural creatures of the planetary magnetosphere," an entire ecology of organized energy rather than aliens from outer space. Could the loas be the most highly evolved form of "energy entities"?

Another was that they were creatures of another reality that existed independent of flesh or even regular matter because it was the realm of "dark matter" and "dark energy," which physics had proven was really there but which scientists had been unable to detect, which sounded like the same thing.

Erzuli herself never gave her a straight answer. Because, or so she claimed, she didn't have any.

What makes you think we know, hon'? We don't remember ever being not here, but what makes you think we know where here is or what it is? Especially seeing as how it doesn't seem to be a here like what y'all have. What we know is we each have our powers, and none of us have bodies, and just like you, what we like, and what we don't.

It was always like that, so this time around, MaryLou tried a different question. *What is the Supernatural Krewe turning Mama Legba into, Erzuli?*

Erzuli laughed. *A candidate for governor of Louisiana, what else? Promising them the sun, the moon, and the stars, whatever they want to hear, when you win the election. Isn't that the way it's done?*

MaryLou had to admit Erzuli had a point there. *But Mama Legba isn't going to win the election.*

So we don't have to worry about breaking any promises we're making, now do we? Erzuli said, laughing again.

MaryLou couldn't deny that made a twisted kind of sense too, and no more twisted than the usual run of politicians who didn't worry about breaking any promises after they were elected either, but just went right ahead and made them. But. . . .

But what are you trying to do?

What makes you think we're trying to do anything, girl? Ever think we just wanna have fun?

Is this candidate act supposed to be the real deal, or is it supposed to be a joke?

Is there a difference? said Erzuli with a laugh.

This wise-girl comeback also made a kind of sarcastic sense, and after all what else could Mama Legba be as a candidate for governor but a satiric comedy act?

Still, the laugh had an edge to it that said something otherwise. But for the life of her, MaryLou could not figure out what.

B ut Montrose promised to promote you to captain even if
he lost and you had to wait two years for him to be elected
mayor to do it, and in the meantime Bradford promotes you
to lieutenant," Luella told Luke over the remains of breakfast
after Little Bruce was off to school. "So what's the problem,
Martin Luther Martin? We've still got our house, you're on
the fastest track to captain ever according to Daddy, you're
the darlin' of the People's Police, you're my ever-loving hero,
we got it made. Or am I missing something?"

"Yeah, Luella. You don't get it. You forget that if Brown
wins, he sends in the National Guard to throw everyone with
an eviction notice out into the swamp, including us, arrest
everyone not obeying all the crappy tight-assed little laws the
People's Police are winkin' and nodding at, and like you say,
I'm the public darlin' of the People's Police but not exactly
Mulligan's golden boy, so I get a load of the shit dumped on
him instead of a lieutenant's badge, and just maybe get canned
unless Big Joe can protect me."

"Oh," groaned Luella.

What Luke didn't dare to say and what Luella didn't have
to hear was that being Montrose's front man spreading the
police strikes upstate had made him Brown's number-one enemy.
So if Brown sent in the Guard under martial law some bright
boy just might figure out something to arrest him for. Wouldn't
he do the same if he were Harlan Brown?

"And Brown's going win, isn't he?" Luella said. It was not a
question.

"Tell me how Montrose can win."

It was not a question either and no one in Louisiana seemed

to have an answer. Luke had done his job pretty well turning the attention of a big enough slice of the upstate vote away from smashing the sinful evils of Godless New Orleans and its deal with the Devil's demons and toward voting against the fear of the National Guard being used to evict *their* peckerwood asses to have Montrose running ahead of Brown in the polls.

But that was before this crazy Mama Legba candidacy had turned the race upside down and inside out. Now Montrose was losing big-time.

Anyone who would still vote for a tight-assed tool of the Loan Lizards like Brown to spite the Devil wasn't about to vote for the Voodoo Queen of New Orleans and her krewe of supernatural demons from Hell instead. Except of course the few upstate yokels who actually believed all the bullshit promises she made and didn't get it that they were jokes.

But Elvis Gleason Montrose had never really been the hero of a lot of the people who were going to vote for him just because he wasn't Harlan W. Brown, and some of them were going to vote for Mama Legba just to throw big gooey pecan pies in *both* their faces, just a good joke, since she couldn't win.

Last poll numbers had Brown leading in the polls with ten days left 37 percent to Montrose's 30 percent and maybe even pulling away, with Mama Legba getting 18 percent and who could figure how much of the 15 percent saying undecided or none of your business, hah, hah, hah, going to go to her.

Some fuckin' joke!

Mama Legba wasn't going to win.

But she was going to elect Harlan Brown.

I should've seen it, shouldn't I? We all should've seen it, or anyway at least one of us should've seen that either Charlie

Devereau had been conned himself or had been in on it from the git-go, but either way we all, and yours truly in particular, had been conned into bullshitting Mama Legba into running not just to promote the tourist business out of the doldrums, but also to elect Harlan W. Brown.

Oh yeah, Mama Legba's freak show candidacy for governor had boosted her national ratings and was already pulling in more tourists during this off-season than had showed up in years. And likewise the advance bookings were no longer feeling any pain to say the least. Charlie's big idea and my big mouth had done *that* job all right.

But when Brown took office and sent in the National Guard and took a hard Christian line against the go-along-to-get-along of the People's Police and Mama Legba's Mad Mardi Gras, the crackdown would come right at the buildup to the high season and a martial law enforcement of the booze, drug, prostitution, and nudity laws, was not exactly going to pack 'em in.

Worse still, much worse for yours truly, was that all that would be a smoke screen for using the Guard to evict foreclosure victims by the hundreds and thousands just like poor ol' J. B.

About the only good thing I could think to think of was that the cabal of political heavyweights I had rented my bordello to for their conclave didn't know that I had talked Mama Legba into running, or I would be in even deeper shit when Harlan Brown beat Elvis Montrose and took office, which it seemed only voodoo black magic could possibly prevent.

Who could have believed that it could? And would?

Until it happened.

It just seemed part of the act at the time. Who would believe such a ridiculous threat?

I was in Lafitte's Landing when the show came on five days before Election Day. If the joint wasn't packed, it was two-thirds full, half of whom who I made for tourists, not bad considering it was the low season.

And of course Mama Legba and Her Supernatural Krewe was up there on the big screen I had put up, if for nothing more than to help move the expensive new drink I called Voodoo Moonshine I had dreamed up—cheap corn liquor, island rum, blood orange juice over a lot of ice in a very tall glass, and liberally watered with club soda.

I was checking on the supply of Moonshine behind the bar and not paying attention to what was on the screen, which I generally didn't do anyway, when it happened.

Suddenly the barroom went dead silent. I turned around and saw that everyone was staring at the screen like cobras at a snake-charmer. I looked at the screen and was spellbound myself, maybe even more so, seein' as how I was probably the only one in the saloon who had seen this before, up close and personal.

Mama Legba had shut up in midstream. Was frozen. Didn't move a muscle. Didn't have anything you could call an expression on her face. Blank. No one and nothing at home. For a very uncomfortable moment that had turned the barroom silent.

Then she began to dance. Not one of those voodoo twitch and jerk dances, but in slow motion, graceful but sinister like a cobra dancing to its own tune, something cold-blooded coming to make a call, something that should only come out at night, something that if it never came out would not be missed at all.

It stopped dancing as it turned Mama Legba's face into a grinning skeleton mask with glowing dead eyes like those of a nighttime alligator caught in a hunter's flashlight. But these weren't the eyes of a trapped reptile. These were the eyes of a reptile trapping *you*.

"I am Baron Samedi," loudly hissed a cold and angry voice that matched those eyes and that humorless grin. "I am death and destruction when that is my mood. That is my mood now. We offer you our rule through our chosen horse among you, Mama Legba. Yet there are those of you who insult us by spurning this great boon. Who even presume to deny that I exist. I am Baron Samedi. I am death and destruction. Defy me and perish. I will show you that we exist."

Tidal waves and tornadoes, whirlwinds and hurricanes, blowing in that voice, I could see *one* skeletal horseman of all the apocalypses riding Mama Legba through the airwaves, I could somehow even *smell* graveyards and corpses on television, didn't everyone in the saloon, didn't you?

"I now command Agau and Simbi, Sogbo and Bade, loas of thunder and lightning, wind and water, ocean and storms, to do as they have never done before, to use their powers together to summon up a storm such as your world has never seen. A hurricane that is more than a hurricane, a tornado that is more than a tornado, a whirlwind that is more than a whirlwind. It begins now in the Gulf, and it will dance slowly up the Delta and up the river to New Orleans. It will drown all of the city to the crowns of the treetops on the highest hills. It will raise a tsunami tidal bore that roars up the Mississippi overflowing all levees, swamping Baton Rouge and inundating the Mississippi flood plain as far as Memphis and beyond. Neither Jesus nor the Army Corps of Engineers can save you from the wrath of Baron Samedi."

MaryLou came back from wherever she was when she was ridden by any loa but Erzuli to hear Erzuli say through her mouth "But we can" to a studio audience and even cameramen who looked totally freaked.

What had happened? Who had done it?

"Baron Samedi is the lord of doom with a bad attitude and more power than most of us," Erzuli went on, "but I'm Erzuli, loa of love, lust, and mama knows best, and right now *I'm* Mama Legba not Baron Badass, and I'm not speaking for his bad boys. I'm speaking for the loas who love ya and want you to love *them*. Besides which, Baron Samedi sometimes lets his bark get ahead of his bite, he just wants y'all to understand that he *does* exist, which he does, and has the power do what he's gonna prove he can do, which he will. So think of what you just heard as a badass campaign speech, like vote for me or I'll kill you. Which he *will* do unless you elect Mama Legba, that's me, that's us, governor of Louisiana. Over to you, Papa dearest."

A t least what replaced the loa Erzuli this time wasn't something fit to almost have even me crossing myself and trying to believe Jesus really *was* my personal savior but something or someone a lot more reasonable, someone I had tried to do business with and succeeded.

"I am Papa Legba, guardian of crossroads, the giver and taker of choices," said Mama Legba. "This is a crossroads and I give you the choice. It should not be a difficult one. You need not believe in Baron Samedi to choose the road to destruction for he is about to demonstrate what will happen if you spurn the road to salvation we offer you by accepting our rule through our chosen horse, Mama Legba. But we who have the power to call up this ultimate tempest have the power to turn it back. You must choose Mama Legba in your own hearts—"

"—on Election Day, y'all," said Erzuli, "just in case you don't get what the Big Daddy of this here crossroads is telling you."

There was a long moment of silence after the Mama Legba show ended in this political carnival act capper, this take on any television evangelist who had ever demanded that we put one hand on our TV sets and the other in our wallets or else.

A great act maybe, better than speaking in tongues or snake-handling, but vote for me or I'll huff and I'll puff and I'll blow your house down, was too far over the top to have the crowd in Lafitte's Landing doing anything but taking a deep breath and then rushing to the bar to drink the fear away and the joke down.

Good for a graveyard chill and a barroom laugh.

But no one was laughing when next morning's weather satellite shots showed that a huge black cloud deck about the size of Texas had appeared more or less out of clear skies in the Gulf of Mexico well west of the Florida coast north of Yucatán casting a shadow of impending doom from horizon to horizon.

It just sat there in the Gulf for twenty-four hours or so doing nothing, "a meteorological phenomenon unlike anything ever seen," as the weather reporters unhelpfully put it.

After Katrina, when both hunkering down in the Superdome and the so-called compulsory evacuation order had turned into chaotic disasters that turned New Orleans into a depopulated ghost town wreckage of itself, the city government had created a so-called emergency evacuation plan which turned two-way Interstates into one-way escape routes out of town.

Fortunately it was never used, since there were only enough vehicles, public or private, to evacuate those who owned cars or who would have won life and death hand-to-hand battles for the trucks and buses. And once the Hurricane Season set in, reducing the city to the Alligator Swamp and New Orleans Proper and making it clear that there were going to be multiple major hurricanes every year, fleeing in and out for months at a time was no longer even a chaotic option, and permanently abandoning the city or hunkering down became the only alternatives.

So what was left of Hurricane Season New Orleans had long since more or less adapted and survived. New Orleans Proper shrank to the high ground and fortified itself against hurricanes like Tokyo did against earthquakes as best it could and the Alligator Swamp built its villages up on stilts and piles high enough to survive the flooding and even Category 6 hurricanes produced no real panic anymore.

But then, four days before Election Day, the big black cloud began to rotate, slowly at first, and then faster and faster, and the Countdown to Doomsday, as the TV weather guys and gals helpfully put it, began.

Three days from Election Day it was two-hundred-mile-an-hour winds around a fully formed hurricane that made a Category 6 look like a desert dust devil. By sundown it was moving slowly but steadily straight toward the mouth of the Mississippi Delta and New Orleans, estimated landfall on Election Day itself.

Call it brass balls, call it the Spirit of the Big Easy, call it just plain crazy, call it faith in Mama Legba and her Supernatural Krewe, who after all had shielded New Orleans from the last Hurricane Season, to do likewise with this thing. Or call it what I called it, no other alternative but to board up what could be boarded up, roll the bones, and keep my saloon and whorehouse open as a well-appreciated and lucrative public service.

Two days before Election Day, the Super Hurricane stopped dead in its tracks well south of the Delta, as if Baron Samedi was actually holding it there as a warning. People were even praying in Christian churches that it was. People were praying to Jesus. People were praying to Mohammed. People were praying to the ghosts of Huey Long and Elvis. People were praying to all of the above at once and Mama Legba besides. All day long and through the night, whatever was holding back the Super Hurricane seemed to be listening.

But the day before Election Day it began to whirl even faster and faster, pulling in on itself, faster and faster, beyond anything like hurricane speed, clouds rotating around its eye at tornado speed and beyond, flashing lightning and cracking thunder, faster and faster, but still bigger than any hurricane in the history of the world, sending flood-bores up the Mississippi even at this distance and over all but the highest levees, turning the Alligator Swamp into a shallow lake.

And then a tornado funnel dropped down out of it, a tornado as wide around as a full Category 6 hurricane and beyond, so enormous and so powerful that where it touched down on the surface of the Gulf, instead of setting off circular tidal waves the whirlpool that formed created a permanent water-sucking fountain sending the seawater *up* into the funnel and into the thunder and lightning of the hovering cloud deck to fall back down as a drenching rain.

When the sun rose and the polls opened on Election Day it was still there, it was already being called the Hurricane Tornado, and it was moving toward New Orleans at a speed that would take it to landfall just downriver about the time that they closed.

21

Colonel Terrence Hathaway had more than once heard it said that, given the state of the world, it was easier to believe in the Devil than in God, and had always denounced this as blasphemy, sometimes only in his own heart, sometimes in a good Christian voice loud and clear.

Until the results came in on Election Day.

28 percent for the Democrat, Elvis Gleason Montrose
35 percent for the Republican, Harlan W. Brown
37 percent for MaryLou Boudreau, aka Mama Legba

But as the commander of the Louisiana National Guard, Hathaway was about to confront this Daughter of Satan in the flesh for the first time.

Mama Legba, the Voodoo Queen Governor of the State of Louisiana.

How could God have allowed this to happen?

Or rather, his faith told Colonel Hathaway to more truly ask, *Why?*

The how of it was, after all, easy, he had seen it on television, and so had most of the rest of the world.

Just after dawn on Election Day, Mama Legba, or rather

the satanic demon who called himself Papa Legba and possessed her at the time, had announced that she would sally forth as the "horse" of her Supernatural Krewe to protect New Orleans from what the news was now calling the Hurricane Tornado as they had from the last Hurricane Season—if enough deluded fools would present them with enough offerings in the form of their votes to elect her, meaning *them*, governor of Louisiana.

Mama Legba, or whatever was "riding her," had then rented a large enough airboat for herself, a foolhardy camera crew of two, and a very brave pilot, and planed south down the Mississippi toward the whirlwind of black cloud, followed at a dangerously close distance by television boats and helicopters broadcasting the event through the longest lenses they had and no doubt praying for the best, like the people of New Orleans watching the coverage.

But to Who?

Or to What?

Terrence Hathaway had been commander of the National Guard since he had retired as a full colonel in the United States Army Military Police. Although he had been technically promoted to brigadier general for pension purposes upon retirement, he preferred to use the rank he had actually earned, because it seemed to him more honorable, less pretentious, and more resonant down here in Dixie.

He had been born on a farm in northern Alabama, far from the famously sin-sodden politics of Louisiana and particularly of the Devil's playground, New Orleans, and had been Born-Again as a Christian at West Point. But his years as the Commander of the Louisiana National Guard and the necessary habitation in the state had educated him in how far down the sides of the Pit people could slide and still remain standing on the Earth.

Buying and selling votes for money, or proclaiming that Jesus Christ was on your side in order to win them, was no big deal in the environs with which Colonel Hathaway was now all too familiar. But for actual *demons* to demand the electorate pray to them for salvation and require the voters to vote for a candidate for governor admittedly possessed by the minions of Satan or else, was a level that no Louisiana politician had previously plumbed.

Save your state and your city at the price of your souls.

And it seemed that a multitude of the Hell-bound were willing to do just that.

The television broadcasts of the woman in star-speckled black robes in the prow of the airboat approaching the Hurricane Tornado across flooded swampland cut away briefly to scenes of frenzied dancing harlots, voodoo ceremonies featuring headless chickens flapping away from bloody knives, crowds of worshippers not falling to their knees before Jesus Christ, but dancing in full demonic possession by and for the pleasure of the Prince of Darkness. And all the while, above crawls showing the projected vote count for Mama Legba rising, while those for the Republican candidate sliding downward a bit and those for the Democrat falling precipitously as Election Day wore on.

Terrence Hathaway had crossed himself repeatedly through all of this, on his knees at home with his wife, praying good Christian prayers not to Satan but to the Lord that these very sights would not tempt his heart.

For as the camera boats and helicopters following Mama Legba's airboat maintained a more or less safe distance from the vortex that rose through the heavens, the airboat itself inched slowly toward it during the afternoon as the exit poll projections showed Mama Legba drawing even with Harlan W. Brown.

By the time the sun began to go down and she had moved slightly into the lead, the live coverage became fixated on the figure of Mama Legba, so perilously close to the Hurricane Tornado, her arms raised and outstretched like the Christ of the Andes and seeming to hold it back as if performing a miracle, Hathaway could not help it—as a Christian he might loathe her as a slave of Satan, but as a soldier, his heart could not keep from going out to such martial bravery.

Mama Legba had a sound feed from a microphone on the boat, yet there was nothing to be heard above the monstrous hissing roar of the storm. But as the sun came down and the talking heads began to call her narrow victory as the polls began to close, someone did a remixing trick, and the Hurricane Tornado was reduced to accompaniment to her mighty amplified voice.

"I am Papa Legba," she boomed in a powerful male voice. "I stand at the crossroads of your destiny. I have offered you a choice and you have made it."

"I am Erzuli," she said in a female voice. "Y'all have spoken, and I hear you, and I love y'all."

Terrence Hathaway took to crossing himself obsessively as the voice of Mama Legba became a satanic chorus, the Babel of a demonic multitude, merging with that of the roar of the Hurricane Tornado itself, blasphemously becoming akin to the whirlwind from which the Lord Himself had spoken to Moses.

"We are Mama Legba. Who you have elected governor of Louisiana."

And then a single voice spoke from the Whirlwind.

The voice of he who had called himself Baron Samedi. He who a good Christian knew by another name.

Did he not?

"I am Baron Samedi. I am Mama Legba who now rules. We all are."

Mama Legba tipped a phantom top hat to the cameras as she did a little bow, and the move put a wink in the next voice that spoke.

"I am Papa Legba. I stand at the crossroads of your destiny. Roll the bones my way, and you don't crap out."

Mama Legba turned to the Hurricane Tornado and snapped her fingers.

once—

And the whirling corkscrew cloud reversed its spin and begin twisting *upward—*

twice—

And the tip of the vortex left the surface of the waters.

thrice—

And the Hurricane Tornado screwed itself into the sky like a film of its birth run backward and disappeared.

Colonel Hathaway had then been certain that, though it had saved New Orleans and much of the rest of Louisiana from destruction, he had seen the work of Satan on television. He had then turned it off and prayed to Jesus for understanding that did not come. And as he entered the governor's mansion in Baton Rouge to confront the price that the Devil had extracted for that salvation in the flesh, he crossed himself and prayed wordlessly for he knew not what now.

Huey Long, a cynical egomaniacal, demagogic governor of Louisiana during the Great Depression of the 1930s, had caused a new governor's mansion to be erected as a half-assed half-scale replica of the White House, because, he had said, "I want to feel at home in the one in Washington when I move in."

For reasons Colonel Hathaway found impossible to morally comprehend, the Kingfish, as this unprincipled mountebank had been affectionately called, was still a blackguard hero in this blackguard state, perhaps because he was the image that the political varmints who infested Louisiana like the nutrias infesting the swamps prayed to during elections.

And his White House was still there, though even the Kingfish might be outraged at its being occupied by the Voodoo Queen Governor. Huey Long might have stolen chickens, but there were no tales of him having slit their throats as sacrifices to Satan.

Like everyone else, Terrence Hathaway had seen plenty of Mama Legba on television, far too much as far as he was concerned, but now that he was actually entering her gubernatorial lair for his first meeting with her in the flesh, he realized that, like everyone else, all he really knew about Mama Legba was just that: a electronically graven image on television.

A demon herself? Possessed by demons from Hell? A direct manifestation of Satan Himself? He knew nothing about Mama Legba's soul at all.

Assuming that she had one.

Did the demons of Hell have souls? Did Satan? Did these so-called loas? Did evil spirits have evil souls or were they soulless creatures? This was too much theology for a simple Christian to truly comprehend, but Terrence had the feeling he was about to find out anyway.

Mama Legba received him in a bureau mercifully unlike the Oval Office in the full-scale Washington White House, and wore a businesslike dark blue suit befitting a female governor rather than a Voodoo Queen. But she didn't really look right in it. She looked like the street busker she had once been uncomfortably stuffed in a uniform she knew she did not deserve to wear, a pathetic shadow of his own daughter Annie in her West Point cadet's uniform, shrunken in stature, in awe of her own office.

As he soon learned, she indeed was.

"What do I call you?" Hathaway ventured. "Ma'am? Madam Governor ... ?"

"Can't bring yourself to call me Mama Legba, can you, Colonel?" she said. "Not that I blame you. Governor Boudreau, Miz Boudreau, or even MaryLou will do, because that's who you're talking to now."

"And may I ask why you ask ... summoned ... me here today ... Governor Boudreau? Just to get acquainted ... ?"

Governor Boudreau sighed. "I suppose you could say that," she said in a sad little voice. "Or maybe just to hear someone in this damn state government call me that. Or say anything to me at all. Both houses of the legislature are still Republican and as far as they're concerned I'm a creature of the Devil, and the Democrats won't have anything to do with me because I screwed Elvis Montrose out of sitting in this office. The old Republican cabinet is still in place and I can't fire them because no one will serve in a government headed by Mama Legba, so if I do, there won't be *any* government."

She shrugged and sighed again. "Look, Colonel Hathaway, who's kidding who? I never expected to be elected, I'm totally unqualified for this or any other political office, I mean I didn't even vote for myself. And the only advisers I have willing to talk to me are my agent Harry Klein, who knows no more about this job than I do, and J. B. Lafitte, the saloon owner and bordello keeper who sweet-talked me into running for governor as a publicity stunt by assuring me I was in no danger of winning."

Colonel Hathaway was surprised and somewhat undone by the sympathy he felt for MaryLou Boudreau, who in person seemed less the satanic Mama Legba, and more like an innocent kid not much older than Annie and way over her head in other people's satanic machinations. And the well-being of the state of Louisiana with her.

"What are you asking of me?" Hathaway said gently. "I'll do what I can. But I have to admit than I'm no politician either."

"But they say you're a real Christian. I admit that I'm not, but I think I'm glad that the commander of the New Orleans Natonal Guard is, because I hope it may help me get the right answer to my question."

"Your question . . . ?"

"Would you obey an order to send the National Guard into New Orleans to forcibly evict people from their homes because the New Orleans police won't do their sworn duty?"

"A bitter question, Madam Governor," Hathaway told her uncomfortably, "and likewise a bitter answer. As an army officer I have often enough had to enforce orders that as a Christian I found repugnant. But to disobey orders I was sworn to obey would be oath-breaking, equally repugnant, and punishable by court-martial."

"That's not what I was wanting to hear. I'm not going to give any such order. But it would help if you made it public that you wouldn't obey it."

Colonel Terrence Hathaway found himself staring at her in naked befuddlement that needed no words.

"I can at least watch the news and while Lafitte may be just a saloon keeper and what you would probably call a whore-monger, he does have plenty of what anyone who worked the Quarter as a street act would call street smarts or he wouldn't still be in business and he wouldn't have been able to have conned me into running for governor . . ."

"So . . . ?"

"So I may not be qualified to hold this office, but I'm able to inform myself, and I've got some down-and-dirty advice, and a human heart too, which is more than you can say for the heartless bastards who control the state legislature and the

Republican lieutenant governor, who are demanding that I order the Guard into New Orleans to not only enforce evictions under martial law gunpoint, but also to take over enforcement of the laws against victimless crimes from the New Orleans police who refuse to arrest people breaking them, and maybe even arrest the instigators like Luke Martin."

"I read the papers and watch the news too, Madam Governor. . . ."

"Then maybe you also know that the legislature is already drawing up a resolution to give itself the power to order it themselves over the head of the governor. . . ."

That was indeed shocking even for Louisiana! "But wouldn't that be unconstitutional?"

"Only if the State Supreme Court said it was, and seeing as this is Louisiana, even they know which side their bread is greased on. But if *you* declared you wouldn't obey any such order no matter *where* it came from, it would be a lot harder for the legislature to get away with it politically."

"You've quite lost me, Governor Boudreau," Colonel Hathaway confessed distastefully. "I'm a military man, not a politician."

"You think I am? This is Lafitte's scheme, not mine. I need you to go public with this, Terrence, if I may, and you *are* a true Christian, are you not?"

"I try to be."

The voice changed, became insinuatingly seductive and supplicating, the voice of the loa Eruzli as heard on television, and the eyes fixed upon him turned MaryLou Boudreau's face into an unholy mask of Mama Legba.

Terrence Hathaway would have crossed himself but for the words it spoke.

"Then tell me as a Christian, luv, could you really throw innocent families out into the muddy streets to make the rich richer? Would you want to stand before your Maker and try to walk through the eye of that needle? Would you really arrest fellow officers for refusing to commit such a sin in order to obey an order from the servants of Mammon?"

The words. . . .

How could such words not touch his Christian heart and his officer's honor?

"What are you asking me?" was all he could say.

"Could you do it? Would you do it?"

Colonel Hathaway prayed for an answer. None was forthcoming. "I will pray that I never have to find out, and that believe me, is the heartfelt truth!"

"Oh, I do," crooned Mama Legba. "And so do we all, hon'. An' all you gotta do to stay straight with your Jesus is let it be known that you won't obey an immoral command to send the National Guard into New Orleans. How's that gonna offend your, whatya call it, warrior's honor?"

Such . . . honorable words . . . such . . . Christian words. . . .

But that which spoke them. . . .

And then, as if his mind was easily enough read, the next words were spoken by a male voice, the voice that called itself Papa Legba, speaking like a fellow officer in another country's army.

"We both know that we're not each other's choice of allies. You believe in Jesus Christ, you believe that I either don't exist or you're talking to Satan. I *know* I'm Papa Legba, guardian of crossroads and standing at a fork in your destiny. *You're* the traffic cop at the crossroads this time, as an MP, you've been here before, now haven't you? And as a Christian, you must believe your God will guide you. It's not the singer, it's the song. So you can't trust the speaker, but can't you know a Christian truth when you hear it, no matter who's doing the talking?"

Terrence Hathaway trembled in his chair. Terrence Hathaway's head began to pound. Terrence Hathaway's heart had never been more deeply troubled.

"How *can* I trust what you say? How do I know I'm not hearing it from the Prince of Liars?"

"You can't," said the voice of Erzuli, "and half the time we all can't trust Papa Legba's words as gospel either. He *is* the Trickster too, after all."

And the face, the mask, of Mama Legba gave him a lubricious wink. "But come on, hon,' if you can't trust your friends, you should at least be able to trust your enemies. And Christian or otherwise, isn't what's right what you feel good after?"

"I'll allow myself to be asked whether I would obey such an order, and refuse to answer one way or the other, at least I can go that far for now," Colonel Hathaway finally found himself saying.

Having to say, for that was all that the conflicting demands of sworn duty, officer's honor, and Christianity could allow him to do.

Stand there and execute a holding action for as long as possible at the current . . . crossroads.

And pray long, and hard, and regularly, that he would never be forced to choose one path over the other.

And pray that if the Lord *did* lay that burden upon his shoulders, Jesus would at least grant him the knowledge of which was right before he condemned himself to whatever he was fated to feel afterward.

22

ow, you may ask, did J. B. Lafitte, saloon keeper and
bordello impresario, end up as the Voodoo Queen
Governor's chief and only political operative? Well,
I could claim it was a matter of guilty conscience aroused by
that phone call from her agent Harry Klein and it would be
true. Up to a point.

"Listen Lafitte, you bullshitted her into running in the first
place, she's up there in Baton Rouge all alone, and no one one
with any kind of political job or hope for one will touch working for her with a barbecue pit fork."

"Including you?"

"I don't know jack shit about Louisiana politics, Lafitte,
and I don't want to."

"And you think I do?"

"Come off it, Lafitte, you knew enough to get the poor kid
into this mess, now didn't you, and the way I see it, you owe
it to her to try to get her out of it," Klein told me, and I could
hardly deny he had a moral point, the sharp end of which did
penetrate what passes for my heart.

"Or else . . ." Klein continued in a threatening tone of voice
that I did not like at all.

"Or else what?"

"Or else the word might get out that you *were* the guy

behind the Mama Legba candidacy, which would not exactly put you in good standing with the Democratic party honchos who are still the power in our fair city, now would it . . . ?"

I didn't like it, but I had to admire it.

As long as Mayor Bradford, New Orleans's next mayor Elvis Montrose, and Big Joe Roody didn't know that, I wasn't in bad odor, but if they found out the part I had played in innocently costing Montrose the governorship, I'd stink like a very dead redfish, and maybe be one besides.

"Pretty good for a guy who doesn't know jack shit about Louisiana politics."

So I took MaryLou Boudreau's call less than an hour later, listened to her woes, realized that if the National Guard *did* take over they'd be mine too, seeing as how my whorehouse and saloon were among those under foreclosure, and put through a call to Big Joe Roody.

Roody had no particular loyalty to Montrose, Bradford, or the Democratic Party, and was happy as a clam who had avoided being served on the half-shell with the way the police union he headed had been making inroads with local upstate forces, thanks to the use he had made of Luke Martin during the campaign.

"Why should I stick my nose in Mama Legba's problems in Baton Rouge? Brown's not the governor, and why should I care that Montrose isn't either?"

"Because it's gonna be *your* membership's asses if the legislature gets away with overruling her and sending in the Guard, Roody."

Big Joe wasn't born yesterday, and he quickly changed his tune when I explained what the Republican legislature was up to.

"I'll call you back after I talk to our lawyers," he told me, and hung up. A couple of hours later, he did. "It might be legal, and it might not, meaning the State Supreme Court might do the deciding, and we both know Louisiana has the best Supreme Court money can buy. We can't let it get that far."

"So how do we stop it?"

"Not with legal eagles, and not with clout in the Republican legislature, which I sure don't have. . . . Looks like we're forced to try moral suasion. Terrence Hathaway is supposed to be a true Christian with a broomstick up his ass, that's the only pressure point we have, you gotta have Mama Legba try to trap him between Jesus and the legislature . . ."

"How is she supposed to do that?"

"Leave my name out of it," Big Joe Roody said, but more or less told me. And I more or less told the governor, and she more or less told me it had more or less worked, though she didn't know how, her "Supernatural Krewe" had gotten through to Hathaway when she wasn't there or something, and I felt no need to ask the next question.

Handling the Born-Again Christian Commander of the Louisiana National Guard proved far easier than a bad boy from the Big Easy could have imagined. When I got through to him on the phone, he needed no coaxing and little preparation. I just sent him the script I had one of my barfly writers crank out in return for a week's free drinks. I then set up a "chance meeting" with a news crew supposedly on the way to cover something else in front of the state legislature building across the street from the statue of Huey Long giving it the postmortem finger, which seemed only appropriate.

The reporter I had coached stuck a microphone in his face, followed her own script, and popped the question.

"Colonel Hathaway, would you send the National Guard into New Orleans if so ordered by the governor, yes or no?"

"The governor has publicly promised never to do that, so

until she goes back on her word in public, that's a question I don't have to answer, and don't want to answer, so I won't."

"But if the legislature passed a bill ordering you to do it?"

"I would imagine that Mama Legba would veto it."

"And if the legislature overrides her veto?"

"You're asking me if that's within their legal powers? I'm no lawyer, that's for the courts to decide."

"And if the courts say it is?"

Good old Hathaway paid attention to the camera for the first time, and spoke to it as directed. "I am sworn to obey the orders of the duly constituted civil authority. But I try to be a good Christian, and it was Martin Luther King who made a lot of us realize that it could sometimes be necessary for a good Christian to break the law and suffer the consequences. I was also a cadet at West Point where we studied the campaigns of Julius Caesar. So I'll tell you what they say he said before the Rubicon . . ."

He paused as directed, turned his back on the reporter, and delivered the line over his shoulder as he dashed away.

"I'll cross that bridge if and when I come to it."

Mayor Bradford had delivered Luke Martin's promotion to lieutenant as promised even though Montrose hadn't been elected governor. After all, Brown hadn't been elected either, and Mama Legba, who had been, had made it clear that she would actually make good on at least one of her many campaign promises and keep the National Guard out of New Orleans.

Nor was Luke really in ill favor with Montrose, who was a lock to be elected mayor of New Orleans in two years, and he wasn't even on the shit list of Superintendent Mulligan, although that had a lot to do with his being the fair-haired boy of Big Joe Roody, and Mulligan being more or less under Big Joe's thumb.

Thanks in large part to Luke, a growing number of local upstate forces were joining the new Police Association of *Louisiana* that Big Joe had created for the purpose of welcoming them into what had been the Police Association of *New Orleans*, which was now the largest and dominant chapter of the statewide police union of which he was also overall president.

And as the price of admission, the local chapters who wanted to join had to accept its formal policy of refusing to enforce any eviction notices on anyone period, and some of them were even buying into the voluntary police policy now called "No victim, no arrest," though only the New Orleans Police Department had taken to officially lettering "People's Police" on their vehicles.

As the head of the expanded union, Big Joe now had much more real power than Mulligan as police commissioner, and even the lame duck mayor couldn't afford to cross him, as Roody had explained to Luke with no little relish.

"The union is now running the People's Police because we really *are* the people's police force now, protecting them from the Loan Lizards, and sticking to 'No victim, no arrest.' We're now the *heroes* of the same people used to hate our guts!"

"We are the law, Joe? That's legal?"

Big Joe had laughed. "Who's going to arrest us? In the real world, the law is always whatever laws the police force in question *chooses* to enforce, not always what the political powers that be *order* the cops to enforce. But now that the people believe we're on *their* side, they're on *our* side, and as long as they are, the likes of Bradford and Montrose, let alone Mulligan, know better than to fuck with the union. The assholes in Baton Rouge may be calling it a police insurrection, but I say it's a genuine popular *revolution*. Though of course, not in public!"

But when word came down from Baton Rouge that the legislature was actually going to vote on a bill to order the National Guard into New Orleans to replace the People's Police on their own sacred turf, and the head counts showed it was going to be a close call, Big Joe Roody wasn't so cocksure, and wasn't about to count on the Voodoo Queen Governor to veto it, seeing as how there seemed to already be a move on to impeach her if she did.

"Time for us to do more than flex our political muscle," he told Luke upon summoning him to his office. "Time to use it to kill that damned thing before it passes. Time to raise up mass demonstrations against it, the legislature, and the National Guard."

"Now you really *are* talking revolution, aren't you, Joe?"

"They give us the name, we gotta play the game," Roody told him. "And if the rats downtown squeak too loud about anything we do, we just threaten to arrest a few of them chosen at random on corruption charges or perversion charges; it's not as if our friendly madams and bordello owners haven't slipped us plenty of juicy footage on all of them in return for services not rendered to the letter of the law."

"You're *enjoying* this, aren't you, Joe?"

"And why the hell not! The unions in this country have been having their asses kicked ever since Reagan broke the air traffic controllers, so why shouldn't a hard-assed union leader like me enjoy finally doing *his* fair share of the ass-kicking!"

"How we gonna do it, Joe?" Luke asked, though he was afraid he already knew the answer. Nor did Big Joe surprise him.

"*You're* gonna do it, Lieutenant Martin! *Captain* Martin if we keep the fucking Guard out of here. Bradford and Montrose will be falling all over themselves to do it to keep you from running against one of them in the next election."

"And how am *I* supposed to do it?"

"No sweat, Luke, you're a natural, and anyway, you'll have a script whenever you think you need it. You're a voice *from* the people, *of* the People's Police, and *for* the people who don't want the National Guard down here, which last time I looked was just about everyone. O'Day'll get you all the coverage you can eat, starting with a kickoff rally in front of City Hall, been there done that, now haven't you, only this time it won't just be cops in the audience!"

And so Lieutenant Martin Luther Martin once again found himself standing under the roof of the rotunda in Duncan Plaza park across from City Hall with a script the gist of which he had more or less memorized.

But this time the park wasn't filled with cops, the cops had cordoned off the entire area between Loyola Avenue and La-Salle Street and between Gravier Street and Perdido Street, to traffic, and the whole area was filled with citizens brought out by mayoral proclamation and a press release from Governor Mama Legba, waving homemade placards as well as the official ones proclaiming "Support Your People's Police," and "No Victim, No Crime." And the bouquet of microphones and thicket of cameras were a lot bigger than what Luke remembered.

"On behalf of the People's Police I want to thank you for your support of our No Victim, No Crime policy, and I'm here to tell ya that we're gonna *continue* to protect y'all from the *real* criminals instead of rousting folks who just wanna have fun and those of you makin' a more or less honest living givin' 'em what they want!"

Luke paused for the shouts and applause, as the script suggested he should, and they came, along with shouts, the waving of placards and fists, and he couldn't tell himself he didn't enjoy it.

"And we all know who the *real* criminals are, now don't we! The banks and the Loan Lizards swindled us with sweetheart loans turned to mortgages which no one works for a living can afford now that they turned the dollar into the superbuck! Stealin' our houses and our shops and our farms and our land!"

Louder applause and cheers, angrier this time.

"Well, your People's Police ain't gonna let that happen here! Not now! Not ever!"

Foot stomping to that. And did he hear the chanting of his own name here and there too?

"Luke Martin! *Luke Martin!* LUKE MARTIN!"

Oh yes it was, and it was getting louder and louder.

That much was what they called on script, but you're a voice *from* the people, wasn't that what Big Joe had told him, *of* the People's Police, and *for* the people, you're a natural.

So why not *be* a natural? Why not just let her rip, and think about it later?

"Now there are upstate sewer rats and Holy Rollers in the best state legislature money can buy, owned hook, line, and stinker by the very same mofos wanna throw your asses into the streets so's they can steal from you what they ain't stolen already. And they're fixin' to send the National Guard into New Orleans to do the dirty work your People's Police will *never* do for them. They *hate* New Orleans! They hate *you*! They hate you for knowing how to boogie! Because they hate boogying! Most of all they hate the People's Police for letting it happen and protecting *you* from *them*!"

Whoo-ee!

Yeah, he could stay on script when it came to getting done what he was supposed to get done, but Big Joe had made it

202 ★ Norman Spinrad

pretty clear that he didn't care *how* what had to be said got said, so he could open up loud and clear however he wanted like a star rapper as long as he didn't forget he was fronting for the People's Police, not some musical act, that he was serving what he was learning to call with a straight face a *political agenda.*

"Now, Governor Mama Legba said loud and clear she's not gonna do any such thing, she's not gonna send in the National Guard, she's gonna let the People's Police be the People's Police, she's on our side, but in a few days from now the bought-and-paid-for legislature's is gonna vote on a piece of shit to give *them* the power to send the Guard into New Orleans with orders to take back this city from your People's Police and enforce their tight-assed upstate redneck version of every pissant law, rule, and regulation we've been keeping from hassling y'all. And arrest a bunch of your good People's Police brothers and sisters for crimes against inhumanity. And throw thousands of you out of your homes."

What he was saying was touching the required political bases, but the words and the music were his own rap, up through and out of him from someplace that had never been alive before.

"So it's time to tell these mofos that anyone who dares to vote for that is gonna find *his* ass out in the street! Because you won't vote for him next time around, and all the money in the world spent to bullshit you on election day won't buy back his seat in the legislature. So your People's Police are asking you to fill this park and Jackson Square twenty-four seven and let Baton Rouge know what's good for them and what isn't! Send 'em the message that if they vote to send the Guard in to mess with the Big Easy they can start collecting unemployment insurance and they had better not open their flannel mouths or show their pig faces in this city ever again!"

Luke paraded off the stage pumping his fist in the air and shouting, "No victim, No crime! Power to *you*! Power to the People! Power to your People's Police!"

And while the words change every time he delivered The Speech, the message and the music stayed the same, and so did the exit line, and the more he did it, the easier it got, and the more fun it got to be, if that was what you could call what Martin Luther Martin was feeling, but if it was, it was a different kind of fun than Luke had ever had before.

Doing well by doing good!

No victim, No crime! Power to you! Power to the People! Power to your People's Police!

They were selling T-shirts with the slogans to the locals all over town and even to tourists in the Quarter.

Luke Martin had not only found a cause he could wholeheartedly believe in for the first time in his life, he had found that there was nothing shameful about losing the sort of cynical innocence that would previously have soured his enjoyment of being the hero of a cause he believed in fighting for. No drug had ever given him a high like this! The look he saw in Luella's eyes these days made him feel ten feet tall and the sex was off the scale.

Whoo-ee!

Doing well by doing good?

Luke was about ready to have it tattooed on his own lucky ass!

Occupying Duncan Plaza and Jackson Square was not in the script Luke Martin had been handed but an over-the-top ad lib that raised the ante big-time. Like one of those Occupy Wall Street or Whatever sit-in protests back in the day, but on steroids and Big Easy style.

The People's Police kept not only Duncan Plaza but all the streets around City Hall closed to traffic night and day and the people kept them filled night and day, not pitching tents and sleeping over, but parading in and out in waves, with posters and banners and all, but also to the music of shifts of street bands, and even some name secondary parade acts.

Three sides of Jackson Square had long since been turned into pedestrian streets, but now the People's Police had closed the whole block of Decatur, the main drag between the Square and the levee, to vehicular traffic too, creating a real mess in the heart of the Quarter. They kept the gates to the Square open twenty-four seven but banned camping out to allow room for the day and night Mad Mardi Gras block party jamming the park, the surrounding pedestrian streets, and Decatur.

Barbecue stands, gumbo stands, beer, whiskey, tequila, moonshine, and mixed drinks in paper cups, loose joints by the handful, hookers in and half out of porn gear, bands and musicians everywhere competing for attention and drawing costumed dancers—sex, drugs, rock and roll, with the People's Police lookin' on collecting cheers, applause, free drinks, and doobies.

No one seemed to know who had done it, but a high stage had been erected on a pipe framework right over the statue of Andrew Jackson in the center of the park, hiding it with red-white-and-blue drapery and the best bands by some mysterious popular choices took turns playing atop of it, accompanied by amateur naked ladies and naked gents.

After checking out the scene, I came up with what the media ended up calling the "Heads On Spears" game. Yup, it was ol' J. B.'s idea, and the Pissing and Moaning Society was happy to pay for it, seeing as how the party was overflowing out into the whole Quarter and the overflow was taking lucrative refuge in our welcoming establishments.

We put up a forest of poles tipped with outsize cartoon papier-mâché spearheads around the bottom of the stage. On each pole was the name and picture of a state legislator with the ol' red crossed-circle stop sign around their heads, though here it was also a target crosshairs for the rotten eggs and tomatoes and putrid fruit that people were encouraged to throw at them for the TV cameras, though the People's Police did draw the line at shit.

Would it have been enough to kill the bill making its way to a vote in the state legislature?

New Orleans and like-minded environs like to think so, but we all always seemed to forget that there are more people out there in the rest of the state who had as much fear and loathing for the wicked ways of the Big Easy as we had for these Bible Belt rednecks, which we of course never called them to their faces when they snuck down here for a sin break.

The truth was that it was still going to be a close thing. Upstate legislators' votes were needed to defeat the bill to invade the city with National Guard storm troopers, as Martin and the like were so diplomatically putting it.

This was not gaining many upstate votes, but Big Joe Roody's rebranded Police Association of Louisiana was working, or maybe creating, a grass-roots cop-brotherhood statewise, and if not that many of the upstate cops were buying into "No Victim, No Crime," more and more local forces had adopted no foreclosures as official policy, and wherever they were, voting in the legislature to send the Guard into anywhere to serve as rent-a-cops for the Loan Lizards would be political suicide.

Even if the bill passed there wouldn't have been the votes

to overturn Mama Legba's veto, that's the way J. B. Lafitte sees it. But we'll never know, now will we? Because Luke Martin went and dumped a mess of live alligators into the nicely simmering gumbo and it overboiled right out of the pot.

23

Luke had been invited or summoned or whatever he might want to call it to Baton Rouge by a personal phone call from the governor herself, MaryLou Boudreau, Mama Legba in human person, not some loa, an honor of a kind, but also a plea for help. So how could he refuse or want to, which he didn't, and even if he did, Luella would never let him hear the end of it.

But what sat behind the desk in the governor's office with the body language of a badass Swamp Alligator and the eyes of a stone-cold killer just wasn't her.

And certainly not the even more stone-cold male voice.

"You've come a long way from the Alligator Swamp, haven't you, Martin Luther Martin, now haven't you?" it said insinuatingly. "You don't go back there much at all these days, now do you?"

Luke shuddered at the voice and squirmed at the truth, which was that he hadn't been back to the hood since he made sergeant.

"I guess I've been kinda busy. . . ." he admitted a tad shamefully. "Has it changed?"

"No, it hasn't changed, boy. Have you?"

"For the better. And . . . and for the greater good."

"Oh, you think they're saying that about you down there? What about *their* greater good, or at least lesser agony?"

"The People's Police don't go down there unless they make us have to. They haven't been, so we aren't. We may not be popular in the Alligator Swamp like we are in New Orleans Proper, but I don't think we're unpopular either."

"Out of sight, out of mind."

"Right."

"As long as they *stay* down there, right? Don't want the likes of your old homies up in Jackson Square or in front of City Hall, now do we?"

"I've been told that it's . . . it's . . . politically counter-productive. . . ."

"Well, as you may notice, boy, I'm sitting here in the gover-nor's chair, and I say it's counterproductive to not let the lower reaches of the citizenry of the city have their voices heard. They'll be on *your* side, now won't they? And I, Mama Legba, governor of the great state of Louisiana, order you to go down into the Alligator Swamp and invite the outsiders in."

Luke was torn in time. The boy from the swamp knew that this was the right thing to do, and the memory of that boy relished the thought of doing it, but the professional officer of the People's Police that he now was did not think it was exactly a brilliant idea.

"I . . . I . . . I don't think the governor has the right to order me around like that," Luke stammered.

"Maybe, maybe not," said the thing inside Mama Legba, "but Baron Samedi has the *power*. And isn't it the sad truth of your world and mine, boy, if you want something done right, you have to do it yourself."

And it was inside him.

Whether Luke had ever believed voodoo was anything more than another cult scam was no longer relevant now, for the next thing he knew, or was allowed to know, he was somewhere in the Alligator Swamp, not Baton Rouge, and he was sitting by himself in a four-seat police department airboat, with the deafening roar of the airplane propeller behind him and the big engine thrumming his bones, and the airboat was banking around a curve in a bayou at about fifty miles an hour, then swerving up onto the mud, and gliding toward a little village just like the one he had grown up in.

And maybe it *was* the one he had grown up in, because this had to be a dream, a dream of the watching of a police airboat chasing gangbangers that had set the boy he had been back in the day on the path to the man he had become.

It had to be a dream, didn't it?

Because he was expertly driving an airboat, something he had never in his life done before.

Or was he?

His hands were on the tiller and throttle, but *he* wasn't moving them, *he* wasn't driving the airboat. He was riding the airboat, but *Baron Samedi* was riding *him*.

And talking to him silently inside his own head.

You're my horse for the duration, boy, so you might as well lean back and enjoy it. It's not as if being a heroic cop roaring through the Alligator Swamp on an airboat wasn't your childhood dream.

What the hell's happening to me? Luke wondered.

Luke found that he didn't have control of a single muscle in his body including the ones that worked his mouth and his tongue. But nevertheless he still was talking to this thing called itself Baron Samedi.

Silently.

Inside his own head.

Whatever you want to believe, Martin Luther Martin. You can believe you're really being ridden by Baron Samedi. You

*can believe you're still that very boy dreaming you've grown
up just as you wanted to. You can believe you really are Lieutenant Martin dreaming this is happening.*

A bone-chilling silent laugh with something fraternal
behind it.

*Or you don't have to believe anything at all. Sometimes I
think I could be something else dreaming it's Baron Samedi.
Sometimes I don't. Who cares? What matters is we're going to
take a ride around the Swamp together, and we are both going
to enjoy it.*

And then the airboat slid into the village, thatched or aluminum sheeting huts and houses up on stilts above muddy
pathways, little knots of the curious following the airboat
until it had gathered maybe a few dozen fisherfolk and farmers around it and a few obvious Swamp Alligators in gangbanger colors.

We can do this two ways, boy, and the choice is yours,
Baron Samedi told him. *Either way, I'm in the saddle, and I'll
drive this thing, you're just along for the ride. But I can do the
talking or you can as long as you say what I want said. And I
think you already know what I want said. And whether or not
you believe in Baron Samedi, Baron Samedi believes in you.
Believes you want it said too. Believes you can say it to these
people better than I can. Because you're one of them and I'm
not. Over to you, boy. You can just be my horse, or we can be
one of those centaurs together.*

And Luke found that he could not deny that the nonexistent son of a bitch, whatever he was, was right, and knew it.
And *he* knew what he was supposed to do. And knew damn
well that he wanted to do it.

"I'm Lieutenant Luke Martin of the People's Police, maybe
y'all heard of me, I been in the news a lot, and I know it gets

through to down here 'cause I was born in the Swamp, blooded in the Swamp, so cop or not, I grew up as one of you."

Snorts and head shakes and cynical sour looks all around.

"The fuckin' honcho of the fuckin' Alligator Swamp police!" one of the gangbangers snarled.

What you doing, boy? demanded Baron Samedi.

What we want to do, Luke told him. *Wait and see.*

"That's right, mofo, I started as a cop down in the Swamp an' I made the Alligator Police the top gang in our turf, and me the honcho of honchos, and made y'all like it or else, an' a lot of you did, so you better listen up, 'cause here I am again, only I ain't just what I was, now I'm Lieutenant Luke Martin of the People's Police!!"

"Our enemies!" another of the gangbangers shouted out. "Zookeepers of the Alligator Swamp!"

"That's right! That's what the cops in New Orleans were. Zookeepers of the Alligator Swamp! Hired guns! Hired to keep the Alligators down in the Swamp an' out of the New Orleans Proper and the Quarter where the fuckin' powers that be say low-life mofos like you don't belong."

They're not liking this.

They're not supposed to. Not yet.

The gangbangers were looking at each other in silent and sullen confusion. What the fuck was this *cop* saying?

"Well, we're not that anymore! We're the *People's Police*! And you're the people too! And we wanna be *your* police too."

That line went over like a wet fart. As it was supposed to.

"Yeah, y'all heard that sorta bullshit a million times, and the New Orleans Police never delivered anything to ya but a kick in the ass and time inna joint, so why should you believe it now?"

Hostile silence, what else?

Now that's a good question, boy, you sure you got the answer? Maybe it's time for Baron Samedi to take over?

You got the power, but I got the answer, Luke told him. *These are my homies, not yours.*

Give it a try then, boy, but it better be good.

"Well, you *shouldn't* believe such bullshit, was I still you, I sure wouldn't! But your People's Police aren't asking you to believe anything. Your People's Police are just promising not to hassle you anywhere in New Orleans, not to keep you out of anywhere, not to bust you for anything but robbery, murder, rape, or violence, *no victim, no crime,* maybe you heard about it, you don't have to believe it, you come up out of the mud and into the party in Jackson Square and the Quarter an' around City Hall an' see for yourself that it's true."

"Or it's a trick to get a lotta people busted!"

"Now why would the People's Police wanna do that when we're askin' for your help?"

Blank silence.

"Cuts both ways, you want us to really be your People's Police too, you gotta be our people too. Power *to* the people gotta mean power *from* the people 'cause there ain't any other place for it to come from, now is there? For sure not from the redneck bastards in Baton Rouge fixin' to send in the peckerwood National Guard to bust cops like me and mine an' rule the whole fuckin' city for the benefit of the mofos that own their asses, the mofos who be stealin' what they can on the high ground, the mofos who wanna keep those dirty dumb-ass low-life alligators in the swamp down here in the mud an' shit where scumbags like them believe savage reptiles like you belong!"

Couldn't do it better myself, so why should I bother? Baron Samedi told Luke. *Baron Samedi hasn't had a horse with a mouth like this since they shot down the Kingfish.*

"Okay, we all know was the New Orleans Police keepin' alligators like us out of places like Jackson Square an' the Quarter an' all, but that was then an' this is now! And now I'm telling y'all that the *People's* Police aren't just going to *let* you there, we *want* you there! We're asking you to go there! We're fuckin' begging you to show those bastards in Baton Rouge that *you too* support your People's Police! We're asking you to help scare the shit out of them! They give you the name, means they afraid of your game! Let 'em know that they try to take our city away from all of us, that they try to take the People's Police away from the People, they seriously piss off people who couldn't care less about nonviolent resistance, they just might have a *real* fuckin' revolution on their hands!"

It's all yours, boy! Baron Samedi told Luke. *I'll be your horse and take you where we both want to go, and you do the talking and say what we both want to say.*

"Power to the People! Power to all of the People! Power from you to us! Power from us to you! Power from all of the People to the People's Police!"

It was a wild ride through the Alligator Swamp, depressing sights and stenches that had once seemed normal, but that Luke had not subjected himself for a long and somehow shameful time, delivering more or less the same speech from the airboat dozens of times, like a ward-heeling politician trolling for votes.

Like a politician trolling for votes?

Might that not be what he was in the process of becoming?

Might that not be just what Baron Samedi wanted to turn him into? Baron Samedi? MaryLou Boudreau? Mama Legba? Weren't they all somehow the governor of Louisiana? And wasn't it *the governor of Louisiana* who had summoned him to Baton Rouge to do her, his, and their bidding?

And wasn't votes what it was really what it was all about?

The decent denizens of the Alligator Swamp were too trodden down in the mud to bother voting for some dry-ground mush-mouth, and the gangbangers lived too completely by the jungle law of the Swamp to trust even the laid-back law of the People's Police, let alone even think about voting. And therefore with zero political clout in bottom-line political arithmetic.

Until now.

Now he and Governor Mama Legba was inviting them into the political game.

Whether the loa inside his head was really letting him say what he pleased as the day wore on or just using his sense of the local lingo to phrase his own rap didn't matter, because Luke believed what he was saying.

Power to the People?

How could he believe that these were not people too when he had grown up as one of them? What would that make *him*?

Maybe this Baron Samedi *was* using him as a mouthpiece for whatever his own purposes were. So what? The Alligators of the Swamp were maybe no longer his brothers but he seemed to be getting through to them, persuading them to ally themselves with their previous worst enemy, to actually try supporting their People's Police.

Maybe the Christians would call the thing in his head driving the airboat an evil demon. Maybe Baron Samedi *was* an evil demon. But when the loa drove the airboat to a landing dock and left Luke Martin to his own devices, it didn't leave him feeling raped by some devil like a punk in the joint but like the horse of a rider who had ridden him to where he too wanted to go.

If that was a deal with the Christians' devil, wasn't it a *fair* deal?

If that wasn't voodoo magic what magic was it?

Or so Luke believed when the sun that went down on the Alligator Swamp came up on thousands of its people already having joined the demonstrators in front of City Hall and the permanent Mardi Gras in Jackson Square. What passed for the solid citizens of the swamp; fisher folk and mud farmers, nutria hunters and alligator hunters, their sons and their daughters, hookers without their pimps, but no obvious gangbangers in their colors in evidence at all.

This, however, did not prevent Luke from being called in on the carpet by Superintendent Mulligan, though things being what they now were, the carpet was in Big Joe Roody's office, not his.

"What in hell did you think you were doing, Martin?" Mulligan shouted at him by way of red-faced greeting.

"Winning thousands of new allies for the People's Police," Luke shot back, whether he really believed it or not. "Putting some extra fear in the bastards in Baton Rouge."

"Jesus Christ, Martin—"

"How do you figure that, Luke?" Big Joe interrupted.

A good question, and Luke hadn't really thought up a good answer beforehand, so he had better bullshit himself one now. "Why do you want to keep the Alligators in the Swamp, Mr. Mulligan?" he ventured, not sure at all where he was going.

"What kind of stupid question is that, Martin?"

"Because you're afraid of them, right? Because you're afraid they'll scare the tourists out of the Quarter and go apeshit in the Zone, right?"

Mulligan began to open his mouth, but Big Joe Roody shut it just by silently holding up his hand. No doubt who was really running the People's Police these days, no doubt at all. It was Big Joe he had to play to, not Mulligan.

"So . . . ?" said Roody.

"So the Republicans in the legislature got the votes to pass the resolution to send in the Guard, but not maybe enough to overturn the governor's veto, right?"

"Right," said Big Joe Roody, regarding Luke now with more interest than anger. "So, Luke . . . ?"

"So it's a close thing, right?"

"Right."

"So if we show that the Swamp Alligators aren't the *enemies* of the police anymore, and that the People's Police aren't *their* enemies anymore and can let them into the whole city and keep them under control . . ."

"As long as we want to?" said Big Joe. "Which we just might not want to do if the legislature sent in the Guard . . . ? We might just stand aside and see how well the peckerwoods do at handling a city full of thousands of these supposedly savage alligators . . . ?"

Luke didn't didn't have to say anything to that. Big Joe Roody had done his thinking for him. Even Mulligan's attitude changed.

"You think we can really get away with that?" he asked Roody. "You think we can keep it under control?"

"You tell me, Dick, *you're* the police superintendent. No victim, no crime frees up a lot of cops to keep the peace, not trying to bottle up the Alligator Swamp frees up a lot more to do their *real* job. And if they can't . . ."

"What does that say about my leadership?"

Roody shrugged and smiled fatuously. "You said it, Dick, I didn't."

Both of them turned their attention on Luke for a long silent moment. And it was Mulligan who finally spoke.

"You grew up there, Lieutenant Martin. . . ."

THE PEOPLE'S POLICE * 217

He didn't have to say more. And Luke, somewhat to his own surprise, found himself speaking from the heart. "It's the gangbangers who are the problem, that's who everyone thinks of as the Swamp Alligators, and even they do more dope-dealing and whore-running than smash and grab. The other Alligator Swamp folks got a bad rap, more of 'em than not grow their own vegetables, catch their own fish, hunt the fuckin' nutria for meat, trade the stuff back and forth, run little stores, got too hard a time stayin' alive to go be apeshit troublemakers. And they mostly won't vote."

"Until now. . . ." said Big Joe Roody. "And somehow I don't think any of them are gonna vote Republican. Could change the state demographics . . ."

"That's the real deal, Mr. Mulligan," Luke said. "You gonna say the New Orleans police can't tell the difference and handle that . . . ?"

Luke may have been making it all up on the spot to save his own ass, but by the time he was through he really did believe it.

And when the Alligators among the demonstrators and tourists did little more of interest to the People's Police watching over them than enthusiastically waving any picket sign passed to them and joining the crowds hurling crap at the pictures of the state legislators, when the few actual gangbangers among them had to be busted for nothing worse than a few fistfights and muggings, and the bill to send in the Guard got stalled in committee, the local media crowned Luke their golden political boy genius.

And when Mayor Bradford and Mayor-to-be Montrose calculated how many new votes the Democratic machine was going to harvest out of the Alligator Swamp the next time around, Luke was promoted to captain forthwith, and Big Joe

Roody swore to him that he hadn't had anything to do with it because he hadn't had to.

Luke had a week to bask in the backslapping and free drinks and enhanced media stardom before the shit, whoever or whatever started throwing it, began hitting the fan.

24

You asking me whether the Swamp Alligators just couldn't be let loose in the civilized and moneymaking quarters of New Orleans without succumbing to the temptations of their fetid criminal natures to rob and loot and generally do what comes natural when the police allowed them to rampage out of their cages, or whether it was ringers and agents provocateurs that started the riots?

Well, that was a political question from the git-go, no neutrals in that foxhole, and it's been like that ever since.

There were many, and still are, who need no conspiracy theory to explain why human apes would inevitably go apeshit on their own. But the bill to send in the National Guard was scheduled for a vote the week it happened, and it was going to be close, and even if it did pass there weren't going to be enough votes to overturn Mama Legba's promised veto. So the rioting in New Orleans was not exactly the gift of the gods to the People's Police, seeing as how it suddenly meant that the bill became sure to pass by a wide enough margin to overturn a Mama Legba veto.

So you'll pardon a cynic like yours truly for believing that even if agents provocateurs might not have been needed, those in the process of trying to send in the National Guard would hardly have left the cashing-in on such a golden opportunity to their own reading of the law of the jungle.

Even at the time, I found it hard to blame the Alligators alone for the damage done to my saloon when the rioting spread out of Jackson Square and into the Quarter. It seemed more than a tad suspicious that it started independently around City Hall and in Jackson Square at the same time, as the sun was beginning to go down on two peaceful scenes, a reasonably orderly and organized political protest and the same sort of thing transformed into the kind of permanent happy carnival that was to give me the idea of the Eternal Mardi Gras much water down the Mississippi later.

A few fistfights break out, someone hits someone else with a bottle, someone snatches someone else's roll of cash, someone kicks over a three-card monte table, someone pulls a knife, is that a gun, wise guys start copping feels, and it starts spreading from dozens of little independent ruckuses, and they pool together like the blood on a slaughterhouse floor, and the smell of it is in the air, and yeah, some of the Alligators snorting it do begin to go apeshit.

And once that happens, the People's Police moves in to try and cool things out, which only makes it worse. The rioters— by now that's what they are, and there are plenty of drunken tourists and drunkenly improper folks from New Orleans Proper among 'em now too—flee, or get chased by the cops, out of the Square and away from City Hall, up the adjacent feeder streets and spread out into the city, where there's goodies in the store windows and booze in the liquor-store windows available for free if you're willing to smash some glass, why not under the circumstances. . . .

And then the TV cameras show up, and everyone tries for their badass fifteen seconds of fame, and the cops are constrained to run around like chickens with their heads cut off 'cause this is chaos for coping with which there can't be a plan, and you got looting and rioting in the Big Easy over no-one-really-knows-what and no one really cares.

Among the participants, that is. Up there in Baton Rouge, they cared a whole lot.

MaryLou Boudreau, aka Mama Legba, aka the Voodoo Queen Governor of Louisiana fretfully fingered the first legislation that had ever arrived on her desk for signature at a total loss for figuring out what in hell to do with it.

The legislature had used the news of the riots to ram through the bill requiring the National Guard to go down there and restore the rule of law and righteous civilization to the so-called Big Easy.

If she signed it, she would break her own word, and New Orleans was screwed. If she vetoed it, she'd be keeping her word, but New Orleans would be screwed anyway because according to Lafitte, there were now enough votes to easily override her veto. Nor could she sit on it and do nothing for very long with rioting running out of control in New Orleans, because the legislature would impeach her and get the lieutenant governor who took her place to sign it.

Seemed like no matter what she did or didn't do, the legislature was going to send the National Guard into the city, and that was going to be like napalming a forest fire from helicopters. Even the middle class of the Big Easy, what was left of it, loathed the National Guard as redneck storm troopers practically from another country, besides which local police forces always went bugfuck or tried to at outside intrusions on their turf.

Why couldn't the assholes see that?

Or worse still, maybe they did?

Well, what am I supposed to do now, Erzuli? Marylou Boudreau found herself pleading inside her own head out of force of habit as she sat there all alone in the gubernatorial hot seat waiting for Colonel Hathaway.

But Erzuli wasn't there. Erzuli and the Supernatural Krewe had done a fast fade into the wings when the news of the rioting in New Orleans reached Baton Rouge.

What can I tell you, hon', this wasn't supposed to happen, Erzuli had told her. *We've got our powers, and you've got your powers. We had the power to hold back a whole Hurricane Season, but we're not any more perfect than you are, and especially when it comes to what you call politics and we call turf battle. And believe me or not, a lot of us are no happier with what Baron Samedi gone and done than you are. He's maybe the strongest among us, but that don't make him the smartest! He may be a wise guy, but that don't make him wise. You know what he said about the mess he's made?*

I suppose you're gonna tell me.

I'm the loa of death, am I not? The loa of necessary destruction.

Terrific!

Look, MaryLou, okay, we got you into this, but you did sorta ask for it, didn't you, and now you're governor of Louisiana, and the show called Mama Legba and Her Supernatural Krewe is over, and your Supernatural Krewe would be way in over our heads if we had any. So you're on your own, hon'.

It's not fair! It's not just! It's not moral!

Fair? Just? Moral? Hey, we just don't understand what those words mean, And maybe y'all don't either.

And I was thinking you were my friend!

You were the best horse I ever had, and I been thinking we had a good long ride together. So I'm givin' you back your freedom, MaryLou. You really gonna tell me you don't want it?

Y ou're going to have to command the operation whether I give you the order or the legislature does," the governor told Colonel Hathaway, "so tell me what to do."

Mama Legba didn't look like a satanic Voodoo Queen now, she looked a lot more like a lost little girl who was in way over her head and knew it.

If Satan had been inside her, if the Prince of Darkness was responsible for this situation, it would seem to have gotten out of hand even as far as He was concerned, and He had fled the scene of His own crime.

This was just one more civilian leader dropping a mess of their own making into the lap of the military. "What are you asking me to tell you? My tactical plans for quelling the riots?"

The governor waved a sheath of paper in his face. "Whether I should sign this thing or not!" she screamed shrilly. "Whether I order you in or let the legislature do it, that's what it's down to!"

"Is it?" Hathaway found himself blurting. "From my perspective, what it's going to come down to is whether I obey the order or not. I've left that an open question—just as you wanted me to, remember, Governor."

"I can't take any more of this shit!" the voice of MaryLou Boudreau cried forlornly. "I don't know what to do and no one will tell me!"

"You should've thought of days like this when you ran for office."

"You think I ever really wanted to be *elected*?"

And then the governor more or less pulled herself together.

"Okay, Colonel, two can play pass-the-hot-potato. As governor of the state of Louisiana, I'm officially giving you the order now. What are you going to do about it?"

I could just resign, Terrence Hathaway suddenly realized. But he couldn't say it, he couldn't say it because he couldn't do it. The temptation was there, but no commanding officer could preserve his honor by walking away from a distasteful, dire, or even suicidal duty with the lives and property he had sworn an oath to protect at stake.

Besides which, they'd only appoint someone else to do it, and the result would be the same.

Or would it? *He* at least would escape blame for whatever that result would be.

Oh no I wouldn't! Terrence told himself. Not the blight on my own soul!

For that had been a most un-Christian thought. No true Christian would hand over this cross to another! No true Christian with the responsibility and unwelcome opportunity to save the people of New Orleans from their own madness could walk away without trying. He might have thought an unthinkable thought, but doing the deed was doubly unthinkable.

His duty as an officer, and a Christian were the same, and that was some brave comfort, but what exactly was that in real world tactical terms?

"What are your orders?"

"I just told you, take the National Guard into New Orleans and stop the rioting!"

"Under what rules of engagement?"

It was a perfectly automatic next question for any commander to ask upon being ordered on a mission. But this time something else was resonating with Terrence Hathaway's military mind, for in his Christian heart, he realized that rules of engagement had more than one aspect.

The military rules of engagement defined the limits of the force, weapons, and tactics to be used, and in a situation like this, also the level of acceptable collateral damage and casualties. But the Christian rules of engagement defined the collective good to be fought for and hopefully achieved by the military action, defined his *moral* duty.

And gaining that clarity of soul began to clarify Colonel Hathaway's mind. "Neither of us wants to do this, but both of us know that it has to be done, besides which, we can't stop it," he told the governor. "But you and I, right here, right now, can, and should, set the rules of engagement."

It was definitely MaryLou Beaudreau who gave him that look of a deer caught in the headlights.

"If you order the National Guard into New Orleans by your authority as governor, you set the rules of engagement," Hathaway explained crisply but patiently, almost as he would to his own daughter. "If you don't, the legislature will, and *they'll* set rules of engagement which will be mass arrests, water cannon, whatever means necessary, arresting Luke Martin and the leadership of the People's Police, bloodbath or not. And there are indications that the rioting may, shall we say, not have been entirely spontaneous."

"Meaning what, Colonel Hathaway? I'm not sure I understand . . . Or maybe I don't want to. . . ."

"Maybe I don't want to understand either, but I'm afraid I do. Because I'm afraid that that's what they really want me to do, and spontaneous or not, the rioting certainly seems to serve what seems to be their real purpose. . . ."

"To take control of the city away from the People's Police in the name of restoring order and use it as cover to make the

National Guard do what they won't? Enforce all those fore-closures . . . ?"

Hathaway nodded. "And perhaps even under martial law. And if the legislature gives the order, it sets the rules of engagement, and if it does, it *could* mean martial law. But if *you* set the rules of engagement right now, I will be legally and morally bound to obey them."

MaryLou Boudreau seemed to be studying him for a long confused moment. But then she seemed to be beginning to understand. "Look, Colonel Hathaway, I know nothing about martial law, or rules of engagement, or any of this stuff," she told him with a certain less than entirely sincere naïveté, "but you do. So why don't *you* just suggest the rules of engagement and I'll just give the order."

"No heavy ordnance. No provocative helicopters. No firing of live ammunition unless fired upon. No mass arrests where there is no mass violence. No enforcement of any law or regulation not currently being enforced by the People's Police. No arrest of Martin or any other People's Police officer."

Governor Boudreau managed a fey little smile. "My, my, my, Colonel, a pacifist soldier."

"A *Christian* soldier," Colonel Hathaway corrected. "I'll be commanding three thousand men or so if you authorize those numbers, and they'll be armed with both lethal and nonlethal weapons."

"Consider it so ordered," said MaryLou Boudreau. "But if you don't mind, I'd like to add one rule of engagement all my own. . . ."

"By all means, ma'am. You're the governor."

"You remain in command of the National Guard troops, but I order you to *engage* with the People's Police. It's still *their* city, not yours, not anyone else's, and you are under *their* command, and not the other way around. And when the

People's Police tell you thank you very much, it's time to leave, they throw you a great big farewell party, and you bring your boys home."

"You mean we only serve as auxiliaries when called upon by the local police authorities?"

"You got it, Christian Soldier. How do you like it?"

"You know what," said Terrence Hathaway with his first smile of the day, "I like it just fine."

25

Superintendent Dick Mulligan made it abundantly clear to Captain Luke Martin that his appointment to "Deputy Assistant Chief of Police," a position that had not existed before the governor ordered in the National Guard, was hardly a reward, not that he had to.

"You need the bullshit title which I've just invented because I'm appointing you the People's Police liaison officer with the National Guard commander, and I'm appointing *you* because you created this mess and richly deserve to be our public fall guy. But don't get the idea that you're gonna be in command of anything, Martin. Your official job is to transmit my requests for National Guard backup to Hathaway, which will be as few and far between as possible. Your real job is to stick to Hathaway like a leech, appear to be the one giving the orders, and use the big mouth that stirred up the Alligators in the first place to somehow herd them back into the Swamp."

"What Mulligan really told you is that he hasn't a clue as to what to do," Big Joe Roody told Luke, as if he had to. "And neither does Bradford or anyone else, me included. So the good news is you're on you're own. And the bad news is that you're on your own."

So much for official orders and helpful advice from Joe

Roody, as Luke stood at the junction of the pedestrian entrance and the oval racetrack itself in the center of the Fairgrounds awaiting the imminent arrival of Colonel Hathaway and his troops.

At least the words from the birds around the Blue Meanie, paranoid or not, were a little more informative.

Cops who had been on duty when it happened agreed that the simultaneous outbreaks of rioting around Jackson Square and City Hall had been too well coordinated to be spontaneous, at least at first. A fistfight, maybe staged, a snatch-and-grab, tables overturned, knives being conspicuously flashed, and it was off to the races.

The department surveillance photos of Swamp Alligator gang members were fragmentary at best, since there were hardly any cameras posted in the Swamp, but not entirely nonexistent. But around Jackson Square there were plenty of cameras and even more so in the Business District and particularly anywhere near City Hall, so it was really odd that on opening day of the riots, there were virtually no matches.

The consensus was that Swamp Alligator gang members had not been present in any significant numbers and certainly not in organized groups when the rioting erupted, but there had been perhaps an unusual number of sightings of known professional perps of the sort that bounced in and out of Angola and would have been readily available for modest fees and reduced sentences forked over by those with the power to do so.

Once the rioting became chaotic and the general looting by the great army of the unemployed and unemployable became general, organized teams of members of well-known Alligator gangs like the Fuck Yo Mothers, the Dirty Dicks, and the Vampire Bastards, some actually sporting the colors, emerged from the Swamp to take advantage of the cover of the general rioting by the needy and greedy to steal what could be stolen, and smash what could be smashed.

Consensus opinion was that certain interests who had the means to make the rioting happen made it happen and were pinning it on the Swamp Alligators in general.

Who might that be?

Whoever wanted the National Guard dispatched to New Orleans on the excuse of stopping it, of course. Whoever wanted to use the Guard to do the dirty work that the People's Police wouldn't do for them. Whoever delivered the paper bags to their flunkies in the state legislature. No one in the Blue Meanie wanted to embarrass themselves by asking the next question when the answer was so glaringly obvious.

The Fairgrounds had been the obvious and maybe only possible choice as the staging area for upward of three thousand troops. Up on the Gentilly Ridge, it was a straight shot down wide Esplanade Avenue to the French Quarter and with easy access to the Central Business District and the City Hall area too. Used to host outdoor music festivals, carnivals, and the like, it was mostly a big empty space when not full of tents, booths, stages, and other temporary structures, except for the horse-racing track in the center. It hadn't been in use when the riots broke out, leaving the sanitary facilities for tens of thousands conveniently intact and empty.

And here came the National Guard, parading toward Luke around the racetrack, led by Colonel Hathaway dramatically standing ramrod straight in the back of an open Humvee as if there were a brass band behind him. There was no band, not even a bugler, no flag, no dress uniforms, just a seemingly endless curving line of Hummers, troop trucks, armored personnel carriers, motorcycles, busses, though at least no tanks or helicopter gunships.

Luke had never seen anything like it before in the flesh,

though who hadn't on television, but the long cloud of dust, the tang of ozone, the gas and diesel fumes, the deafening growl and grumble and buzz of all those engines, the smell and gut-rumbling vibration of the real deal, were surprisingly overwhelming.

And as the parade drew closer, he saw that these were indeed army troops in combat gear, not civilian police puffed up on steroids, or at least that's what these despised peckerwood weekend warriors looked like, wearing camo fatigues, body armor, and helmets, carrying assault rifles, Plexiglas shields and taser-billies, and what were maybe even machine guns.

Hathaway led his troops right past Luke, and around the full oval of the racetrack, which seemed like an outrageous deliberate insult that set Luke's blood to boiling, until he came full circle round, and Luke realized that what the colonel was doing was using the racetrack as a convenience to deploy his full force behind him before calling for a halt when his vehicle had come around again to where where Luke was standing.

Hundreds of military vehicles came to a halt behind him, their engines rumbling and growling in neutral like so many threatening lions.

Colonel Hathaway descended, marched up to Luke, and stopped, looking as if he couldn't decide whether to salute him or not. So Luke saluted *him* with a sarcastic click of his heels.

Hathaway was not amused.

"This is not an invading army, son, despite current appearances," Hathaway told him frostily. "I am martialing my men in good order at our base camp. When on off-duty shifts, my men will return to bivouacs here."

Hathaway then surprised Luke by offering his hand and seeming to take his bullshit official position quite seriously. "I'm Colonel Terrence Hathaway, United States Army Retired, with a long career experience commanding Army Military

Police, so it's not as if I'm entirely new to carrying out policing orders."

And then he shrugged. "But I must freely admit that I have
no experience quelling urban riots and restoring order in an
American city, nor ever thought I would have to. So I intend to
obey the governor's rules of engagement to the letter. Which
are that you will not directly command any National Guard
unit or choose what unit to deploy where. But you may request deployments from me and suggest what I do with them.
And frankly, given my lack of tactical experience in these
matters, I will regard those requests and suggestions as orders
unless I believe they are crazy."

Luke didn't know whether to be flattered or appalled, not
knowing jack shit about this sort of thing either. But he *did*
have his own orders, to ride Hathaway around the city, stick
to him, and somehow use this show to calm the waters he had
turned into a class-five human hurricane when Baron Samedi
had been *riding* him.

"Well, Captain Martin?" Colonel Hathaway demanded.

Well . . .

Well, what?

Well, about the only experience *he* had ever had corralling
and more or less taming Swamp Alligator gangbangers was
as the unofficial honcho of a little squad of cops that came to
be known as the Alligator Swamp Police, so it seemed like he
should think gang logic as he had back in the day. If for no
other reason than he didn't have another idea in his head, and
no one, not even this army colonel seemed to have anything
else to offer.

"Well, I guess we have to start by showing the colors,
Colonel."

"*Showing the colors,* Captain Martin?"

"Gangbanger for what you'd probably call showing the

flag," Luke told him. "It's been my experience as a police officer, Colonel Hathaway, that the first thing you've gotta do when dealing with gangs is show them who rules, that *you* got the power, and if they give you any shit, you will use it."

"A show of superior force . . . ?"

"Never had to do it with full-scale riots before," Luke said. He nodded toward the thousands of troops neatly lined up and effectively at his command, if Hathaway really was taking him seriously. "But then again, never had this much force to show."

26

I s this kid some kind of military genius in the raw? Colonel
Hathaway found himself wondering. They certainly didn't
teach these tactics at West Point.

The first thing Captain Martin ordered up was a formation
of a thousand infantry in trucks and APCs, and in combat
gear, not riot gear; body armor, assault rifles, no shields, no
taser-billies. He and Martin led this force down Esplanade
Avenue, a broad residential boulevard, from the back of an
open Hummer, which would have seemed excessively dangerous in Hathaway's opinion were it not flanked front, rear, and
both sides by People's Police squad cars, sirens blaring, as if it
were the president's armored limousine.

Down Esplanade, which seemed untouched by the riots,
right on Decatur, which ran past the French Market to the eastern end of Jackson Square, and was an unholy mess. The French
Market was a long linear outdoor mall purveying produce,
restaurant food, tourist gewgaws, and the like, and though it
looked quite thoroughly sacked and trashed, there were still
looters rummaging through the remains for what might be
left.

The sights and sounds of a thousand motorized infantry in
full combat gear sent them fleeing in every direction like cock-
roaches in a dark kitchen when the light is turned on. Hatha-

way would have ordered a few squads to give chase and take prisoners but Martin said no.

"The idea is to make no arrests at all if possible."

Hathaway would have detached a few squads to guard the French Market, but Martin again vetoed the deployment. "What's the point in guarding someplace where there's nothing left to steal?"

Jackson Square and the streets surrounding it, on the other hand, though also thoroughly trashed and looted, were quite deserted except for St. Louis Cathedral facing the main entrance gates to the park, where a small and pacific-looking crowd was gathered on the steps. Store windows fronting on the pedestrian streets had all been smashed and the stores emptied of their fancy goods. Temporary stands, kiosks, bars, and the like lay overturned and in ruins. The park itself was a junk heap of more of the same, plus bandstands, tents, and garbage, and the whole area stank of spilled beer, piss, and stale marijuana smoke.

"Looks like the morning after one hell of a party," Hathaway observed.

"Because that's what it is," Captain Martin told him. "So let's get it started again."

Here, Martin had him dismount two hundred soldiers and deploy them surrounding the fenced park and the street entrances to the Square, assault rifles at the ready, and pointedly pointed outward.

"I don't get it, Captain, there's no one and nothing left here. What are we supposed to be guarding?"

"Folks who just wanna have fun," Martin told him, grabbing a bullhorn and climbing up a ladder to the high bandstand in the center of the park thrown up over the statue of Andrew Jackson now hidden under garishly patriotic bunting.

"I'm Captain Luke Martin of your People's Police, I'm in

command here, and the good old boys with the rifles are friends of ours here to help your People's Police make goddamn sure that no sons of bitches spoil the party again! Looters will be shot! Muggers will have their skulls cracked! Anyone who don't know how to behave at a Big Easy party will not be allowed in! So come out, come out, wherever you are! Clean up the mess so's you can make a bigger an' better one! Bring back the booze and the beer and the doobies! Start the music! Let the good times roll again! That is an order from the People's Police!"

And to Terrence Hathaway's astonishment, it was obeyed.

Slowly, tentatively, people descended from the Cathedral steps, past the soldiers, and into the park guarded on their behalf. The Cathedral doors opened and more people emerged and passed through the gates and into the park. Some of them carried instruments and began to play "When the Saints Go Marching In." People started singing it. Hathaway almost found himself singing it himself. People crept tentatively down the side streets and into the Square. More bands began to play. Other songs. Raps. Gospel. A few people began to dance.

Colonel Terrence Hathaway found tears welling up in his eyes. And though he could not quite understand why, he knew that they were good Christian tears. Jesus would have wept such blessed tears Himself.

So far, so good, but restarting an interrupted mini Mardi Gras bash in New Orleans was not exactly military rocket science, or, as Luke had once heard a fellow officer joke in the Blue Meanie after one too many or maybe just enough, the police are not here to break up the wild party, the police are here to *preserve* the wild party!

However, pacifying the French Quarter couldn't be quite such a cakewalk. All the streets of the grid were too narrow and too thoroughly clogged with drunks thoroughly plastered on the bottomless glasses of freebies commandeered from the saloons and the even lower life preying on them for the same tactic to even be tried, let alone work.

On the orders of Mayor Bradford transmitted through Superintendent Mulligan, the New Orleans police, heavily outnumbered citywide by rioters, had been broken up into disconnected squads that were spread out thin guarding so-called high-value targets—major hotels, car dealerships, major appliance and electronics stores, department stores, museums, jewelry stores, the dwellings of the rich and well-connected, police stations, firehouses, and of course City Hall itself.

In the Quarter, where only a hundred or so cops had been deployed, they were so heavily outnumbered by the hordes of drunks and stoners, all too many of them of the belligerent variety cruising for a bruising, that they would have just made themselves targets if they made any futile attempts at controlling the chaos.

So they had withdrawn from most of the area, and Bourbon Street in particular, primarily for their own safety, and in favor of guarding the high-end art galleries, antique stores, and boutiques of Royal Street against the forays of professional burglars and looters.

Even the eight hundred or so combat-ready troops that Luke had remaining at his disposal would have not been able to clear the streets without firing blanks into the air at the very least, and if they did, they'd probably end up having to defend themselves with live ammunition. And even if that succeeded without the kind of bloodbath that could turn drunken rioting into enraged insurrection, there simply wouldn't be enough troops to protect the hundreds if not thousands of bars, strip joints, music halls, restaurants, and porn emporiums afterward.

But between Esplanade Avenue and Canal Street and between Rampart and the Mississippi levee, there were less than two dozen street exits from the French Quarter.

"So, if we can't chase them all out and defend the Quarter afterward," Luke told Hathaway, "we make them afraid we won't *let* them out, and when we finally do, the exits we guard get turned into gateways we control like the *entrances* to a theme park or a football stadium."

"Empty out some of the vehicles except for the drivers and three or four riflemen as guards and use them as mobile barricades . . ."

"You got it, Colonel. . . ."

"Send in infantry from four sides before we do, and just parade them in force *inward* toward the center . . ."

"Then turn them around, menace the rioters with their weapons and drive them toward the exiting streets . . ."

"Which by then have been been barricaded . . ."

"Leaving them feeling trapped like cattle in a slaughterhouse corral . . ."

"And *so* relieved when we show mercy and release them!"

"Brilliant, Captain, absolutely brilliant," Colonel Hathaway told Luke, and he actually saluted.

Colonel Hathaway had understood the theoretical brilliance of the tactic readily enough, but it seemed like a miracle when they actually pulled it off without a single military or civilian casualty.

After dispatching the Humvees to guard the exits, he divided most of the remaining troops into four columns of a hundred and twenty soldiers each, four ranks wide and thirty ranks

deep, each led by a sergeant with orders to keep them marching in good parade ground order, with their weapons shouldered,
but raised in the air every hundred steps at a forty-five-degree
angle. A quarter of the rifles were loaded with blanks, which
were to be fired in the air every other time they were so bran-
dished.

The tactical rules of engagement were not to respond to
verbal taunts, not attempt to clear drinking establishments,
not make arrests, not attempt to clear the gutters unless the
parades were impeded.

Live ammunition was to be used strictly in self-defense.

It was never needed.

The jam-packed mobs of drunken and stoned-out rioters
hastily evacuated the gutters at the sounds of marching boots
and the sight of troops in full combat gear approaching them
to take control sidewalk to sidewalk.

Much empty braggadocio and foul language was then
rained down on the troops from the angrily overcrowded sidewalks, but no one was drunk enough to try to impede the crisp
and orderly march of formations of combat-equipped troops
parading down the gutters with their weapons regularly raised
in unison, and even that faded away when they started firing
blanks salutes as if at a military funeral.

When the four columns converged at the crossing of Tou-
louse and Bourbon, were brought to a simultaneous parade
rest, and then nicely executed about-faces and reversed direction, few of the drunken hordes were so inebriated as to fail
to get the message, and there was general panicked flight in
all four directions up the other French Quarter streets away
from them.

When they found all streets out of the Quarter sealed at the
periphery by infantrymen atop Humvee vehicles aiming assault rifles squarely at them, panic turned to fear. As the sound

of marching feet and fusillades of gunfire approached from the rear, fear turned into outright terror.

When the engines were started and escape routes were cleared, they fled the French Quarter as fast as their wobbly legs would allow them.

Rather than a miracle, Colonel Hathaway really knew full well, a new military tactic not presently to be found in any West Point textbook or Military Police manual. Perhaps it should be. Perhaps he should write up a report and submit it to the proper authorities.

Or perhaps not.

Upon second thought, Colonel Hathaway realized that perhaps he hadn't really learned a new military tactic after all. Military personnel had carried it out, and carried it out well, but this had been a *police* tactic.

A *new* police tactic?

It was not quite Terrence Hathaway's area of expertise, but he had never heard of anything like it being employed before, and certainly not to such perfect effect. And he was *sure* that what Captain Martin Luther Martin had done at Jackson Square could never have been done by anyone other than an officer of the New Orleans People's Police.

No, neither of these tactics had really worked a *miracle* and Terrence Hathaway doubted very much that Captain Martin would disagree.

But was there not something rather Christian about them?

27

In a few short hours, the entire French Quarter had been pacified and secured, and by the time of the 5:00 P.M. news, the live coverage of Jackson Square coming alive again and the Quarter cleaning itself up and preparing to open up for business as usual behind National Guard entrance checkpoints was the top local and regional story, and even a national feature.

Dick Mulligan was all over it like a fly on horseshit, taking full credit for his own brilliance, and Luke Martin would have been sorely pissed off if he had dreams of running for something. But since he didn't, he really wasn't, and it seemed a fair enough deal, keeping Mulligan from coming down on him for exceeding his nonexistent authority. And when Mulligan got on the horn to tell him he now really *was* in charge tactically as long as he went along with the fiction that he was only transmitting the superintendent's own orders to Hathaway, Luke felt he was getting the better of it.

But as the convoy emerged from the Quarter onto Canal Street and ventured a few blocks up it, Luke realized that pacifying Canal and the Central Business District was not going to be another parade-ground cakewalk.

Canal Street ran all the way up from the French Quarter

levee of the Mississippi through the width of New Orleans Proper to City Park Avenue. It was wide, it was the city's main shopping street, high class, skuzzy, and everything in-between for much of its length, meaning overloaded with tourist attractions, hotels, bars, restaurants, department stores, shops, and all sorts of other juicy targets for mobs and looters.

The overextended New Orleans Police were deployed all along Canal in small isolated units guarding the high-class stuff and of necessity allowing the looters and rioters their fun and games with everything else, and ditto or even more so, in the similar environs of the Central Business District downriver from it.

And as Luke knew, as any New Orleans cop knew, as any citizen of the city knew, as any Swamp Alligator knew, this was the key to the whole situation. The French Quarter was compact, self-contained, now pacified, and the heart and soul of the tourist industry, without which New Orleans would long since have gone the way of Detroit without the auto factories or Las Vegas without legal gambling. But if the Quarter was the soul of the economy, the Central Business District was the big stomach of the Fat Cats That Be and Canal Street was the gullet that fed it.

So protecting these business interests, like it or not, had to be the priority even for a force that now called itself the People's Police. The Central Business District was just what the name said it was, the actual headquarters and the symbol of the Fat Cats that everyone who wasn't one hated, and Canal Street was lined with stores, shops, and emporiums with their tantalizing show windows smashed open and inviting those formerly on the outside to come on in and help themselves.

The hell of it, as far as Luke Martin was concerned, was that while his current self-interest and duty as a cop lay on one side of that divide, his old Swamp Alligator's back brain was insisting that his gut loyalty lay on the other.

"Over to you, Colonel Hathaway," he said unhappily. "Stop the looting on Canal and clear the Central Business District and the rioting will fade away, but I've got no bright ideas of how to do it. . . ."

And I'm not exactly sure I want to.

It was simple enough for an officer of the People's Police to come down foursquare on the side of the People on the French Quarter side of Canal, where you didn't really have to think about *which* people you were supposed to serve, but on the business side *which* people's interest you were supposed to protect started getting *political* and Luke did not find himself liking it.

But Colonel Hathaway apparently saw it strictly as a military professional. "A much larger scale operation than what we've done so far, but more straightforward since we've got the overwhelming force with which to do it."

Luke glanced backward at the force they were leading, no more than five hundred men by now. "*We do?*" he said dubiously.

"At the Fairgrounds, not here," Hathaway told him. "I've two thousand or so troops up there doing nothing. I divide them up into three eight-hour shifts and divide each shift into say sixty ten-man platoons or so and parade them up and down Canal Street continuously at about ten miles an hour in Hummers and trucks spaced a half block or so apart. Where looters are encountered and don't flee immediately, blanks are fired from the vehicles at them. If that doesn't send them fleeing up side streets, a platoon dismounts and chases them up side streets firing live ammunition over their heads until they are completely dispersed. I don't think much more will be required, do you, Captain Martin?"

"I don't see how . . ." Luke admitted glumly.

He could see how the tactic would achieve its objective easily enough, but that didn't mean he liked it. There was something missing, and yes, damn it, something . . . *political.*

"What's bothering you, then . . . *Luke,* if I may?"

"It'll look too much like . . . a military takeover of the center of the city . . . *Terrence* . . ."

"Well, it rather *will be*. . . ."

"And I'm here with you to make sure it won't look like . . .
like . . ."

"Martial law?"

"The deal is your troops must be clearly seen to be under the
command of the People's Police, not an invading army. . . ."

"I have no problem with that," Colonel Hathaway told
him. "So you pull the police units away from stationary guard
duty where they will no longer be needed, and put a police
squad car in the lead of my troops and at the rear of the parade and interspersed between the vehicles, lights flashing, and
sirens blaring all the while. That should do the trick, don't you
think?"

"And a good one, Terrence," Luke said with a grin. "Turn it
into a kind of armed Mardi Gras float parade."

Hathaway laughed. "Too bad your People's Police don't
have a brass band."

"You know, we just might. And if we don't, Mulligan can
probably round up a volunteer band somewhere, though they'll
probably be playing moldy old Dixieland. Riots or not, this *is*,
after all New Orleans."

After the orders were radioed in, they led the column down
Loyola to City Hall, appropriately enough as Luke was now
beginning to see things, not far from the ass end of Canal, where
the scene around it was all too politically clarifying and all too
politically repellent.

City Hall itself was cordoned off by maybe a hundred cops even though no looters or rioters were to be seen, only three television trucks set up on the street fronting the main entrance. Duncan Plaza, across the street from it, which had been the center of the permanent giant block party in the surrounding streets, was now empty and surrounded by hundreds of cops keeping it that way. The surrounding area, lacking a lively bar scene or very many stores worth looting, was pretty much deserted.

Colonel Hathaway shook his head with a disgusted frown. "What would you call *this* deployment, Captain Martin . . . Luke . . . ?"

"*Political* . . . Terrence . . . ?" Luke suggested.

"A cowardly and dishonorable waste of troops I'd say. . . ."

"There's a difference?"

Hathaway made a sound somewhere between a grunt and a laugh that was neither.

"What do you suggest?" Luke asked more seriously. *A lot more seriously.*

Hathaway nodded toward the television trucks, now turning their cameras on them and their troops. "Well, it might make an interesting point for the cameras if we replaced the police guarding the politicians cowering hiding inside City Hall with Guardsmen," he said dryly. "Though I suppose we can't make a show of having their weapons pointed inward instead of outward, much as we might like to, now can we?"

"I suppose not," Luke answered in kind. "Much as I'd like to. But . . ."

"But?"

"But I'll tell Mulligan we have to keep say a hundred cops in the park twenty-four seven and he's gonna have to negotiate an expensive work rule exception with Big Joe Roody because they're going to be the same cops camping out there for the duration. And I'm going to tell Superintendent Mulligan that he has to do it because you're insisting on it."

Hathaway just looked at him as if he had gone crazy. "I am . . . ?"

"Oh yes you are, Terrence, else you will refuse to obey my order to do the same thing with a hundred of your own men. And then they'll all be missing the fun."

"*Fun?*"

"Oh yeah, camping out in Duncan Square Park's gonna be duty we both gonna have plenty of your guys and mine fighting for."

"I suppose if this is a joke, Luke, I'm now supposed to ask why?"

Luke laughed. "Back in Jackson Square, I remembered a line I heard from a party animal cop in a bar. The police are not here to *break up* a wild party, the police are here to *preserve* a wild party. Or in this case, start it over again."

I'm no military man, no cop either, and neither are most of the citizens of New Orleans, but you don't have to be a ballplayer to know a perfect game when you see one pitched and appreciate the brilliance of the performance.

Well, at least a no-hitter.

The People's Police and the National Guard had not only quelled the rioting without anyone getting killed or hit by live ammunition, they had managed to turn a public relations disaster for the national reputation of New Orleans and therefore the tourist industry into a citywide celebration of the triumphant spirit of the Big Easy that had folks from all over wanting to come on down and join the party that seemed like it could go on forever.

Jackson Square stayed one continuous carnival of bands, street acts, drinks, doobies, strippers, hookers, doin' it in the road, and dancing in the streets in and out of homemade costumes, a permanent little people's Mardi Gras without the floats or parades, drawing overflow into the Quarter, and Lafitte's Landing, and saloons like it, like the real deal did leading up to Fat Tuesday.

Down in Duncan Plaza, Captain Martin and Colonel Hathaway had put together a gypsy encampment, music festival, and retro love-in, presided over and godfathered by the National Guard and the People's Police right under the nose of City Hall, and then allowed it or rather encouraged it, to spread out into the surrounding streets as a giant block party.

"The People's Police are not here to *poop* the party, we're here to *preserve* the party, y'all come on down!" as Luke Martin put it in one of his TV interviews, to the delight of the Chamber of Commerce, who picked it up as a primo advertising slogan.

But it was the continuous parade of the National Guard up and down Canal Street through the center of the city that was the capper.

It started with just troops in military vehicles and People's Police squad cars with lights flashing and sirens blaring, but within hours there were marching jazz bands at either end, and what with New Orleans's long tradition of spontaneous so-called secondary street parades always popping up when enough folks felt like it, there were soon more bands marching along on the sidewalks, and the police cars kept their lights flashing but turned off their sirens.

Dancers in their secondary parade glitter and feathers began weaving in and out among the Humvees and squad cars, and neither the cops nor the Guardsmen did anything to try to stop them, not with pretty girls blowing them kisses and tossing them flowers, and folks of all races, genders, and religions handing them joints and drinks.

It didn't take long for homemade secondary parade floats to join in, and finally a few of the major Mardi Gras krewes even joined in with their fancier floats that after all were just sitting in their warehouses doing nothing.

What with all those floats, dancers, and party animals joining the parade through the breadth of the city, Canal got pretty crowded, and some of the bands and secondary parade dancers, and their floats, spread out into the main surrounding avenues, and it all began to seem like it might never end.

And hey, why should it?

Oh yeah, it was indeed the inspiration for what I would sell to Disney and the rest of them later as the Eternal Mardi Gras.

Oh yes, I did, let J. B. Lafitte finally set *that* story straight!

Dick Mulligan tried to claim credit for ordering Luke Martin and Terrence Hathaway to do everything they had done, but everyone who was anyone and even most folks who weren't, knew that was bullshit, and pathetic bullshit at that.

Martin and Hathaway went along with Mulligan at least to the point of not publically contradicting him, but when Mayor Bradford, doing his own piece of scene-stealing, presented one of those giant cardboard keys to the city in front of City Hall to Colonel Hathaway for Mission Accomplished and Now Go Home—hint, hint, hint—Hathaway handed it to Martin, not Mulligan.

Now, unlike Mulligan, I freely admit that *they* were the geniuses who created what evolved into the Eternal Mardi Gras, not me. But you've got to give J. B. Lafitte credit for being able to be inspired by the vision of what I saw happening, like Saul seeing the light on the road to Tarsus, and naming it too.

Mardi Gras all year round!

The . . . *Eternal* Mardi Gras!

All over New Orleans!

Mama Legba's X-rated Mad Mardi Gras spring, fall, winter, maybe even early summer, every season but the Hurricane Season!

No victim, no crime!

Anything goes!

Y'all come down whenever you like, and stay at the permanent party as long as you want!

More tourist hordes flocking to New Orleans *all year round* than ever it in two measly weeks in the winter during the so-called real thing!

Big time corporate money financing big budget floats, and parades twenty-four seven all year long except during the Hurricane Season! X-rated casino shows! X-rated *theme parks*!

Paying big taxes pumping steroids into the city budget and greasing many palms with heaping handfuls of superdollars! Sopping up unemployment with thousands of full-time, almost year-round, jobs! Transforming the economy of a city sinking into the swamp into a city that could hire the Dutch to turn swampland into pay dirt!

And J. B. Lafitte putting it all together and dipping his wick into his fair share of the proceeds. Doin' well by doin' good and vice versa, as I see it, an' if you don't, why don't you just take your tight-assed business elsewhere?

When Mayor Bradford had given the commander of the National Guard the key to the city with a municipal pat on the back and a Mission Accomplished, it had been a none-too-subtle hint to remove the troops from the city. Everyone knew it, and all that remained was for the governor to sign the order.

So why hadn't she done it yet?

A lot of people and most of the press smart-mouths figured she was waiting for a proper triumphant farewell parade past cheering crowds out of the city to get organized, and that would have made sense to me, if I hadn't known better.

But I did, because it wasn't parade planning holding up the order, it was the speech to be given announcing it. I knew this because I was working on it with MaryLou Boudreau.

I had long since given up thinking of the governor as "Mama Legba" because there was no one or nothing else but MaryLou Boudreau left in the governor.

And that was the problem. MaryLou Boudreau wanted to act like a real governor but she didn't know how.

MaryLou Boudreau was the grandchild of bayou hippies, the daughter of Quarter street buskers, and nothing more than a failing street act herself before the Supernatural Krewe made her the Voodoo Queen Governor of Louisiana, which wasn't what you would exactly call a graduate course in the downs and dirties of Louisiana politics.

Governor Boudreau had pleaded with me to come up to Baton Rouge to help her with the speech because she had no one else to confide in. "But please don't bring a writer; with your help, I intend to write it myself."

Why didn't that come up waving bad-sign red flags the moment I heard it?

She hadn't even written anything when I arrived.

"What's the problem, Governor Boudreau?" I told her, maybe a little pissed off at being dragged up to Huey Long's miniature White House. "You sit here behind this desk, smile at the camera, praise the People's Police without having to mention Mulligan, Bradford, or Martin to avoid any political problems, and praise Hathaway for a job well done because there's no political problem with that, and then you can praise the people of New Orleans for being so cool."

"And *then what*, J. B.?" MaryLou bleated, a lot more like a kid trying to squeeze pearls of rescuing wisdom out of her daddy than a governor.

"Then what?"

"What do I say?"

"What do you say . . . ? You say, by the authority vested in me as governor of the state of Louisiana, I hereby order Colonel Terrence Hathaway, commander of the Louisiana National Guard, to withdraw his troops from the City of New Orleans by such and such a date. I don't get it, MaryLou, you needed me to ghost-write that for you, or just hold your hand?"

"I want to say *more* than that, J. B. I know I'm not qualified to be governor, but here I am, and if I can't really do the job like it should be done, at least I'd like myself a lot better when I look in the mirror if I could tell myself I *did* something with it. . . ."

"For who?"

"For the people who got conned into voting for me. For the people of Louisiana."

"Like what?"

She shrugged. "I was hoping you could help me with that, J. B.," she said softly and forlornly enough to touch the heart of a whoremonger who didn't have one made of gold.

I found myself trying to imagine what I would want to do if I were in her shoes, and came up short, but I sure knew what *I* wanted to see done from the vantage of standing in the shoes I was actually wearing.

"Nothing any governor, president, or *any* politician in the United States of America could do would be more appreciated by more people than having the hovering black thundercloud of foreclosure permanently lifted from over our property and houses and farms and business premises," I told her. "You want to do something for the people of Louisiana who voted for you, or for that matter, who didn't, you do that!"

MaryLou Boudreau's face lit up like one of those cartoon antique three-way bulbs had appeared over her head and been shifted from 30 watts to 150. "Yes!" she cried. "But . . ."

"*But?*"

The bulb had been turned down to about 75.

"But hasn't that been done already, J. B.? The New Orleans People's Police won't evict anyone, the little upstate forces, most of them, won't do it either, and under the rules of engagement I worked out with Colonel Hathaway, neither will the National Guard, so just about no one in Louisiana's being evicted already—"

"Yeah, but it's not *legal,*" I told her. "Nobody's being *evicted,* but only because there's no police force that will throw us out, so the Loan Lizards might as well use their foreclosure notices as toilet paper. But no one under foreclosure has *legal title.* We can live in our houses, work our businesses, farm our land, but we don't *own* them. We can't sell them, we can't pass them to inheritors, and if some future governor wants to or some future legislature gets it passed, they can send in the National Guard to do the dirty work, and like Yogi Berra said, it's déja-vu all over again."

"Oh . . ." moaned the governor. "Couldn't I get some law passed like just *giving* y'all this . . . legal title . . . ?"

"The legislature would just tell you to shove it up your ass!" I told her. "But . . ."

"But, J. B.?"

I could feel something percolating in the back of my brain, and it wasn't Café du Monde coffee. If *I* had one of those three-ways above my head, it would be going up from 30 to 100.

"But you're gonna be governor for four years, during which *you* can tell them to shove it up *their* asses if they trying it again and the people, aka the voters, would most all be with you. So for those four years the Loan Lizards sitting on all that paper won't be making a dime off of the mortgages they're holding! They're not collecting interest payments, they can't sell the properties, and no one would be crazy enough to buy the mortgages. They're sitting on hundreds of millions of dollars in useless paper. . . ."

And that was when the lightbulb over my head got so bright and hot it exploded.

"How far are you willing to go, Madam MaryLou Boudreau, governor of the great state of Louisiana? You willing to play a game of political hardball so down and dirty it'll make Huey Long and Fast Eddie Edwards look like pitcher and catcher on a high-school girls' softball team?"

"Try me," said Governor Boudreau.

"You got one secret superpower as governor that as far as I know even the Kingfish never threatened to use during the Great Depression. It's called the power of eminent domain."

"What's that?"

"The state, meaning you, can at least in theory seize private property for the public benefit, like to build a road, or a levee, or a reservoir, or something . . . so you could in theory use eminent domain to seize everything under foreclosure from both the people who possess it physically like me, and the banks and other species of Loan Lizards sitting on the useless mortgages. . . ."

"I could really do that?"

"Maybe . . . on the grounds that as things stand now, the state government, meaning the people, is losing millions in property and income taxes this way. . . ."

"But . . . but why would I want to . . . ?"

"Because you then sell clear title to all the property back to the folks like me for the princely sum of one dollar!"

"But that's outright thievery! Isn't it, J. B.?" Governor Boudreau said, without exactly sounding outraged about it. "Could we really get away with it?"

"Maybe, maybe not . . . but it sure would be a credible threat because it would all be tied up in the courts for years and years . . . so the Loan Lizards might just be amenable to an alternative they'd be in no position to refuse. . . ."

"Which is?"

"Which is retroactively index the dollar value of the mortgages and payments to the deflation rate and future inflation or deflation rate of the dollar."

"In English, please. . . ."

"The whole reason millions like me are in the fiscal shitter in the first place is because we bought into low down payment mortgages denominated in fixed numbers of dollars, and when the buck got turned into the superbuck so did the numbers on the mortgages, meaning we owed five or ten times as much in buying power dollars as we bargained for and couldn't hope to keep up the monthlies. . . ."

"So the idea is to turn it around to what people thought they were buying into in the first place . . . ?"

"You got it, Governor."

"And the Loan Lizards might buy into it because—"

"—because 20 percent of something is more than a 100 percent of nothing."

"Why J. B. Lafitte, that sounds like political *blackmail*. . . ."

"Such an ugly word, Madam Governor. . . . Why not think of it as, shall we say, rough justice without the tar and feathers?"

"Well . . . when you put it that way . . . I love it!"

Well, the scenario might have been my idea, but while J. B. Lafitte might often enough be accused of being a little too big for his britches, I wasn't so full of myself as to think I could actually write a speech like that, and Governor Boudreau even less so, so we hired a legal ghostwriter to do it, gave her three days to get it done, and scheduled the speech for Jackson Square, a much more media-friendly venue than the Baton Rouge Governor's Mansion.

28

MaryLou Boudreau had never ridden in a helicopter before the flight down from Baton Rouge to the New Orleans Fairgrounds, and she had never ridden on a Mardi Gras Krewe float as the queen of a parade through cheering crowds, and now here she was, standing beside Colonel Terrence Hathaway in the back of a National Guard Hummer, leading a kind of Mardi Gras parade, waving to the cheering crowds lining both sides of Canal Street.

Hathaway had given the bulk of his troops forty-eight-hour passes, withdrawing most of the military vehicles, so that the perpetual Canal Street parade was now more of a traditional secondary parade writ large and seemingly permanent, dominated by marching bands, homemade floats, costumed dancers, and just plain folks joining in.

But plenty of the at-liberty Guardsmen in their uniforms were mixed in with the rest of the revelers, enjoying their unexpected popularity as heroes of New Orleans, and the ones he held back to ride the Hummers, decked out now in makeshift red-white-and-blue bunting to show the National Guard flag on this triumphant parade, were feeling no pain either, as women tossed them flowers, men handed them drinks and joints, people even tossed Mardi Gras throws *up* at the troops riding the Hummers.

Bands on the sidewalks followed the parade along all the way down Canal to Bourbon Street, and when it turned left into the Quarter, a voice that was not a voice spoke to Mary-Lou inside her own head.

Whoo-ee! What a parade!

Erzuli! You're not gonna—

No way, hon'! You deserve this, sister! You were the greatest mount ever, girl, you're the queen of this here parade, and this is your hour to enjoy riding your own horse.

Bourbon Street was jam-packed all the way to St. Ann's, so crowded sidewalk-to-sidewalk that a jazz band had to spontaneously jump out in front of the lead vehicle to slowly plow its way toward Jackson Square. People in costumes, people more than half naked, people dancing in the street to the music blaring out from the bars and saloons.

People dancing as if . . . possessed?

Is that the Supernatural Krewe out there . . . ?

Well, of course it is, you expect us to miss a party like this! Don't we have a right to celebrate? Ain't this our party too, if you don't mind? And even if you do, hah, hah, hah!

Not at all, Erzuli. You know, in a way, I missed y'all.

Ya know what, hon', we all kinda miss playin' Mama Legba too!

Right on St. Ann's, past the church, and the parade came to a halt in front of the entrance to Jackson Square Park. National Guard troops formed the right side of an honor-guard aisle from the entrance to the base of the tall makeshift stage hiding the statue of Andy Jackson in the center of the park with People's Police doing the honors on the left.

MaryLou and Colonel Hathaway sashayed to the base of the red-white-and-blue-draped stage while a brass band played a Dixieland version of Beethoven's "Ode to Joy," and climbed up the ladder to the top as the crowd cheered.

From where MaryLou now stood, it looked as if all New Orleans was there cheering. For as far as her eyes could see, within the gates of the park, in the pedestrian streets surrounding it on three sides, packing broad Decatur, lining the levee beyond, every space that could be filled was filled with cheering and waving humanity.

Glancing at Colonel Hathaway, she was amused to see that he was standing there at rigid attention with a wooden expressionless face, as if scared shitless. For a moment, MaryLou Boudreau wondered why *she* wasn't.

But hey, hadn't she been a street busker playing this very venue to crummier and far less enthusiastic audiences? Hadn't she been a TV star called Mama Legba? Wasn't she standing there as the Voodoo Queen Governor of Louisiana? If she wasn't all of that in this golden moment in the spotlight, who was she?

What's to be afraid of, girl? The stage is all yours, and so are they!

"Are we having a good time yet?" Mama Legba said into her hidden lavaliere mike, and the amplification turned it into a mighty roar.

The crowd roared back, shook beer cans over their heads in salute, waved spliffs, roared back, and she knew that she had them.

"Are we letting the good times roll?"

Enough people shouted "Fuckin'A!" to allow it to be heard through the wall of joyous noise.

"Three cheers for the People's Police of New Orleans!"

The cheers were enthusiastically forthcoming.

That much had been entirely spontaneous, but now it was time to more or less follow the speech script she had more or less memorized.

"I hereby proclaim that as long as I am governor of Louisiana neither the State Police nor the Louisiana National Guard will ever again be called into New Orleans to dispute, violate, or nullify the full policing authority of the People's Police of New Orleans, including their refusal to be used to enforce eviction notices and their right to maintain the policy of no victim, no crime!"

The cheers this time, were even louder.

"And I will send to the legislature a bill legally extending the policy of no victim, no crime, and the nonenforcement of eviction notices by any police authority, to the entire state of Louisiana!"

Not much more than polite applause to that one, not that she expected any more, given that this was New Orleans.

"Not that we all expect what we've got right now in Baton Rouge to pass anything like that . . ."

That laugh line was scripted, wasn't very funny, and didn't get much more than cynical snickers.

MaryLou Boudreau, who was Governor Mama Legba, turned to Terrence Hathaway, who was commander of the Louisiana National Guard.

"By the authority vested in me as governor of the state of Louisiana, I hereby order Colonel Terrence Hathaway, commander of the Louisiana National Guard, to withdraw his troops from the City of New Orleans."

That much was in the speech script too, but Governor Mama Legba who was MaryLou Boudreau added a little ad lib of her own.

"You've got ninety-six hours to do it, Colonel Hathaway," she said, and turned to face her live and broadcast audience. "That gives y'all four days to show these boys a good time worthy of the City of New Orleans to thank them for a job so well done!"

And then, when the cheering was done, it was time to get down to business.

"Now, when I was running for governor of the great state of Louisiana and it was supposed to be a joke, and I knew I wouldn't win, I could promise the sun, the moon, the stars, and free drinks on the house for everyone for ever and ever, without being accused of breaking those promises, and I seem to remember I also promised to save everyone in danger of being evicted from their houses or farms or places of business because of legal foreclosures on their mortgages. Well, thanks to the People's Police of New Orleans, and Colonel Hathaway, and the Police Association of Louisiana, that's one campaign promise I've actually been able to keep!"

Cheers, mixed with laughter, mixed with grunts, adding up to uncertain confusion.

"*So far,*" said Mama Legba. "But it's not permanent because it's not *legal.* Nobody's being *evicted,* but only because no police force will throw them out, but no one under foreclosure has *legal title.* Y'all can live in your houses, work your businesses, farm your land, but you don't *own* them. Can't sell them, can't pass them on to your kids, and if some future governor wants to or some future legislature gets it passed, they can send in the National Guard to do the dirty work, and you will all be out on your asses!"

Muttery grumbly silence.

"Well, I'm gonna do something about it!" declared Mary-Lou Boudreau who was Governor Mama Legba. "I'm gonna give those greedy Loan Lizard sons of bitches the chance to do the right thing," said Governor Mama Legba who was Mary-Lou Boudreau, "and if they don't—"

—*sledgehammer blows riding up her navel to her chest*—

—*the pop-pop-pop firecracker fusillade sound of high-powered rifles*—

—*a ribbon of pain coming on like the stabbing of many knives*—

—*screams, shouts, her knees buckling, coughing up blood,*
falling forward—
    —*into the arms of Colonel Hathaway—*
    —*his stricken and furious face the last thing she saw—*
    —*as the darkness closed in—*
    —*and her head mercifully exploded.*

29

The assassination of Mama Legba on live national television was probably a greater shock than even that of JFK, the quick series of high-powered rifle shots, her chest and belly suddenly spurting blood as she fell, Colonel Hathaway reaching out to catch her, the final shot smashing into her forehead spattering brains and blood, all seen not in some grainy black-and-white home-video, but in close-up high-definition color.

The closest thing, I suppose, was the fall of the Twin Towers on 9/11, hammered into people's brains by endless repetition with days of nothing else on television. But there was something at least as powerful and somehow even more heartbreaking about that close-up of Colonel Hathaway, his uniform dripping gore, tears running down his cheek, his jaw clenched in rage, holding the broken bloody body of MaryLou Boudreau in his arms and carrying her to the lip of the stage, and then hoisting Mama Legba above his head with what seemed like superhuman hysterical strength.

When the shock wore off the media started asking who had bought this obviously professional hit and why?

Well, the obvious big winner was George Hockenberry, but no one could take that seriously because no one who had ever even heard of George Hockenberry could take *him* seriously.

Who in hell was George Hockenberry?

That was what most folks wanted to know.

George Hockenberry was the former lieutenant governor and now governor of Louisiana, that's who.

And having Hockenberry suddenly become governor was for sure not the advent of a previously major player like Lyndon Johnson.

Hockenberry had been an upstate state senator for more years than anyone could care to remember. No one cared to remember because Hockenberry had never done anything memorable, having risen to the unofficial status of Senate Republican Bagman a decade or two ago, and having been awarded the lieutenant governor nomination as a sort of gold watch. Being the long time distributor of corporate and grayer largesse, ol' George was popular with his colleagues and the real world party leadership, but ol' George was beginning to lose a few of his marbles, and the lieutenant governorship was a retirement home, an office he was likely to die in without doing any damage, requiring nothing more than collecting his salary, unless a sitting governor died in office before he did.

But now she had.

We soon got a good dose of what replaced her.

New Orleans was in outraged mourning; he wouldn't dare show his ass here, so his first public appearance the day after the assassination was before the legislature in Baton Rouge. He blamed the assassination of the Voodoo Queen Governor on anarchist communist Arab drug-dealing Mafia dons, or some such thing equally incoherent, and accused the "so-called People's Police," which he reminded us, sounded like something in the Soviet Union, which he seemed to have forgotten no longer existed, of colluding with these evil forces to bring about chaos in order to establish a godless atheist socialist dictatorship.

His first move was to declare martial law, and his first order under it was for the National Guard to remain in New Orleans to restore an order that had long since been restored, enforce the letter of every cotton-pickin' law on the books, and arrest Police Superintendent Dick Mulligan, Deputy Assistant Police Chief Martin Luther Martin, Joe Roody, anyone else above the rank of lieutenant in the People's Police wearing their uniform in public and attempting to play cops and robbers, and if he opened his Democrat mouth about it, Mayor Douglas Bradford too.

The lunatic had inherited control of the asylum.

For the next twenty-four hours the city waited fearfully to see what Hathaway would say, what the National Guard would do, while Colonel Hathaway arrested nobody, and said nothing except that he was proceeding with standard redeployment preparations, whatever that was supposed to mean.

While this was not going on, it became clear that Governor Hockenberry was not in control of anything or anyone including himself, but had simply graduated from being the senatorial bagman for the Louisiana chapter of the Powers That Be into being their puppet-show lead.

An emergency bill sailed through the legislature giving Hathaway forty-eight hours to begin making the arrests required under Hockenberry's martial law order, enforce the letter of all laws as God and the property rights of the Loan Lizards intended, or be removed as commander of the National Guard.

Coup who?

Coup *you*, suckers!

"What are you gonna do, arrest us?" Luke Martin asked Colonel Hathaway as he, Hathaway, and Big Joe Roody sat at a corner table in the Blue Meanie, closed down this morning to host this needfully secret meeting. "And Superintendent Mulligan too?"

"That's my orders, Luke," Terrence Hathaway told him. "Instead, here I am, sneaking off to have a beer with y'all."

"At least you're not one of those born-again teetotalers," Big Joe said.

Hathaway grimaced. "This situation would drive Carry Nation herself into the bottom of the whiskey jar. What am *I* going to do? What are *you* going to do if I try to arrest you?"

Luke had been pondering the answer to that one since Fuckinberry had declared martial law without coming up with an answer.

Hathaway sighed, shrugged. "The real operational question is what are the People's Police going to do if I try to carry out the governor's orders?"

"Meaning what would Mulligan order?"

"*Please!*" Hathaway said. "We all know that Superintendent Mulligan will do what it takes to keep his job and his butt out of the stockade. That's why you're here, Mr. Roody, and he isn't."

"Meaning what am *I* going to tell my membership to do?"

Hathaway nodded.

Big Joe put it to Luke. "Speaking as an officer in the People's Police but a member in good standing in the Police Association of Louisiana, New Orleans chapter, what would you do if Mulligan ordered you to surrender and I said resist?"

"You mean, which side am I on?"

"I mean, which side are you on. Which side would your brother officers be on?"

"Yours or Dick Mulligan's?"

"Mine or Dick Mulligan's."

"You have to ask that, Joe?"

"I've got to ask *someone*, Luke. . . ."

Luke thought about it. He thought about what Luella would probably say now. He thought about what his son would say about him years later, whatever happened. He thought what the kid in the Alligator Swamp would have wanted him to say then, what that boy inside him wanted him to say now. He thought of what the people of New Orleans would say. He thought what the cops of a previously despised police force would say in the packed Blue Meanie.

Who was he kidding?

There was only one choice.

"No retreat, Joe, no surrender."

Terrence Hathaway both knew and feared what Luke Martin's answer would have to be as soon as Roody had asked the question. He had come to respect this young police officer, believed that he was a man of honor, if not, or not yet, a Christian. And as a man who strove to be both, Terrence Hathaway would have been disappointed in him had he answered otherwise.

But that answer had put him in the most terrible quandry he had ever faced as an officer and a Christian, as a Christian soldier as MaryLou Boudreau had once called him.

As an officer in the United States Army, he had sworn an oath to obey the orders of the chain of command reaching up out of the army all the way to the president, no matter how repugnant, or indeed stupid and counterproductive, he found them personally. Without military honor dependent on fealty to that oath, no democracy could long survive the scorn of the military for policies of the elected civil authority, as had been proven over and over again in the past throughout Latin America, Africa, and indeed most of human history.

Disobeying such an order was close to staging a military

coup. Therefor disobeying such an order was tantamount to treason.

But he was not an officer in the United States Army now. Well, not exactly. Not unless the National Guard was federalized by order of the president. And Governor George Hockenberry was not the president. And he was clearly a madman. A madman apparently being used by evil powers for evil purposes. And to obey his order would clearly have dire consequences. Might even result in gun battles between the Guard and the People's Police.

As a Christian, was it not therefore his moral obligation to disobey such an order?

Which side are *you* on, Terrence Hathaway?

"Well, Colonel, are you going to obey the order of the nutcase in Baton Rouge or not?" Joe Roody demanded of him. "You gonna force the issue and arrest us right now?"

"Damned if I do, and damned if I don't," Hathaway told him.

And "damned" was an accurate description in this case rather than a cuss word. Damned as a Christian if he obeyed Hockenberry's orders to commit a terrible sin, and damned if he didn't for violating his oath as an officer.

"The King of France, with ninety-thousand men, marched up the hill, and then marched down again. . . ." Hathaway muttered.

"*What?*"

"For now, I'm going to keep my troops engaged in snappy parade ground exercises until I can certify that they are ready for the mission. After all, most of my troops are currently on liberty in the city and sleeping off last night's hangovers, and without proper sober MP squads, it could take quite a while to collect them all, marshall them at the Fairgrounds, dry them out, and return them to fitness for duty."

During which I must pray as I have never prayed before for a miracle.

A moral miracle.

W ho leaked the text? How much money went to who for doing it?

Even now nobody knows, but of course there are endless conspiracy theories.

That the ghostwriter has never been found is certainly suspicious, but then it had to be printed out, and taken to the governor's office, and so forth, and could have been copied anywhere along the way, so the devil could have found well-paying dirty work for any number of hands.

Why, I've even heard it whispered that *I* did it! After all, I had my own copy, which I ended up releasing afterward, so I certainly *could* have done it. But why *would* I? Follow the money! I had a lot more to lose than to gain.

The only way I can explain why, even though I knew what MaryLou "Mama Legba" was about to proclaim, is that New Orleans was in such a state of dread at what Hockenberry was calling down on the city, such a state of conspiracy theory turmoil, and so was I who knew the lady personally, that it took me a while to ask myself the obvious next question.

Why was MaryLou gunned down before she could finish the speech?

And as soon as I found myself asking myself the question, I knew the obvious answer, and I knew that ol' J. B. was in danger of a lot worse than having the National Guard throw me out in the street without a means of financial survival.

MaryLou Boudreau had been shot down to keep her from serving out her term, to keep her from using her executive power to forbid the carrying out of evictions by the National Guard.

Because the next thing she was going to do was make the threat of using her power of eminent domain to blackmail the Loan Lizards into writing down the principle and monthlies on all the loans into affordable superbuck numbers.

I knew this because I supervised the writing of the script with her.

Whoever had ordered the assassination must have known it too.

And I had a copy of the script.

Did whoever knew what was in it know that too?

I sure did not want to find out the hard way!

What in hell was I supposed to do?

It didn't seem like destroying the script would protect me from anyone who knew that I knew what was in it.

The brave and righteous thing to do would be to make a bunch of copies and release it to the press come what may, and to my credit, I've got to admit that the thought did cross my mind.

But on second thought I realized that even if that didn't get me killed, a lot of folks might believe that I had just made it up myself, which, of course, was kinda true. I could leave town and run away to Mexico or Brazil like I'd do if this were a movie, but in a movie the problem of what the hero does for money usually does not come up.

And while J. B. Lafitte may have been a lot of things and may have been called a lot more, a hero was not one of them.

But there were two real heroes of the people in New Orleans at the moment: Captain Luke Martin and Colonel Terrence Hathaway. Hockenberry had ordered the arrest of Martin, but Hathaway was the one he had ordered to make the arrest. Under martial law. Hathaway was currently a hero of the people with a giant cardboard key to the city to prove it.

And Governor Hockenberry had made him the law.

Colonel Hathaway had taken his sweet time calling his troops back to the Fairgrounds, given them their own sweet time to recover from their partying, and then given them much more parade ground marching back and forth to get into pointless spit and polish order than they needed or wanted, playing for time.

And praying to Jesus to enlighten him as to what to do when time ran out.

Arrest Martin, Mulligan, Roody, and anyone in the People's Police refusing to stand down, and begin evicting citizens from their homes at gunpoint and perhaps precipitate chaotic armed confrontation?

How could any Christian possibly do that?

Disobey the direct order of the duly constituted civil authority, however evil it might be, however dire the real world consequences?

Resign?

No, he told himself, I can't just fob such dishonor off on whoever they replace me with.

Hathaway had still neither been able to square this moral circle on his own nor received an answer from On High to his fervent and fervently desperate prayers, when, of all people J. B. Lafitte, a saloon keeper and pimp, made his way through the encampment and to his tent to present him with a possible answer to those prayers.

But in the form of yet another conundrum, this one practical and legal. Or so at least it seemed when he read the full text of what Lafitte claimed was MaryLou Boudreau's interrupted speech.

"I don't understand what you expect me to do, Mr. Lafitte, I could keep you here under protective custody, but—"

"Don't you get, Hathaway?" Lafitte demanded shrilly. "*This* is what she was killed for! MaryLou Boudreau was murdered to keep her from making this threat in public! To keep her from serving out her term and making good on it! Doesn't that make your fuckin' good Christian blood boil?"

Terrence Hathaway thought about it.

Could this be a Sign from Jesus? God worked in mysterious ways His miracles to perform, so could He not send the moral miracle he had prayed for via such an amoral sinner? Certainly the Lord had done such things before. Certainly if Lafitte was speaking truth, his paramount duty, both as a Christian and the responsible police authority under martial law was to arrest. . . .

Arrest *who*?

"This may be clear evidence of motive, Lafitte, and I am willing to proceed on the belief that it is in theory, but I ask you again, what would you have me do?"

"Arrest whoever bought the professional hit, what else!"

"And who is that?"

Lafitte stared at him silently.

"Oh . . ."

Hathaway stared back. Hathaway nodded.

"Well, you were in the Military Police, weren't you? Can't you—"

"My experience with detective work is zero, and I am now in command of the National Guard, not even a real *military* police force, and I very seriously doubt that there is a homicide detective among them . . ."

"Well then, the People's Police—"

"I'm under orders to arrest their leadership and any of their officers attempting to exercise policing functions. . . ."

J. B. Lafitte had no answer to that.

"Look, Mr. Lafitte," Hathaway told him gently, "I know you must be frightened. I would be if I were in your shoes, and I am willing to keep you under protective guard here—"

"That's the best you can do?"

"That's the best I can do without even having a suspect to arrest."

Lafitte regarded him with something that seemed like anger, then contempt, then fear, then what seemed to be fear overcome by a bravery that Terrence Hathaway could not but find admirable.

"Well, Colonel Hathaway, that may be your *best* but I haven't yet done my worst," Lafitte told him. "And back in my high-school baseball days, our unofficial team motto was, when all else fails, play dirty. And I'm from New Orleans, my man, and believe me, ol' J. B. knows how."

30

Well, this was the Big Easy now, wasn't it? This was semisecret Party Town for the weasels in Baton Rouge, wasn't it? I was a bordello owner, wasn't I, one among many, and didn't we all keep video of the weirder kinks of our political guests for use where and when doing what was good for business required a little . . . political leverage?

So I hightailed it back to Lafitte's Landing, closed the place down, convened an emergency meeting of the French Quarter Pissing and Moaning Society and while waiting for arrivals, phoned as many other of my fellow whoremasters and madams, high and low, as I knew, which was just about all of them in town, and told them what was needed, namely juicy footage of state legislators in perverse pornographic action.

Someone that one of us had the goods on had to know something, right, wasn't a detective commonly called a dick?

Well, I guess you don't have to imagine there was plenty of it, but let me tell you, you'd have to be a real dirty bird to even *imagine* some of it. We had the means to control enough votes in the legislature to repeal the law of gravity. But we were stymied until Charlie Devereau slunk into the joint uninvited. About as welcome as a friendly visit from an IRS agent until he told us why he felt constrained to seek our forgiveness and redeem himself in our eyes.

"Hey, look, guys, I might have been fool enough to have been responsible for running Mama Legba in the first place, but y'all know damn well I live and die with the tourist trade just like you, and I sure don't want an asshole like Hockenberry screwing it up—"

"So?" I demanded sourly. "We don't have the time to listen to your bullshit, we don't even have enough time to spare to beat you up!"

"Then shut up and listen, will ya! Two state representatives dining in one of my establishments got roaring shit-faced drunk, maudlin babbling drunk, and before I had finished gracing them with the ol' genteel VIP 86, they blubbered out the terrifying secret they had unsuccessfully tried to drown out of their pinhead brains—"

"Which was—"

"Which was a secret meeting of maybe a dozen representatives, a couple of senators, the usual mouthpieces of You Better Not Ask, and the then lieutenant governor. A day or two before Mama Legba's scheduled speech. . . ."

"*So what?*"

Charlie stared me right in the eye. "So they had a copy of the speech, J. B."

"Oh shit. . . ."

"This savvy conclave was called to figure out what to do about it, and had come up dry, until George Hockenberry, who was anything but dry, rose far enough from his stupor to offer up his shit-faced unfunny sarcastic suggestion.

"'Too bad the Klan ain't around to just solve our problem with a 12-gauge shotgun or a stick of dynamite, hee, hee,' he had drooled. ' 'Cause if I wuz governor, hey, right, *no* problem.' "

"You don't suppose—"

"You think they really—"

Everybody was talking at once, so I had to shout them down.

"It doesn't matter."

That shut up the barroom babble. Was *my* barroom anyway, now, wasn't it?

"It doesn't matter," I told them. "These two guys testify, we got the goods on Hockenberry for conspiracy to commit murder."

"You don't really believe—"

"Doesn't matter if Hockenberry doesn't end up convicted. These two jerks sign paper with the charge written on it, it's sworn testimony, and Colonel Hathaway will happily arrest Hockenberry and let the courts settle it in their own sweet snail's time. And what do we all do in the Big Easy when we need some sworn testimony?"

That, no one needed to be told. And sure enough when we went through our collective whorehouse footage, we had more than what we needed on the two guys who had spilled the beans in Charlie's restaurant, and better than merely disgusting, some of it was humorously pathetic, gorilla suits, chocolate syrup, bananas, an' all.

Even so, I insisted that we pass the hat to buy them a judge who would guarantee them immunity for their testimony, it might even be sort of legal, so it shouldn't be unreasonably expensive.

"Come on, guys," I told them, "this is the Big Easy, now, isn't it? Go along, and get along."

Was this manna from Heaven? Terrence Hathaway asked himself when J. B. Lafitte returned to his headquarters with the deposition papers. Were these documents actually an answer to his prayers?

Sworn testimony by two eyewitnesses, along with an utterly evil motive that would make the arrest morally correct, politically correct, and a distinct personal pleasure.

Answer to good Christian prayers from a whorehouse pimp?

God works in mysterious ways, His miracles to perform. And after all, He is omnipotent. So how can it be blasphemy to suppose that the Lord might be able to contain an occasional mordant sense of humor?

"As a temporary officer of martial law and a permanent Christian gentleman, I somehow believe that I have a need not to know how this testimony was obtained," he told J. B. Lafitte in something of the same spirit.

"I somehow believe you are right," J. B. Lafitte told him. "So what are you going to do about it?"

"My duty under the very martial law decree laid down by the governor of Louisiana, which is to enforce the laws of both man and God, and arrest George Hockenberry for conspiracy to commit murder, and I care not a swamp nutria's ass that they just happen to be one and the same."

"Like the Good Book says, 'God works in mysterious ways His miracles to perform.' "

"Why, Mr. Lafitte, I didn't know that a . . . bordello impresario could quote the Bible."

"Why, Colonel Hathaway, I didn't know a Christian soldier could have a sense of humor."

31

Colonel Hathaway might have been a Christian soldier and all that, but he soon proved that a Christian soldier could have political street smarts and media smarts as well, but then again, you just might be able to say that about Jesus, too, given the history of the last couple of thousand years.

In an admirably publicly humble manner which was also cunningly political by my lights, Hathaway didn't go up to Baton Rouge to make the arrest himself. He just sent a small unit commanded by a mere sergeant to the Governor's Mansion to arrest Governor George Hockenberry on charges of conspiracy to commit murder. And it was done a little after midnight, and the news media was not informed beforehand, so there was no coverage until morning and the first footage that was seen was that of Hockenberry in a cell.

Hathaway, after all, had been an Army Military Police commander, and though I've mercifully had not personal experience being arrested and hustled off by MPs, I would imagine this was how they'd do a VIP version, especially when arresting one's own superior.

Hockenberry was under arrest, but he was still governor or so he claimed, and this in a state where Earl Long had remained governor while in the state bughouse by firing medical directors thereof until he finally hired one cynical enough to certify that the governor wasn't crazy in order to keep his job.

So Hockenberry fired Hathaway from his jail cell.

Or tried to.

"I had hired two outside civilian lawyers, one from New Orleans, who knew Louisiana constitutional law, and one from Chicago, who was known as a political operative, so I figured that together they could walk me through the legalities," Governor Hathaway told me over lunch about six years later.

Which they had.

Sort of.

Terrence denied Hockenberry's legal right to fire him on the grounds that he was no longer governor because he was under arrest for murder, and therefore the state of Louisiana did not have *any* governor with the legal power to either remove him or lift the state of martial law.

While teams of expensive lawyers were having a high old time duking that one out with the meter running, Terrence announced that as far as he and *his* lawyers were concerned, the legal last orders he had were those issued by Mama Legba moments before she was killed by order of the cabal headed by Hockenberry.

Which was to withdraw his troops forthwith from New Orleans and return policing powers there to the People's Police, leaving him in charge of policing powers in the rest of the state under her no victim, no crime, no forced evictions, rules of engagement, which had never been rescinded and could not be because Louisiana did not have a legal governor with the power to do so.

Which he then proceeded to do, parading them ever so slowly up toward Baton Rouge, while the secretary of state was arguing that *he* was now the governor under the current constitution, and the legislature was threatening to write a new one tout suite so that *they* could grab the power to appoint a new governor and fight among themselves as to who among them it would be.

Marching on Baton Rouge was *never* meant as threat of a military coup, Governor Hathaway still insists, with an almost straight face.

"How could there be a coup against a duly constituted civilian government that did not exist, J. B.? I was simply following my last orders from the last one that did, that of Mama Legba to withdraw the National Guard from New Orleans and maintain martial law and order until Louisiana somehow managed to come up with one."

"Uh-huh, Terrence, but of course if the folks in the state legislature just might believe that a long leisurely march by armed troops upriver in their general direction just might be meant as a warning. . . ."

"*They* might believe that, J. B., but *I* couldn't possibly comment."

"No political intent, huh, *Governor* Hathaway . . . ?"

"Not unless carrying out my officer's oath to obey my last orders from a legally constituted civil authority and my moral duty as a Christian to pick up the righteous torch struck from the hands of that martyred lady and carry it forth counts as *political intent.*"

That much I am sure was and is 100 percent sincere. But political intent or not, there sure were political consequences, what with the legislature backing down and turning turtle, the State Supreme Court twiddling its thumbs, trials, and appeals, and appeals of appeals, and constitutional battles, and so much legal confusion and political battles that for four fondly remembered whole years until the next gubernatorial election, the only functioning law was martial law, and the de facto head of what government existed was the Commander of the National Guard and administrator thereof, Colonel Terrence Hathaway.

"I never intended to run for governor," Terrence Hathaway kept insisting with a straight face during the election campaign. "All I intended to do was my sworn duty to preserve the necessary rule of law and order under the rules of engagement given to me by Governor Mama Legba."

"And threatening to invoke eminent domain under martial law if the Loan Sharks didn't start negotiating down mortgage debt and monthlies, Colonel Hathaway?"

"My Christian duty to complete the righteous deed that MaryLou Boudreau was *martyred* to keep her from fulfilling. And Christian or not, and whatever else she may have done in life, I believe that Jesus has cleansed her soul for that one brave and noble deed, and if there is a Heaven, and I do believe there is, she is in it. How could I do less than pick up the torch from that fallen heroine? The Bible condemns usury, does it not? *Jesus* ejected the money-lenders from the temple, did he not? Could I do less if I had the power when entrusted with the power?"

And even now, I still believe him. Who wouldn't? Who wouldn't *want* to believe him? Even a card-carrying cynic like me finds it impossible not to believe that Governor Terrence Hathaway has always been and still is a sincere Christian, even if I'm not and never have been.

For four years, Louisiana was under what the upstate Bible Belters started calling Christian martial law. For four years, under the People's Police no victim, no crime was the law in New Orleans, and for four years, under Terrence Hathaway's Christian martial law it was the law in the rest of the state, too, as he continued to carry out Mama Legba's so-called rules of engagement.

For four years, Terrence Hathaway, incorruptible Christian soldier, was the de facto go-along, get-along ruler of what folks like me started calling the Free State of Louisiana.

Elvis Gleason Montrose got elected mayor of New Orleans on schedule, campaigning to formally make what was now called the Eternal Mardi Gras permanent. He graciously allowed Dick Mulligan to resign as police superintendent before he appointed Luke Martin to replace him to the delight of the People's Police and the police's people, maybe under pressure from Big Joe Roody.

Mama Legba's former one shot Mad Mardi Gras, rebranded as the Eternal Mardi Gras by yours truly, went yearwide except for the Hurricane Season, a big, big boost, for the tourist industry, which, thanks to increased tax money take by Baton Rouge as well as New Orleans, even began to help the upstate economy.

Under Hathaway's threat of eminent domain, the banks started grudgingly bargaining down mortgage principle numbers and therefore monthlies to prices the mortagees could afford in return for clearing titles.

About that time, with the help of Charlie Devereau, some of his big-time Chamber of Commerce buddies and my small-time ones in the French Quarter Pissing and Moaning Society who we let in on the deal, we put together a syndicate to buy up a big piece of the eastern Alligator Swamp piecemeal.

Then, what with the profits being racked up from the Eternal Mardi Gras by lesser outfits, and a cock-and-bull story that heavyweights from Bollywood and Shanghai had already approached us with plans for the world's first X-rated theme park, I didn't have too much trouble convincing the Mouse to buy our swampland from us at a fat profit and add a "Eternal Mardi Gras Land" as an X-rated adults only addition to Big Easy Disneyland.

Of course, Disney being Disney, they did screw us a little on the deal by not telling us that they were going to hire the Dutch to put up those mighty Hans Brinker twenty-foot sea-walls and giant solar-electric windmill pumping stations to turn what they bought from us at what turned out in the end to be a cut-rate price and turn it it into primo real estate for a lot more than a Disneyland.

The rest is show biz history, as the X-rated saints and sinners came marching in with one hand in their pants and the other reaching for their wallets.

By the time of the next gubernatorial election, the Republicans and the Democrats were fighting with each other like cats and dogs to get Hathaway to be their candidate for governor.

Terrence refused both of them but finally allowed himself to be drafted as an independent, promising to do as much as was necessary and as little as possible, and as he actually put it, "continue to let the good times roll."

Of course, he won in a landslide.

And that's how the Eternal Mardi Gras, with its sex, and drugs, and retro Dixieland, with its corporate financed Hollywood and Bollywood budget floats, its year-round days of wine and roses, raised New Orleans out of the muck and mire to its present fame, fortune, and glory as the Born-Again Big Easy.

And that's the story of how little and how much goodness had to do with it. J. B. Lafitte has enough *enjoyable* sins on his soul without adding the sin of false modesty, and I claim my share of the credit, in dollars, euros, pounds, and all major credit cards.

But for my money, and these happy days I've got plenty of it, as far as I'm concerned, as General George Washington was the father of the United States of America, so was Colonel Terrence Hathaway the father of the Free State of Louisiana.

And that says it all.

Or does it?

I saw that Voodoo Queen Float again yesterday. I've seen it more times than I can count, whoever's ever been to the Big Easy these days hasn't? It circulates through the city every day of the year except during Hurricane Season. It's got naked girls and boys galore tossing Mardi Gras throws and plastic Mardi Gras doubloons good for free drinks, fucks, spliffs, and shows at participating venues. They say Disney owns it, or at least built it, because of the state of the art double life-size audio animatronic Mama Legba in Voodoo Queen stripper's gear taking it all off every half hour, but the Mouse, he ain't talkin'.

And every half hour, when she's down to her nipples and pubic hair, she tosses a few of the very special coins, the ones that get a dozen or so lucky people out of the crowd and onto the float if they dare, to take part in the audio-animatronic voodoo ceremony replete with audio-animatronic dancing headless chickens, and to allow some kind of wizard loa virtual reality program to dance them around like like happy horses on Jimsonweed.

Maybe.

But this time around seeing the show got me thinking.

What if there is no program?

What if it's the real deal?

Mama Legba has gone to wherever Terrence Hathaway may think she is, but her Supernatural Krewe boogies on in New Orleans forever?

What if this Eternal Mardi Gras is just what the loas intended?

Wasn't that the deal Luke Martin made with Mama Legba and her Supernatural Krewe live on television?

If they're riding their dancing horses on that float, they exist, don't they? If they exist, haven't they gotten just what they want? If they exist, and they showed up to take it, wouldn't we give them the key to this city?

If they exist, maybe they had it all the time already.

If they exist, isn't New Orleans and its Eternal Mardi Gras their party too? If they exist, they sure are getting along in proper improper Big Easy style, so why not go along and enjoy being their rides?

Does that mean you have to believe in voodoo?

Who gives a swamp nutria's ass?

No one wants to rain on anyone's Mardi Gras parade in the Big Easy.

Y'all come down and see what I mean.